GHOSTS & LIARS

THE IMPOSSIBLE JULIAN STRANDE PART TWO

KATHRYN ANN KINGSLEY

First Print Edition: March 2020

ISBN-13: 979-8-64573-646-0

ASIN: B084NFB7PM

ACKNOWLEDGMENTS

As always, my thanks, my love, and my condolences go to my husband who put up with my dumb ass when I had to bash this story out in one and a half weeks.

Thank you to my editor, Lori, who puts up with me and my new "word rut of the week."

But once again, thank you to all my readers. Thank you for enjoying my silly stories with strange, villainous male leads. Without you, I wouldn't continue writing. Thank you. And I hope you enjoy the second half of Julian Strande.

THE IMPOSSIBLE

JULIAN STRANDE

THE GREAT MAGICIAN

MR. KELLAR Says:
"STRANDE is the greatest
Magician the World has ever known."

1

Julian Strande was an impatient man.

He had always been that way. Often, he had been accused of being brusque or impetuous. He had always wanted the next thing *now,* like the greedy, thirsty creature that he was. It had been true in life, and it was still true in death.

Over a hundred years had passed since his heart had beat its last. Since then, he had hoped his restlessness had tempered. After all, he'd seen no recent evidence of it over the past several decades. But now he saw that was very much not the case. It had only been replaced with boredom.

His eagerness had been tempered only by the fact that there was nothing he desired.

Now...that had changed.

Alice.

Placing the tip of the sharpened steel rod against the glass, he used his straightedge to score the surface in a carefully placed line. After repeating the motion a few more times, he lined up the piece of glass with the edge of his table and, taking a small mallet, carefully tapped away at the surface until it broke alone the line and the shards fell away.

Picking up the piece, he examined it carefully. It had to be perfect. He carefully placed it down along the pattern he had drawn and ensured that it was cut correctly.

Every detail had to be in its place. This project was the most important one he had ever undertaken in either his life or afterlife, save perhaps the construction of his estate. He had already thrown out more pieces than he had completed. A single tiny chip or an imperfection in the glass was enough to make him hurl it into the trash.

The curves and delicate pieces were the ones that gave him the most trouble, as could be expected. But in the graceful lines of the leaded glass were what gave the whole project its elegance. When he soldered them together with copper, they would create a stunning piece of stained-glass.

She would love it. He knew she would.

Oh, Alice.

His heart soared at the mere thought of her. The image of her in his mind when she received his gift—when she used it—gave him immense joy. And stoked the fire in him to a fever pitch. It quickened both his impatient nature and his desire for her.

Julian Strande had never been in love as a living man. He hadn't had the desire nor the inclination. Between his travel, his art, and his darker magical pursuits, he hadn't had the time. He had always overlooked relationships for the next step up the ladder in his career and his rise to power.

But he had reached the pinnacle of both the day his heart ceased to beat. He had ended on the ultimate high note—burning out his life like a firework in the sky. He left an impact that would linger for a thousand years. Or so he hoped.

He had known being dead might be dull. He had not predicted it would become so terribly lonely. It came as an utter shock to him, since he had never wanted companionship in his living years. But in the vacuum left behind by his need for greatness, it crept in like an insidious poison.

That was why he had chosen to turn his home into a museum. Perhaps inviting in the public would help stave off the vacuous solitude. He invited them, and so they came.

But the swarms of people who trekked in and out of his house like a carnival ride and the veritable carnies he employed to operate it never did anything to help. He never felt a connection to any of them. They were only noise. Endless noise.

It was admittedly slightly better than the silence.

Slightly.

And then she came to call.

He had not known what to expect when he placed the ad in the papers in every city in America. He had hoped he would find someone to amuse him for a time. He had shockingly few responses, most of them commenting about how they had found it by chance as they "typically only looked online for jobs." *Pah.*

He appreciated technology and understood it perfectly well. Phones and computers were interesting enough, but they lacked imagination to him. There was a simple pleasure to be found in doing things *his* way. Gears and pulleys. Smoke and mirrors.

Dark and impossible magic. *Real* magic.

He was the Impossible Julian Strande. He had taken that moniker for two reasons. One, it had a wonderful ring to it. And two, it was true. Again and again, he had been hounded by his colleagues for any hint as to how he could perform the tricks that had astounded and fooled so many.

Even the greats could not fathom the inner workings of his illusions.

Because they were not illusions.

They were real.

Now they all lay dead in their graves. Carter, Thurston, Kellar, Bancroft, Edmund, that lout Houdini, and all the rest. How he *hated* Houdini. Their souls moved on to wherever they were taken, and their influence on the world left only in their legacies.

He wondered if Houdini had ever really tried to answer the call from one of the seances that was held every year in an attempt to summon him. It was a curious thought. Perhaps he had wished to appear but could not. Or, more likely, his desire to prove spiritualism false kept him away.

Houdini had always been such a cynical bastard.

Julian forced himself to focus. He was going to break more of the emerald green leaded glass if he was not careful. The glass he had purchased to match her eyes so perfectly would be the main feature of the monogram he was creating to sit prominently in the center of the masterpiece he was sculpting.

The internet was not without its uses.

He might have been a curmudgeon when it came to technology, but he was also an ardent neophile. Well, as much as he could keep up with it. It all seemed to be in more of a rush than he was. The fact that he could order quite literally anything to be delivered to his door was too convenient to ignore. Especially since he could not leave the property.

The phone calls came in answer to the listing in drips and drabs, and he found most of them disappointing. There were none, save one, he had wished to meet in person. And he was so very glad he had made the decision to invite her in. He remembered her standing at the foot of his stairs, gazing up at the fourth-floor tower, her large green eyes caught in wonder and wariness.

The memory of meeting Alice for the first time made him smile as he smoothed the sharp edge of the glass with a piece of sandpaper. She had looked up at him with such curiosity. He had been surprised by what he had seen in her. Beauty, yes. But also untapped potential. A woman who had been ignored by society and relegated herself to mediocrity.

There was no greater curse than that.

He had vowed free her from that cage. She would know who she truly was. And as he had begun to dig and peel away the layers, what a stunning, captivating, *naughty* little creature he had found.

Now he was grinning. He had desired her from that very first second. He had wished to pin her up against the wall the moment he had seen her. But that would likely have scared her off. No, he needed to ease her into the reality of his...condition.

The excuses came easily after so many years of practice. *I'm ill. My house is a disaster. I have agoraphobia. My car is in the shop.* People were so quick to dismiss that which they did not want to believe. "Charles" was only one name in a growing list of those he had adopted so he could walk his house during the day unchecked and run his own business the way he saw fit.

Who was going to accuse him of actually being the impossibly powerful ghost of Julian Strande? No one. They would be carted away in a straitjacket for their trouble. No one had ever batted an eye. The guides who worked his home were never there for long enough to spot the problem. He would shut down the museum for a few years on claims of maintenance, fire the staff, change his name, and begin again.

"Charles" was a lie. As had been "Arthur" and "William" before him.

And soon...Alice would know the truth.

How he wished to tell her himself, to rip back the curtain and show her how the trick was done. But she needed to find out on her own. If he forced it on her, she would shatter. Or worse, she would not forgive him. She would climb into her car and speed off for the horizon, and he would lose her forever.

He could not let that happen.

The thought of her leaving him burned a hole through his soul. Even the image of the idea made him ache. He did not know what would happen to his mind if she abandoned him.

He loved her.

More than life—or afterlife, as the case may be—itself.

This newest project of his was hidden in one of his many secret chambers, one not even Alice would be able to find. She was fiendishly intelligent, but he was a genius.

Not to mention...this room didn't have doors.

Convenient thing, being able to walk through walls.

And while he would invite her to see every room and uncover every secret before long, these darkest places of his house he would keep to himself until she was ready. Until she was truly his.

They had spent so many days and nights in each other's embrace. She was his perfect match. He had never been happier than when he was in her arms. Soon, she would know that she loved Julian Strande.

Soon she would know there was no Charles Mensonge. He was so terribly happy she did not speak any French.

He was confident she would accept him once she knew the truth. She might think she loved "Charles," not Julian, but as Charles, he did not play a persona. Charles was not a character; he was merely an alias. Soon, she would understand that the ghost and the man were one and the same. Soon, she would revel in the wicked things he, Julian, could truly do to her.

The memory of her locked in his puzzle box, arching into his touch, moaning and gasping out his name, made him pause in his work to shudder in bliss. Soon, she would understand what a man in his unique condition could do to a woman. And he knew she would welcome his devilish pleasures with open arms. She was a wicked thing. She may not know it about herself, but he could see it clear as day.

He groaned at the ideas that raced through his mind of what he could do to her.

He really was an impatient man.

Loving her as Charles was hardly disappointing, he had to admit. But anything that did not reach its true potential was a crime in his eyes. And oh, to what heights he could take her.

The piece of stained-glass he had cut was perfect. The curl of the embellishment on the letter was flawless. Prideful, he placed it down with the rest. The lettering was nearly complete. Then, once he had all the parts, he would begin to assemble his gift to her. The most important gift he could ever give her.

A wedding gift.

A very personal, very special wedding gift.

"When I find you, you owe me a surprise." That was what Alice had said to the empty air when she vowed to solve the puzzle of his existence.

And what a surprise it would be.

He let his finger trace the monogram as if he were a fountain pen. Two letters, curled around each other like vines, made to mimic his own prolific logo.

A.S.

Alice Strande.

"You will be mine," he whispered to the empty air. "You will be my bride."

IT WAS LATE SPRING, and she could finally sleep with the windows of the carriage house open. There was nothing quite like being able to let fresh air in for the first time after a thickly cold winter.

Something about it made everything cozier. She could bask in the breeze underneath a warm blanket. Her current company didn't hurt, either. Charles had essentially moved into the carriage house with her. They were hardly apart anymore, and she couldn't have been happier for it.

She was lying in his arms, her head on his chest. It was late morning on a Sunday. He had started to take the day off with her or working only in the afternoon so they had more time to spend together.

His fingers were slowly tracing the circles of a blue and lavender swirl on her shoulder. He loved the large tattoo she had, and often made a point of kissing along its entire length. Not that she'd ever complain. He was incorrigible, and she loved every second of it.

"I'm always surprised you have so much ink," he murmured down to her. "A shy, introverted girl like yourself. I suppose people are often more than what they seem."

"Books by their covers." She smiled and shut her eyes, enjoying the feeling of him against her. Warm. Comfy.

"What made you get it?"

"I guess I wanted to remind myself not to be boring. To not always do what's expected of me. I was always trying to do what I was told, and I suppose I wanted a part of me to be unexpected. *Alice in Wonderland* is a masterpiece to that effect. I've loved the story since I was a little girl. My aunt used to read it to me all the time. She was in her late forties when they adopted me, and I don't think she knew what else to do with me."

"I admit I've never read it. I've seen the Disney cartoon."

"I think you'd really enjoy it. I'll loan you my copy. I've had it since I was little. It's one of the few things I own that I really treasure."

"You'd trust me with it?"

"Of course."

He kissed the top of her head. "I'd be honored."

"I always identified with the Alice from the book. She was always wishing her life could be something special, or that she could go where she could be someone important. She leaves the world of expectations and goes somewhere she can be free. I always wanted that."

"It's also a dangerous world, isn't it? With the Red Queen and the Jabberwocky and all that."

"It is. But what fun is a world where everything is safe?" She put her hand on his lower abdomen. "A little danger can be fun. And sexy."

He grunted. "God, I love you."

She laughed and pushed herself up onto her elbow to lean in and kiss him. He lifted his head to meet her, and the hand on her lower back pulled her firmly against him. She knew very well what she was doing.

When he grabbed her wrist, she tried to yank out of his grasp. It was all playful, and a dance they had done many times before. He growled and rolled over. She fought, and he fought back. But before long, she found herself pinned on her stomach with both her wrists trapped in his hands close to her head.

He kissed the hollow of her ear slowly. "I love you, Alice."

"I love you too."

She gasped as he bit down on her shoulder, and she let her eyes slip shut. She pressed her body up against his, seeking out some of the glorious friction she knew was about to follow.

He snarled and leaned his weight on her, stopping her squirming. "For once in your life, stop fighting, would you?"

"Never."

"Good girl."

THEY LAY TANGLED in the sheets once more, her body curled up against his. Julian smiled at her. She wasn't asleep but basking in the glow of what they had done. He would never tire of the feeling of being buried inside her, or of watching her exultation as they brought each other bliss.

He ran his fingers through her hair slowly, combing the long blonde strands. Her heartrate was only now simmering down, and he forced his to match.

He wondered if "normal" ghosts could do what he had mastered—remembering what it was to be human and alive in all ways. What a cold and empty existence it must be for those who could not. He had a fashion of an eternal, if stationary, life. He pitied the dead who lingered but could not do the same. For him, it was reflexive as riding a bike. He could eat and drink. He could cry tears. He could bleed. He could make love.

And how he wished to do the latter again, and again, and again. But the poor girl had her limits. There was something to be said for the aftermath and of the quieting of a sated hunger. The afterglow was beautiful and wonderful in its own right.

His stomach growled.

One hunger was replaced by another.

Alice laughed in his arms and leaned her head in to kiss his bare chest. "All right, all right, you fiend. I'll feed you. You're worse than my cat."

He chuckled. "I worked up an appetite. Do you blame me?"

"Not in the least. Waffles or French toast?"

"Why not both?"

She laughed louder and climbed out of bed. She picked up her pajamas from the floor where he had thrown them, and he watched as she slipped them on. He enjoyed every second of the view and was a little sad she was no longer naked, but he understood cooking like that was unwise.

"Waffles and French toast it is. You really are a food vacuum."

"I'm not the only vacuum in the house. You can suck like a—"

She threw a pillow at him, whapping him across the face and breaking off his salacious comment. He found himself laughing along with her and tucked the pillow beneath his head. He would get up in a moment, but he was comfortable for the time being.

"You're an ass, Charles."

"Mmhm." He wouldn't deny it. He was. Besides, she loved his commentary. She always had. "You love my ass."

"Yeah, yeah."

"Don't worry. It's mutual."

With a shake of her head, she left the room. He stretched out his long limbs and lay there with a broad smile. He took up most of the bed if he tried—something she was very eager to comment on.

Soon you'll be in my bed instead. It's much bigger. Much better suited for the two of us. He'd have to launder the sheets soon.

And dust.

His fourth-floor rooms were sadly neglected. Very soon, he'd be carrying her over the threshold. He would have to make sure the place was ready to welcome home his new wife.

Very soon, Alice. If I have anything to say in the matter.

And I am the master of my domain, aren't I?

2

THE MYSTERY of Julian Strande was not going to defeat her. *You might have been a genius, but I'm...um...persistent. That's good enough, right?* She smirked to herself as she tapped away at her computer.

She was almost done with the very first map of the Strande Estate. She was capturing the last few details of the basement. And it was there she had discovered her first lead into trying to figure out what was going on with the thirty-feet-in-diameter "mystery hole" in the middle of the house.

It spanned all three floors and the basement. A perfect circle in the very center, like a cylinder, stretching all the way up. She wished she could see what was on the roof, but the only way to see it was from the tower of Julian's apartment, and Charles had insisted that it was strictly off-limits.

If she weren't very painfully aware that the ghost of Julian Strande was not only *very* real, but always watching, she would have picked the lock and gone up there in a heartbeat. But with the threat of a wrathful spirit of a powerful magician—who practiced real magic, from the looks of things—she thought better of it.

The only clue she had to the mystery of the giant gap in the center of the house was sitting across from her now. She had her laptop propped up on a stack of boxes in the basement. She was staring at the clue. It was sitting there—a lock to a door she was desperate to open.

It was an old upright player piano that was battered by time and neglect. The ivory keys were yellowed and cracked. The stain of the wood was dark and unmaintained, looking nearly black in the dim lighting of the naked bulbs along the ceiling.

The stained-glass emblem on the front, emblazoned with the ubiquitous J.S. monogram, was dusty and clouded.

Most importantly...it was built into the wall. The wood projected back into the stone. No amount of tugging and yanking on it budged the instrument in the slightest. She knew; she'd tried. A lot.

It was also the only hint to an entrance to the empty gap in the middle of the house that she had seen. She had scoured every square inch of the walls on every floor trying to find a hidden passage. She found a few others in the process. Doors and alleys between rooms that even Charles said he hadn't known about. The place was riddled with them. They arced between rooms in patterns and pathways that made no sense. Some led to narrow stairs that switched between floors with no discernable pattern.

Julian was a genius. No doubt about that. But he was also maybe, just maybe, a little bit insane.

And now she was staring at the lock to what she was certain was the answer to the whole mystery. That broken player piano. She walked up to it and pressed every key on it. Each one answered with a hollow *thunk* or a click. She had tried to open the piano to fix it or to see if there were switches on the inside she could trigger, but there was no way to get inside of it that she could see. No panels or latches. It was built to be inaccessible, or perhaps it had been assembled from the other side. But that was impossible. There were no other entrances into the thirty-foot chamber. If somebody built it from the other side, they would have either died inside or been able to walk through walls.

Like a ghost.

She sighed.

She'd considered taking her jigsaw or a hammer to the piano, but the looming promise of an angry ghost was enough to dissuade her. She had to solve this mystery the hard way. She knew he wanted her to find him; he'd said as much in his notes to her. But he would want her to do the legwork.

No cheating.

There were other big gaps in the house, mostly in the basement. She had no idea how to get to them, although it wasn't from a lack of trying. She would have to save those for another time.

Chewing her lip, she ran her hand along the stained-glass window in the face of the upright piano and thought over what she had to work with. Julian's journal was a wealth of information, but she couldn't access even half of it yet. The hint he had given her on the note tied to the second wooden rose had been a start, but she quickly hit a dead end.

It wasn't a simple cypher, which would be one letter per symbol. That'd be too easy, oh no. Julian Strande would never let something be so simple. It was a cypher built on top of a shorthand system she couldn't quite figure out. Only certain letters seemed to be combined with others, but she couldn't figure out which ones they were.

She counted her clues.

She had his journal, but it was still a mystery.

She had her map of the house, which was growing more detailed with every passing day. She was still working on building a three-dimensional model of it to print like a doll-house for Charles as a surprise. She was about halfway through the digital model. It didn't have all the bells and whistles, but because it was going to be quarter-inch scale, she didn't have to worry about capturing every piece of trim and decoration.

Modeling the infinity tower over the foyer had been a *bitch.* But it was worth it. Turned out it was only three stories tall, despite the fact that it looked like it soared up hundreds of feet. That had been her suspicion, but it was nice to know for sure. Now that she knew Julian could do *real* magic, she hadn't been quite certain it hadn't actually been some weird interdimensional, pocket-reality...thing.

She also had a single sheet of music Julian had given her a few weeks ago. He had drawn it for her.

A proverbial lightbulb went off in her head. "Oh, my god, I'm an idiot!" She tore upstairs as fast as her legs could take her, running past Greta and a few of the other guides.

"What's on fire?" Greta called after her.

"Nothing! I'm fine!" She rounded a corner and nearly collided with Charles.

"Whoa! Whoa, there. What's all the hubbub?" He caught her shoulders and laughed.

"I think I figured something out. I have to go get something. I'll be right back—meet me downstairs by that weird piano." She slipped out of his hands, smiling at him, beaming. This might solve it! Maybe Julian had given her the solution, and she hadn't realized what it was for. She kicked herself for sitting on it for this long.

After nearly dropping her keys on her porch, she ran into the carriage house, barely stopping to pet her cat, who was very put out that she hadn't come home early for his sake. "Sorry, Loki. I'll feed you later." She snatched the piece of hand-drawn sheet music from her growing stack of notes and repeated the run back into the house. When she skidded to a stop in the basement, Charles was already there, leaning against a post with a deeply amused look on his face.

She was huffing, and she had to stop to catch her breath. "What?"

"You're adorable when you're excited."

"I think—I think I know how to open that." She pointed at the piano.

"Open it?"

"I think it's a door. I think it's the way into that gap in the center of the house."

"Oh..." He studied the piano with renewed interest. "I guess that would make sense. Weird. And you think that piece of music he gave you is the key?"

She placed the sheet music on the piano and, putting her hands on the keys, played the notes and chords. Well, she pressed the keys. They didn't make a sound save for the hollow clunks and ticks. When she finished the tune, she held her breath.

And waited.

And waited.

Letting out a rush of air, she sighed. She played it again.

And waited.

Nothing happened.

"Damn it!" She pounded her hands on the keys and hung her head.

An arm slipped around her shoulders as Charles hugged

her to his side. "I'm sorry."

"I should've known he wouldn't make it that easy. I should've guessed he'd make me work harder for it." She picked up the sheet music and glared at it, as if it were the paper's fault she wasn't smart enough to figure it out. "I bet if I posted this shit on the internet, a bunch of puzzle nerds would solve it in a day."

"Why don't you do that, then?"

"Because...I want to be the one to do it. Julian's left this for me and nobody else." She let out another long, beleaguered sigh and leaned into him. "I don't know why he picked me, but I don't want to fail at this."

Charles kissed her temple. "I bet he finds you as sexy as I do. Correction, I know he does, from what you've said he's done." He snickered. "He's probably basking in the attention this way instead of what he'd really love to get from you." His hand trailed down to her ass and squeezed.

"Hey!"

"All mine, Uncle Julian. Mine. Not yours. Remember that."

She swatted at his chest and laughed. "Yeah, yeah. What've I said about taunting the dead guy?"

"Fine, fine." He poked a few of the piano keys idly. "I think you're right, though. I think this is a lock. It makes total sense. I've never really thought of it as anything other than some more weird junk in the basement."

She slipped away from him to put the sheet of music on top of her laptop's keys. Furrowing her brow, she studied it again, hoping she might see something in it she hadn't seen before.

Wait. What the hell is—

With a gasp, she plucked the paper up again.

"What? What is it?"

She pressed it to her computer screen.

"Julian, you *asshole!*"

"What did you just say about taunting the dead guy?" Charles was standing next to her now, peering over her shoulder.

Watermarks. The paper was watermarked! She couldn't see them without the backlight. When she had placed it on her keyboard, the glow of the keys had been enough to reveal a hidden symbol over one of the notes. Now, pressed up against the backlight from her screen, she could see each arrangement of the notes had a glyph attached to it.

The letter combinations suddenly made sense. The missing letters from the cypher weren't words. His shorthand symbols were *chords!* And he had given her barely enough to start figuring out the pattern. "Holy shit, Julian, thank you. You're the best." She was grinning from ear to ear and couldn't wait for her shift to end before she started plowing through his journal again.

"I thought you said he was an asshole?" Charles teased as he kissed her cheek.

"He can be both." She turned to kiss his lips instead and hooked her arms behind his neck. "Must be another thing you get from him."

"Hey. I am not an asshole. I'm a jerk, a jackass, a tease, a freak, and I'm insufferable." He listed off all her most frequent playful insults. "But not an asshole."

"Okay, fine. I'll give you that." She leaned up to kiss him again. She was so excited. That, and she loved to kiss him.

"Wanna fuck on the creepy piano-door thing?" he murmured against her lips.

"I'm still on the clock."

He sighed heavily. He knew what that meant. It was her only hard and fast rule regarding their relationship. Nothing happened while she was technically being paid to be his employee. It never stopped him from asking. Again. And again. And again. "What if I gave you the rest of the afternoon off to work on your new puzzle?"

That was incredibly tempting. "I still think I'd rather not hump on the old piano." When he pulled her against him, she laughed and gently nudged him away.

He shrugged it off. "You still get the afternoon off. You won't be able to focus with that new clue buzzing in your head."

"Really?"

"The broken things'll be waiting for you tomorrow. They aren't going anywhere."

She was smiling like an idiot again. "Thank you!"

"Anything for you. Now, shoo, and go find Uncle Julian. Maybe he'll shut up once and for all if somebody finally solves his stupid riddles."

Picking up her laptop, she shut the screen with the sheet music trapped in between it and the keyboard. She kissed him on the cheek as she left, heading back to eagerly begin cracking the code.

"CHARLES" watched her walk away from him, and he smiled wistfully. He would miss these days when they were over. He loved watching her face light up with joy with each new revelation. The game he played with her was a diabolical one, but he loved it too much to give up.

And it was necessary.

He walked up to the old and broken-looking player piano and let his hand trace along the top of the lid. It was not in disrepair. It was precisely as it had always been. He had designed it this way very much on purpose. So important, so obvious, but so easy to overlook. Nobody paid any mind to junk in some dusty old basement.

Soon, his game would be over. Perhaps in the next week or two, she would crack his little code. She would learn the whole of his secret, and he would be able to reveal himself for what he really was.

The greatest joy in an illusion was the reveal. The punchline. The moment all the setup culminated to create. And this was his greatest trick of all. Watching her discover it would be absolute ecstasy for him.

And not long after that, he would have an eternity of new games to play with her. This one might end, but so many more lay before them.

Come find me, my little rabbit. Come play with me.

I'm so impatiently waiting for you.

SHE WORKED TIRELESSLY into the night. Charles had complained at her long enough for them to order some pizza. Two, as usual. One for him, and a few slices of the other for her. He was asleep in bed behind her and had tiredly asked her not to stay up too late.

She had agreed, but the hours were slipping past her like seconds. The mystery was starting to unravel before her eyes, and with every thread she chased, the knots began to come undone. The marks on the notes were the beginning of a pattern. It wasn't the whole solution—Julian wanted her to work for it—but it was enough to unlock the system.

Each of his shorthand symbols was a chord. The key of the music was set by the sheet music he had given her. D minor. Of course, he'd write his music in the minor key.

When she had those words sorted out, it led her to the next. A minor. And then the next was C minor. F minor, and then she had the whole scale.

She'd cracked his code. Bit by bit, page by page, she translated all the symbols of gibberish into the Excel document she was using to track it. Each symbol she found had a letter or letter combination associated with it, and in the next cell over, she filled in the answer of what it meant.

She had transcribed the entire journal using that method into a little piece of software she had noodled up. She wasn't a coder—it was a terrible program, and it was buggy as shit—but it would do. Once she was done translating every symbol, or close to it, she could hit *enter* and watch it spit out a translation.

Maybe. If it didn't crash.

It usually crashed.

The hours rushed by. She knew she should sleep. Her eyes were more tired than her brain, and the glow of the screen was starting to do weird things to her. But she didn't care. She was so close to having her answer and to finally cracking Julian's journal.

It was at around three in the morning when she had finally done it. Once she knew where to start and she could start to see the pattern, everything else fell into place. Her spreadsheet was done. Every symbol had its matching answer.

Her finger hovered over the key. Once she hit *run*, that was going to be it. Unless it crashed. But if it succeeded, she'd have her answers. Something told her it was only going to lead her on another goose chase. Julian was a puzzle wrapped in an enigma and boxed in a myth. She didn't think this was the end of her search.

She honestly hoped it wouldn't be.

The idea of it being over was what made her hesitate. There was so much fun in the solving—in the doing—that after she had finished, she worried she was going to feel hollow. It was like the letdown that always hit her after Christmas. All the hype, all the anticipation, and then it was over.

Something told her, deep down, the solution to this mystery was going to be one that would change her life. She didn't know why. It was that edge of a cliff she lingered on as well, wondering what would happen if she ever did find Julian.

What would he do?

Charles had suggested he might finally rest in peace once someone had solved his code. She highly doubted that. Julian didn't strike her as someone with unfinished business. He didn't strike her as someone who left anything undone. If he wanted to rest, he'd be resting. He wouldn't rely on some dorky girl from San Jose to help him. He was doing this for fun.

They were playing poker. But what was in the pot? What was she gambling with?

She shook her head. Her mind was wandering. She was exhausted. She'd run the program and get a few hours of sleep since it took some time to process, anyway. The journal was long with all the symbols packed in tightly and in odd places.

I'm being a coward. I've always been afraid to take risks.

She looked over her shoulder at Charles's sleeping form. He had shown her the value of gambling. He had done so much to pull her out of her shell in the five months since they had met.

A little danger is a good thing.

She turned back to her keyboard and hit *enter.*

3

The Discoveries of the Impossible Julian Strande
Or; The Faustian Tale of a Magician's Curse
Or; How I Sold My Soul

A FOREWORD.

How did I sell my soul?

How did I do it, you ask?

That is the first question I expect you to demand of me, so here it is.

I didn't.

I never once summoned Lucifer from his fiery depths to look into eyes as black as pitch and sign a contract bound in blood. There were no laughing imps in the corners of the room who might mock me as I signed away my immortal soul.

Neither Beelzebub, nor Mephistopheles, Bael, nor Mammon, Leviathan, nor Asmodeus give a single rat's ass about a human soul. Not even mine, and I carry myself in quite the highest regard, as you might expect. Very high regard indeed. But in hell, I suspect a human is worthless currency.

I'm sure that is a disappointment to whomever might be reading this.

Good on you, by the by, decoding my little piece of work. I can't imagine it was the sole work of a single individual. I hope it took many generations of effort from many brilliant minds to uncover what I have laid here. Otherwise, I would not be as much of a genius as I expect that I am, and we can't have that, now, can we? But I digress.

So how did I create my impossible illusions? How did I discover real magic? How was I able to walk through solid walls, disappear in the blink of an eye, and conjure apparitions from the ether? Simple. I did not sell my soul, gentle reader.

I sold my life.

In parts.

For that is the fuel that drives the magic of the damned. That is the kindling upon the flame. That is the cost one must pay to ink into the fabric of the universe one's sheer will. I paid for my power in drops of blood. In the length of the wick of my life's candle, I spent my body in pursuit of it all.

And I would gladly—very gladly—do it again.

I write this journal in my last days. The deed is done. The price is paid. I am dying. I have perhaps a few more sunrises to go before my body is cold and still.

But I do not plan to exit this world, my gentle reader. Oh, no. Not I. I shall linger on until the sun burns this world to dust. I shall stay here and guard my mausoleum until madness takes me. I shall keep my soul on this plane. I do not wish to embrace the ever-after. Hell holds no interest for me.

But perhaps, someday, my house will be destroyed. Come wrecking ball or earthquake, or plague of fire, and my home might be destroyed. With it will shatter my greatest achievement. Think upon my words. While my body may break as the vessel for my soul within a few more ticks of the clock—another eagerly awaits to accept it instead.

I know the next question you would ask me. I can hear it clear as day. "Why, Julian? Why sell your life for power?"

If you must ask me such a thing, I fear you shall never understand.

I tired of lingering in the shadows. I could see this world in a way no others could. Where others may seek to define this world as linear, as black and white and flat upon a page, I saw it in its full glory. I perceived the world in all its mighty dimensions, and I would control them all.

If you have found this dusty tome in the shelves of someone's collection, then I write this guide for you. If you have found this upon the bookcase of my own home...you will not live long enough to see the dawn.

This is my warning to you, gentle reader. If you continue any farther through these pages and my soul still clings to the joists and rafters I designed for the express purpose to cheat not death, but life—run.

For there will be nothing to save you from me.

JULIAN PRETENDED TO BE ASLEEP. He always did. He rested, but not in the same way as he had when he was a mortal. But he would happily lie here, holding his blissfully unaware betrothed, and pretend. It meant she did not suspect him as he watched her work eagerly into the early morning hours at solving her puzzle. Correction, *his* puzzle.

He watched her fingers hesitate over the button he knew would run her ingenious little translation program. Why? Why did she pause? Did she sense the danger in climbing farther down the treacherous hole he had carved for her?

Do it, little rabbit. Come play with me. Come see what I have done.

Her finger struck the key, and he had to fight his desire to smile. She yawned, stretched, arching against her chair, then climbed into bed beside him. He let himself murmur in false disturbance of sleep and rolled over to hold her, slinging an arm eagerly over her torso to pull her against him.

She smelled like lavender. He would never tire of it. Nuzzling his nose into her hair, he felt the warmth of her body against his. He would covet her until the end of time.

Slowly, her breath began to smooth. Before long, she was in the rhythm of sleep. He slipped away from her then, careful not to disturb her. He disappeared from the bed entirely, vanishing his body into nothingness. She didn't move.

Gathering himself back together, he pulled out the chair from the desk by the wall and sat at her laptop. He did hate the way electronics tingled on his fingers, but it would be worth it for this.

He watched as the program began to translate his works, page by page, word by word. She had done it. His wicked little girl had solved his puzzle. He had given her only the necessary blocks—that which made it possible. She had done the rest.

He sat and watched as it printed out the words he had written. It was in a "text document." He had to use them from time to time. Or worse, to send...*emails*. He hated them. But they were necessary. Slowly but surely, the world was pulling him into the modern ways.

When it finished an hour or so later, he was quite impressed. Smiling like the malicious fool that he was, he lifted his fingers to the keys and added a little note for her at the very end. Vanishing back into nothingness, he slipped back into the bed and took shape once more. The slow gathering of weight didn't disturb his beautiful prize.

Imagine the fun we'll have together when you know who I really am. When you pull back the curtain and find the surprise that's waiting for you.

Imagine the fun we'll have when you are free to be what you are meant to become.

He placed a kiss, slow and passionate, against her shoulder. He couldn't help himself. It seemed he was caught in the perpetual need to have her. But she had worked herself to exhaustion, and she needed her rest. After one kiss, he forced himself to stop and simply enjoy her presence.

There will be plenty of time to ravage you later.

He smiled.

And I will.

ALICE AWOKE WITH A STARTLED SNORT. Her printer was running. What the hell? Charles whined loudly from beside her, clutching her and burying his head into her shoulder. He hated getting up early, and she couldn't say as she blamed him.

Why *the fuck* was her printer running?

She nudged away from him to climb out of bed. He groaned and buried his head under the pillow, pressing it down over his face in a clear attempt to blot out both the sound and the morning light.

Rushing over to her computer, she saw it was printing... the journal. Her translation program had finished. But why —how—how did it start printing on its own? She scrambled to stop it but was too late. By the time she got to the printer utility, it had already finished. It was tightly packed and double-sided, so it only wound up being fifty pages or so.

She sat in the chair and looked down at the pile of papers. She turned it over and stared at it in astonishment.

I did it. I really did it. I translated the book!

She ran her fingers over the title then eagerly began reading the forward.

"Seriously?"

She looked up over at the bed, Charles snapping her focus. He was sleepily glaring at her as best he could, but it only managed to come off as adorably disgruntled. She smiled. "Sorry. It printed itself."

"Uh-huh. Sure, it did." He yawned and plonked his head on the pillow. "Have you been at it all night?"

She checked the clock and saw it was eight in the morning. "No, I got a solid four and a half hours of sleep in there."

"Great." He yawned again, grunted, and accepting the inevitable, climbed out of bed. He always distracted her whenever he was shirtless. She couldn't help but enjoy the view. Long, lithe, and not nearly as skinny as he might appear at first glance. He was that damn tall. Not to mention, he was graceful. He moved with practiced skill. He was a magician, after all. But he seemed not to notice her staring as he trudged toward the door. "I'll make coffee."

"Try not to burn it this time. I don't even know how you manage. It's automatic."

"Where there's a will, there's a way," he mumbled as he headed downstairs.

Chuckling, she turned back to her printout and eagerly began to read.

It took her the better part of the day to make it through Julian's journal. It was fascinating. She could barely put it down. Charles gave her another day off so she could devour it. He said she was going to be reading it anyway, so she might as well feel like she could.

He had gone up to the house to do *his* job, though, and left her to it. She was sitting on her sofa, surrounded by papers. She had begun to circle all the interesting parts as she made her way through it. She had to stop herself from highlighting everything.

It was an instruction manual. Julian was eager to explain why all the other great magicians—both on stage and off—were idiots. They never bothered to piece everything together. Each of them thought they had all the answers and never bothered to look at the bigger picture.

It was the parts detailing how he designed the house that she paid the most attention to. Not that she wasn't interested in how to summon green flame from the palm of her hand, or to summon and capture spirits, but they weren't going to lead her to the answer of where Julian had hidden his body in the house.

Now she knew *why* he had built the house the way it was. The whole thing was designed to capture souls and to keep them contained. But she was over two-thirds of the way through, and still she had no other answers. He hadn't yet mentioned the void in the center of the house. He only described all the books he referenced and all the bits and pieces he used. He confirmed he never drew out plans for the house. He only told the workers each day what they would be doing next, and painstakingly oversaw the construction himself.

But pieces still seemed to be missing. Information had

been left out of the book. When she reached the end, she froze.

Something was written there, a few lines down from the end of his journal.

"Come find me, Alice. You have everything you need. If I might give you a piece of advice, do not approach this from the top down. –J.S."

She referred back to the journal, but she didn't find anything added at the end. The text ended right where the translation seemed to have finished working. The added sentences were put in after her program had run but before it had been printed.

She remembered the printer running on its own.

She sighed and shut her eyes. It hadn't run on its own; it had been Julian. Naturally. She shook her head. She read through the whole book again and took more notes, adding to her sheets where he had drawn magical circles. They seemed interspersed through the book with intention. He hadn't placed them there randomly. Julian didn't seem to do anything by chance. This was all very careful planning.

She only had to put the pieces together.

Put the pieces together, she furrowed her brow. Where had she read that? She flipped through the pages until she found where he had mentioned the "other great magicians" and how they had failed to do exactly that.

She remembered the other books in the fourth-floor apartment. Books like *The Magus*, the *Black Pullet*, and the *Grand Grimoire*. Of course! She shuffled all the papers together, grabbed the journal and her laptop, and stuffed them into her bag.

Right when she was heading for the door, her phone rang. She picked it up. Charles's photo appeared. She had taken a shot of him holding Loki up by his face. The cat had his paw planted flat on the man's nose, and she thought it was the cutest thing ever.

"Hey," she said.

"I have to drive into town for an errand, then I should head home and grab my mail. I'll be back in a few hours, okay?"

"No problem. See you soon. Love you."

"Love you."

And with that, she tucked her phone into her pocket and headed into the house. It was a little after closing, and the guides were still packing up to leave. "Lock up behind you, but leave the lights on," Alice called to Greta as she passed. "I'll be here for a little while."

"Gotcha. Have a good night."

"You too."

Greta waved goodbye. She had been promoted to "manager on duty" recently, and she picked up the mantle easily. She liked the girl, and as far as she could tell, it was mutual.

Alice hummed to herself excitedly as she headed up to the study on the third floor that hid the bookcase that was, in truth, the door to Julian's fourth-floor apartment.

She hesitated before pulling the book that would release the mechanism. She took a step back and chewed her lip. She hadn't been up here alone since...since he had invited her upstairs.

Her face went warm at the memory of what Julian had done to her when she had been shackled in that magic box prop. She had climbed in willingly. She had wanted it. She had wanted Julian. But now, that had changed. She was spoken for.

"Julian." She pulled her bag tighter to herself. "This isn't an invitation to mess with me. I'm not up here because I want to bang you. I'm trying to solve this puzzle, and I think you still have some pieces of it upstairs. Understand? No funny business. No getting handsy."

The bookcase clicked open on its own, swinging into the darkness beyond. She shivered and sighed. She didn't know if that was a yes or a no, but she knew it was all she was going to get from him. She walked up to the open doorway and fumbled for the light. Flicking it on, the stairwell lights sputtered to life.

Climbing the treacherous stairs to the attic, she could see barely well enough in the twilight outside to find the lights on her own. Turning them on, she blinked.

The place was...clean.

Dusted, at any rate. The glass on the counter was gone. His cigarette case of cloves was no longer there. The lights came on easily and, checking them, they had been replaced.

"Weird."

Charles must have come up here to organize and tidy up. He'd said he wanted to do as much the last time they were up there. Shaking her head, she went into the parlor where she had found the journal the first time. Crossing through the dining room, the plates that had sat there for a hundred and twenty years since Julian's disappearance were cleared away. Everything looked polished, like a maid had come through.

Charles wasn't nearly that thorough. He was always rushing whenever he cleaned, and she suspected he probably lived like a hoarder. That was the only reason she could think of that explained why every time she asked to see his house, he made excuses. He was an eccentric guy. She knew it and accepted it about him. He was always going to have those parts of himself he didn't want her poking around in, and she let it be.

Setting down her notes on the parlor coffee table, she

went up to the books. "Thanks for letting me poke around, Julian. I know you're a private guy. I saw your warning on the first page, and I'm glad you've let me try to do this. I don't know how many people you've killed who got too close."

"Only a few."

The whisper in her ear made her jump nearly a foot in the air. She hadn't heard or seen anything from Julian in months. She whirled and saw nothing in front of her. Only empty air. But she knew it wasn't true. She put her back to the shelf and waited. Nothing happened.

She suspected the rumors of the disappearances of people in the home weren't myths. She didn't want to accept the fact that Julian was a murderer, but she knew she was fooling herself when it came down to it.

Chewing on her lip again, she nodded. He was a killer. He had taken lives. But he didn't seem interested in murdering *her.* Lord knew he'd had plenty of opportunities, including right that very moment. It was possible he would change his mind the moment she found his body—and she was certain it was a when and not an if—but for now, she felt safe.

As safe as one could around a ghost who had...um...her face went warm at the memory, and she coughed, turning back to the bookcase. "Thanks again."

Something pressed into her from behind, and she had to brace herself on the shelves to keep from eating one. She felt hands resting on her sides. Warm fingers stroked her through her clothing—no, not through, *under.* Julian could touch her as if her clothing wasn't even there. She had forgotten how unnerving that was.

"What do I get in exchange?"

"Knock it off." She pushed back, and it felt like a solid wall. He didn't budge. "Julian. No."

The feeling of him vanished, and she let out a sigh of relief. He could force her if he wanted to. She couldn't fight him. She knew she'd be helpless if he tried to pin her down and have her. But he respected her enough to not go that far. She was more than a little grateful.

"Thank you. It's not you. It really isn't. I'm with Charles."

Silence.

She turned back to the books and began to pull all the tomes of black magic she could find. There were more than a few. Walking to the table, she set down the stack and began to flip through the first one.

About a third of the way through, she found a notation in the margins. Julian's code. Hah! She knew it! Picking up a pencil, she wrote the symbols down into her notebook. She took a photo of it on her phone, recording the page, the name of the passage, and what book it was in.

About an hour later, her phone rang. She picked it up and put it on speaker. "Hey, Charles."

"I'm back. Where'd you go? The lights in the carriage house are off."

"Fourth floor."

"What? You aren't screwing Uncle Julian all over the furniture, are you?"

She laughed. "No."

"Has he tried?"

"Yeah. And I said no."

"Hah, take that, Uncle Julian! More for me. Can I come up there and do it for him instead?"

"No, no. I'll finish up for now." She laughed and closed the books. When she went to pick up the stack and walk away, something slapped them out of her hands. They fell all over the floor, loudly tumbling over each other. "Shit!"

"What happened? You okay?"

"Yeah. I don't think Julian wants me borrowing his library."

"I'll be up there in a heartbeat. I'm pulling into the parking lot."

"I'm on my way down." She picked up the books and stacked them on the coffee table. "Message received, Mr. Strande. You're a one-book-at-a-time kind of library, and I have your journal."

Ghastly laughter seemed to echo through the house, but she wasn't quite sure. She had begun to believe everything was his fault lately.

She flicked her phone off speaker and pressed it to her ear, shouldering her bag with her notes and her laptop, and heading for the door. "I was thinking we could order from that new Chinese place that opened in town and—"

"Yes! Yes. I love Chinese food. I don't think I've had it in *years.*"

"I'll see you in a second. I'll meet you in the carriage house."

"Roger that."

She hung up and slipped her phone into her pocket. It was when she went to flip off the light switch that she felt a hand press against the back of hers. Warm. Firm, but not forceful, it trailed invisible fingers over the back of her hand and up her wrist before it slowly closed around it.

She could have pulled away. He gave her the chance. She didn't. The ghost held her wrist tightly enough that she could feel her own pulse thump against him. Louder and faster now than before.

Hot breath pooled against her cheek, and she turned her

head away from him reflexively. It didn't stop her from feeling the kiss he placed against her cheek. *"I am not a patient man."*

And with that, he was gone. She shivered and quickly flicked off the lights and left the apartment without a single glance behind her.

She didn't want to see if he was standing there waiting for her.

4

WHY WAS HE NERVOUS?

Why in the ever-loving *hell* was he nervous?

He was dead. He had been dead for a very long time. He had cut off portions of his life and spent it on power and immortality. He had fashioned a house designed from the foundation up to keep his soul inside it for all eternity. In these walls, he was not only a king, he was a god.

But he was nervous.

He was fidgeting like a schoolboy, fussing with his clothing. He had buttoned his vest wrong four times before he forced himself to breathe, stop, and try again. It was Friday night. He had a show in half an hour, but that wasn't why he felt frantic. He had performed thousands of times by this point in his existence. Never once was he worried he would fail to entertain the crowd or that his illusions wouldn't land.

Looking in the mirror, he inspected his reflection. He was as he should be. Blue and brown eyes staring back at himself. Not the hazel lie he maintained in order to keep suspicions at bay. He was dressed in his finest. He had pulled it from his wardrobe, dusted it off, and smoothed the lines of the tuxedo. He hadn't worn this in many, many years.

But tonight was a special occasion, after all. Tonight was going to be a very special show indeed.

Picking up a small box from his dresser, he slipped it into his pocket and disappeared, taking all of it with him. The box, its contents, his clothes, everything. Sometimes it was terribly convenient being a ghost. The only downside was he couldn't walk the world like a mortal man. That said, he found he really did not care. It was well worth the exchange.

Especially since the invention of cable television.

The crowd was gathering in his theater. They were already taking their seats. Alice was in attendance. She had yet to miss a single show, as she had promised. He smiled, ephemeral and invisible, bodiless and intangible as it might be, as he pressed down through the floors of his home toward the theater.

Alice. Oh, Alice.

Tonight will be a very special performance.

Alice stood by the back wall and watched from there. She had only counted one or two shows in the dozens she had seen since she began working at the Strande Estate that hadn't been sold out. There wasn't a seat in the audience that didn't already have a butt in it, and she felt bad taking a chair that could go to a paying customer, no matter how many times Charles offered.

She really didn't mind standing, anyway.

The show, as always, was fantastic. Charles was so

goddamn talented, and he always took her breath away. She hated to admit that the sight of him in his Julian costume did terrible things to her. It always twisted a knot in her stomach every time she got a chance to have her way with him—or more often, vice-versa—in the outfit. Something about him seemed to come unhinged when he wore the old clothes and put in the contacts. Something about pretending to be his great-granduncle gave him the freedom to express his darker side.

And, Christ, she loved every second of it.

After the last trick of the night, the crowd gave him a standing ovation as they almost always did. Only a few Saturday matinees had ever been too lazy to give the man the applause he was due. After he took a bow, he raised his hands to quiet the crowd.

"I have one more special treat for you all this night. One more trick I would like to perform. But this is a trick that, hopefully, I will ever only get to do the once. I will also admit I haven't practiced it at all. So, please be patient with me if I am not my usual, casually magnificent self." The crowd chuckled at his joke.

He took the center stage and smoothed his palms down the long lines of his suit. She hadn't ever seen him wear that one before. It was a full tuxedo that looked like it dated from the turn of the twentieth century, complete with coattails. Nobody should ever wear a cummerbund and look good, but damn if he didn't pull it off.

"I will need an assistant for this trick. But not merely any assistant. Ms. Monroe, will you please join me on stage?"

Alice blinked. What the hell was he up to now? The follow spots swiveled to find her, and she squinted against the light. The crowd applauded, and she realized she was stuck. She had to go through with this. She walked down the aisle nervously. She had only done this once before, and she had hated every damn second of it. He reached down to her and helped lift her up to the stage.

He flicked off his microphone and pulled her to stand in the center of the stage with him. "I promise this won't be like the last time you were on stage," he muttered to her with a playful grin.

Her face went warm, and she knew that had been his goal. Shooting him a glare, she shook her head and dismissed the comment. The last time she had stood on this stage, it had gone...uh...differently than she assumed it was going to go this time.

Flicking the microphone back on, he urged her to stand in front of him so they were facing each other parallel to the stage. "I need you to think of the happiest moment in your life, Ms. Monroe. I need you to close your eyes and focus on it. As hard as you possibly can."

Not knowing what he could possibly be up to, she shut her eyes. "Okay."

"Harder. Try to summon it with your mind. Think on the moment you were the absolute happiest in your life. Hold it on your hand and try to make it real. Try to summon it from the fabric of the universe."

The crowd gasped. She fought the urge to open her eyes and see what kind of amazing illusion Charles had conjured. She nodded and tried to focus. The happiest moment of her life sprung to her without warning. Sledding with her family on a trip up north to Washington. Mom, Dad, and her sister. Before the car accident that took them away. She was little, maybe five or six. But the snow was thick and fresh, and she remembered screaming in laughter as the world whipped past her on the toboggan. "Okay. I have it."

"Now, open your eyes and tell me if this doesn't beat it."

Opening her eyes, she felt like her heart stopped in her chest. Charles was on a knee in front of her. In his hand was a small black box, and in the fabric was a jeweled ring. A diamond with amethysts and emeralds surrounding it. Purple and green twined around a sparkling jewel in a beautiful, asymmetrical twist, mirroring the Art Nouveau style of the home.

Charles was smiling up at her, tears shining in his mismatched eyes. "Ms. Alice Monroe, will you marry me?"

"Yes—" she gasped as she held her hand out for him as he slipped the ring onto her finger. She was shaking so hard he could barely manage. "Yes! I will."

The crowd roared with applause. He stood, and she nearly knocked him off his feet as she threw her arms around his neck and kissed him with every ounce of love and happiness she had ever felt in her life.

He had asked her if this beat her previous happiest memory in her life.

It did.

It was late into the night before they finally could leave each other alone long enough to breathe. She was lying atop him, her body covered in sweat. She had attacked him with a vehement passion she hadn't known she had. He had responded in kind. She hadn't even let him take out the damn contacts.

The mismatched eyes were a little hot, she admitted to herself, although she'd never tell him that out loud. Something about it added a layer of mystery to him. A layer of something a little unsettling that thrilled her. And he hadn't seemed to mind in the slightest. When she had asked if he wanted to stop to take them out, he had chuckled and merely thrown her over the sofa to have his way with her.

Again.

She felt like she had run a marathon, and from his huffing breath, she knew he felt the same. She kissed his cheek and pushed up from the sofa, stretching her back, feeling it pop.

"Where're you going, fiancée of mine?" He smiled up at her, his fingers twining with hers.

"Shower. And getting some water. Maybe not in that order."

"Mmhn. I suppose I should join you." He stretched as well, looking every bit the sated jungle cat, and let out a low growl. "God damn, Alice. You know how to ride a man until he's sore."

"You did most of the work there, bucko. The rest isn't my fault." She chuckled and walked into the kitchen to fetch two glasses of water. She handed him one and chugged her own before heading to the bathroom. "I'm going to go clean off."

"Walk slowly. I'm enjoying the view. I'll be in there with you in a second."

She laughed and put her glass down on the counter as she passed it. "I don't know if I can go another round, Charles." She shot him a narrow and playful look before she left him in the living room.

"Pansy." He folded his arms behind his head and shut his eyes. "Fine, fine. I'll wait until you're done."

Shaking her head, she climbed into the shower and enjoyed the hot water on her skin. She cleaned herself off, glad to be rid of the sweat that was fine while it was warm but was going to get clammy as it cooled.

She marveled at the ring. She didn't take it off. She didn't want to. She leaned against the tile wall and ran her finger along it with a dreamy smile. *I'm going to get married. I love him. I love him so much.*

Cleaning her hair, she rinsed herself and turned off the water. Right when she turned the handle, she heard a squeak. The sound of a finger against the glass of the shower door. She turned with a smile to tease Charles for being unable to stay away and blinked. No one was there.

She saw writing on the door. She opened it and stepped out, not caring for the puddle she was going to leave on the floor. Closing it, she swallowed the rock in her throat.

A heart was drawn on the glass. Inside it read *"J.S. + A.S."* A.S.? What did that mean?

Alice Strande.

She felt her blood run cold, even before she read the writing that was scrawled underneath it in a handwriting she was beginning to recognize as Julian's. *"You're mine."*

Alice screamed.

WHAT A TERRIBLE AND wicked thing he was.

He had proposed to her in his true shape, as his true self, because he could not stomach the idea of her agreeing to marry Charles, and not while gazing into his mismatched eyes. Even if she believed she was marrying someone merely wearing a costume, she would know the truth soon enough. He needed her to marry *him,* not the lie. That said, scaring her in the shower had been too much fun to pass up. It had been too delightful an opportunity to ignore.

And how she had screamed. She had run into his arms and took shelter in his embrace. What a joy she was.

He delighted in her fear as much as he delighted in being the one to soothe it. He cradled her in his arms after helping her put on her pajamas. He had played the angry and concerned fiancé, vowing that she was safe and that "Uncle Julian" was only playing games. That it must be his way of congratulating them.

Alice had her head burrowed into the crook of his shoulder as they lay in bed. A cool breeze drifted through the room, carrying the fresh smell of the spring outdoors. The combination of his warmth and the chill air was calming her down.

He began to hum a quiet tune to her, further calming her. The poor thing was already almost asleep. It was quite late, well after two in the morning, and she was exhausted. He smiled up at the ceiling as he felt her struggle to stay awake in his arms. But she couldn't keep it up, and soon her breathing was regular and smooth.

"I meant what I said," he whispered, quiet enough that she couldn't hear him. "You'll be mine very soon." Leaning his head down to kiss her forehead, he smiled. "Only a little more work, and you'll find me. Keep looking, my love. You're so close."

So very close.

And then our fun will really begin.

5

After the message on the shower door, Alice refused to go up to the fourth floor on her own. Not even when Charles said it was fine. She insisted on dragging him along with her after hours one day. She needed to translate more of the symbols in the books, but she didn't dare walk up there on her own.

It was only inviting disaster.

Charles flicked the lights on and whistled. "Whoa, Uncle. Nice job sprucing the place up."

"I thought it was you." Looking around the place, it seemed like more work had been done to overhaul the space. It looked like the wood trim on the walls, and the furniture had been oiled.

"When've you known me to clean?" Charles snickered. "And I don't like it up here. You know that."

"Why's he doing this?"

"Maybe it's his way of saying you're welcome up here." Charles sat in one of the chairs. This time, there was no giant cloud of dust in his wake. "Maybe he's getting used to the idea of company."

"It's clear what he wants from me. And it's not anything I plan on giving him." She went to the parlor to pull some books from the shelf and brought them back to the living room. Setting them down, she began flipping through them, searching for Julian's notes.

"I don't think he's threatening you. Has he ever gone too far?"

"No. He tried the other day, and when I told him to stop, he did." She'd admit that much. She knew Julian could be doing far worse things with her. Ever since she told him to lay off, he obediently had been. Leaving her creepy notes was the most benign thing the ghost could probably do. "But I don't want to encourage him. It might make him do something awful."

"Like what?"

"I don't know. He might hurt you because he's jealous."

When Charles didn't answer, she looked at him. He had his fingers curled over his mouth, and he was watching her thoughtfully.

"What?"

"I never thought of that."

"I have. And it's a nightmare." She focused on the books. She wanted to find all the hidden writing as fast as she could. "I don't know what I'd do if I lost you." She choked up without meaning to.

"Hey. Hey." He moved to sit on the sofa next to her and pulled her into a firm hug. "I'm not going anywhere. Now, or ever. No matter what happens." He kissed her forehead gently. "I'm always going to be here with you."

Resting her head against his neck, she smiled and shut her eyes and let herself enjoy his presence and the rich and spicy smell of cloves that seemed to cling to him. She patted his leg and nodded when she felt better. "Thank you."

"Of course."

She went back to hunting through the books. It was slow going, sadly. She knew she couldn't get them all in one night. Julian had a great deal of tomes on magic. She probably had to comb through the rest of his books to be sure she didn't miss any.

Picking up a stack of papers, Charles leaned back in the sofa and kicked his feet up onto the coffee table. She'd tease him about it, but she knew it'd do no good. She'd fussed about him putting his shoes on the furniture in the carriage house, and he'd listen, but it lasted all of about seven seconds.

He leafed through the translation of Julian's journal with idle curiosity. "Man, my uncle was a freak, huh?"

"Apparently."

"I bet all those other magicians would shit bricks if they knew he was cheating and had real magic. Especially Houdini. Those two bastards hated each other, both being from Wisconsin and all."

"His rivals would probably want to do the same thing if they could."

"I don't know. Selling off your life piece by piece? Every time he used this shit, it killed him a little. That...that's some serious dedication to being rich and famous."

"I wonder if he regrets it."

"I doubt it. He could probably burn this place down if he wanted to."

"It's amazing what people will do for power, isn't it?" She sighed. "But I guess I can't blame him. Not really. I've never been anything special. If I had the chance to be something —I don't know. It's tempting. I don't think I'd do it, but I can understand why he did."

"You're special." Charles stroked his hand through her

hair slowly, tucking it behind her ear. "Don't talk like that. You're very special. Look at you, solving this puzzle when no one else has."

"I'm only able to solve it because he's given me the answers."

"No, he gave you the bits you needed to be able to solve it at all. You're doing the brunt of the work. You've put the rest of this together on your own." He traced the backs of his fingers across her cheek before resting his hand on her shoulder. "You're incredibly special."

Alice chuckled and shook her head. "You're supposed to say that. And besides, I think Julian killed everyone else who started sniffing around. He wants to bone me, and that's the only reason I'm still alive."

Charles laughed. "Well, I can't blame him for wanting to screw you, that's for sure." He sat forward and rested his chin on her shoulder, his arm draped around behind her. "Lord knows I can't seem to get enough of it."

"I'm going to stop you now. No. Not up here. Not on his bed, his sofa, his table, his piano, none of it."

"Damn." He grunted. "You're learning." He leaned back against the sofa, disgruntled.

When she turned to look at him, she found him smiling at her with a twinkle in his eyes. He was only pretending to be upset. He had cheered her up—again. He was very good at that. "Let me finish looking through this book, and then we can go. It's going to take a few trips up here to look through all the books."

"Oh, good. More of me sitting here, watching you flip through all this, while we *could* be screwing like rabbits." He let out an exaggerated sigh. "Oh, joy."

She slapped him in the stomach without turning to look at him, and he cackled.

"Now, let me concentrate."

He kicked his legs up on the sofa as he twisted sideways, draping himself along the cushions and behind her. "Wake me up when you're done."

"You can't possibly take a nap in the twenty minutes it'll take me to—"

Charles let out a loud, comical, and entirely fake snore.

She rolled her eyes and considered changing her mind.

Maybe Julian *should* push him down the stairs.

THE NOTES JULIAN had left in each of the books made no sense to her. Not at first. It took several days of finding them and translating them before she could even wrap her head around what she was looking at.

Each note on a page was a pair of numbers.

4, 7.

9, 12.

34, 2.

And so on.

She had begun generating a list of them, but she had no clue what to do with them. It seemed like nonsense. But it *had* to have meaning. It had to. Julian wouldn't go through all the trouble of hiding the symbols if they weren't clues to something.

On and on the list went, adding more sets of numbers to the pile. It was days of finding the numbers, translating them, and adding them to her list before she shrugged, and for lack of any better ideas, hit *graph* on the tab in Excel.

She had nearly shot coffee out her nose when she saw the result. Charles had laughed at her like she was an idiot. She probably was. She didn't care.

It was a pattern!

She didn't know what the hell the pattern meant, but it was definitely there. The points were drawn around zero in the very center. It looked weirdly familiar, but she couldn't place it. It was also very clearly incomplete. She needed to find more of the points to finish it.

A puzzle in a puzzle in a puzzle. *Thanks, Julian.*

She often found herself staring at the array of numbers, trying to make sense of it. As if glaring at the graph would help her solve it. She eagerly added more to the graph each time Charles was patient enough to sit up in Julian's apartment and watch her dig through every book the man owned, hunting for more hints. It was slow going.

She'd probably have found them all, but her time in Julian's apartments was limited. She had to wait for Charles to sit there with her. Like hell if she was going to risk sitting up in those apartments by herself.

Julian would take that as either an invitation or an opportunity, or most likely both.

Another week passed before she suddenly realized what the graph meant and what all those little dots represented.

That morning, she had started her work printing the three-dimensional model of Julian's estate. It was finally complete enough to begin printing it for assembly. She had been about to start running the basement parts. She planned to make each floor removable, as well as the exterior walls, so it could be peeled apart like a dollhouse.

When she was loading up the machine with the filament, it had struck her where she had seen the array of dots before. Scrambling frantically though her notes, she found the transparent printouts she had made of each of the plans of the house, one for each floor. She had gone to FedEx and printed them as black lines on clear plastic so she could see how each floor related to the previous one. It was the only way to make sense of it. The floors rarely connected to each other in a straight line, let alone the rooms.

She pulled up the graph on her computer screen and scaled it what she figured might be about the right size. Adrenaline rushed through her system. She looked up at the wooden head of Julian that still sat on the shelf by the far wall. "You clever bastard. You sick, ingenious, clever bastard."

Taking the transparencies, she stacked them together into a pile so she could see the whole house as one element, each floor laid onto the previous one. She held them up to her screen, pulling them a half an inch out until it all lined up.

The number sets weren't points on a graph. *There were points on a map.* Points on a map of the house itself!

She had been thinking about the graph in two dimensions. But it wasn't. They were points on a graph in *three* dimensions. She thought she had been playing regular chess with Julian this whole time and discovered she hadn't even realized there were boards above and below hers.

She remembered the warning in Julian's foreword of his journal. *"Where others may seek to define this world as linear, as black and white and flat upon a page, I saw it in its full glory. I perceived the world in all its mighty dimensions, and I would control them all."*

She groaned. The answer had been there the whole time, staring her in the face. He had given her everything she needed, and her own slow-ass head took that long to put it together. She had been thinking about his clues entirely the wrong way.

She ran the print operation on her computer and sent the new graph off to print from her networked setup in the carriage house. She would have to go up and get it. She was way too eager to start figuring out what those points on the map might actually mean. She knew she still didn't have them all, but it was a major lead.

She shut the door of the workshop behind her and turned—right into Charles. "Gah!" She jumped, startled, and put her hand to her chest. Damn it all. He would never stop sneaking up on her.

"What'cha doing?"

"Nothing." She lied, badly.

"I hear your printer going. What're you working on?"

"It's a surprise." She knew better than to tell him it was a part for a repair. He was fascinated by the work she did fixing up the mechanisms in the house, and she often found him poking around in the cabinets after she was done.

"Oh?" His face lit up. "Can I see?"

"It's a surprise, Charles." She laughed. "That defeats the purpose."

"I told you about me and surprises. I always peek."

She poked him in the chest. "Not this time. It's big, it's special, and I've been working on it for months now. Don't you even dare."

"But—"

"No peeking. Just this once. You can open every other gift I ever give you early if you want, but—"

"I have. You need to hide them in better places."

She glared and kept talking. "But not this one. Please? It means a lot to me."

His shoulders fell. "All right. For you. Because it matters to you." He bent his head to kiss her forehead. "You're late for lunch."

"I had a breakthrough." She held up the transparencies

that were tucked into her notebook. "I think I finally figured out what all those numbers he left in his books go to."

"Oh?"

"They're coordinates to the house. I don't know what he's calling out on the map yet, but I know it has something to do with why the house is built the way it is."

He blinked a few times. "Well, shit. That's incredible. Pretty soon, we can finally drop his moldy ass in a hole and call this job done, huh?"

She laughed. "I don't think he'd want us to move his body."

"What's the whole point of finding him, then?" He pulled her into his arms, lazily wrapping his arms around her waist.

"Because...I don't know. Because it's a puzzle worth solving." That was a really good question, and one she didn't really know the answer to. She had always felt the need to solve mysteries, but this one had gripped her. Not only her mind, but her soul. She felt intensely invested in it. "It's like Mount Everest. When somebody asked a climber why they wanted to go up it, they said 'because it's there.'"

"Mmhmm. I don't believe you." He grinned. "I think you want to find Uncle Julian to prove a point."

"What point would that be? That he's a jackass and this whole thing is needlessly complicated?"

"We know that. I think you want to find him because you want to prove to yourself you can do it. I think you want to show yourself you're smart enough. That you have value."

Shyly, she tucked her head onto his chest. He wasn't wrong. It wasn't the whole answer, but it was some of it. "I know, I know, you don't understand why I don't feel special in life."

"I get it. I think it's a big reason why Julian sold off his life for power. He did all this to feel like he had meaning, and now you're unraveling the mystery for the same reason."

Maybe that was it. She shut her eyes and cuddled into him. "Thanks, Charles. For a guy who always seems to stick his foot in his mouth, you're pretty good at saying the right thing."

"Speaking of putting things in my mouth, *food.*"

She laughed.

He really was impossible sometimes.

JULIAN WATCHED his pretty little rabbit inch closer to the solution. He had wondered if she would discover the meaning behind the numbers he hid in his possessions. He had scattered the answer throughout the pages for several reasons. First and foremost, he wanted to ensure that someone needed the whole set to solve his riddle.

They would also need the house to be intact. They would need a map of his home. They would need his complete collection. If even one piece was missing, one page of one book, they would never find the answer.

Anyone brave or foolish enough to wish to find his corpse, and the secret to his "immortality," would have to assemble them all right under his nose. He had left the clues in case the spell that powered the building ever faltered and failed, sending his soul to the void. It was his last will and testament, should his soul ever pass beyond.

He had never imagined he would let someone unravel his work underneath his watchful gaze. He had never imagined in a thousand years that he would be eagerly anticipating the moment she saw him—the real him—and learned the terrible truth of it all.

Poor girl. Poor little thing. I wonder what you will think when you lay your eyes upon my corpse and realize I have been beside you this entire time?

He couldn't imagine it would go over smoothly. He was already bracing himself for her ire and her wrath. But it would blow over with time. She loved him, and he her. And love conquered all, didn't it?

His wedding gift to her was nearly complete. He had only a few more pieces to solder together with copper before it would be finished. In his haste, he shattered two pieces of glass, and now he forced himself to slow down. It would be some time before she would be ready to receive it.

One thing at a time, old fool. One thing at a time.

First, she must find you.

Then she must accept you.

Only then will she be ready.

6

Julian Strande really *was* an impatient bastard.

He found himself fidgety. He wanted this done. He wanted to reveal the trick once and for all. He felt like he was standing behind the curtain of his very first performance, waiting for the velour to part and for the real show to begin.

It was not that Alice was slow-minded. Not in the slightest. She was speeding through his riddle far faster than he could have imagined. No, it was not her fault he felt ready to crawl up the walls. It really was his. He wanted her to solve it so the rest of their "lives" could begin.

He longed to hear her say the words, *"I love you, Julian."*

He could picture them in his head. He could hear it in his mind. He wanted to hear the words slip past those beautiful lips of hers. Even better, she might do it with him buried to the hilt inside her. To see her gasp and cry out in pleasure as she professed her love would be the happiest moment of his life or death.

Until the event he was creating that would inevitably follow, but that was another matter entirely.

Day by day, she sat in his home, searching through his books for the clues she needed. There were only a few more for her to comb through. A few more coordinates to find. Then she would realize there was one more puzzle before her. One more step.

He had dusted and cleaned—he, of all people. He had oiled the furniture. He had replaced the lights and mended the drapes. His home was going to be populated soon. She would leave that carriage home she shared with "Charles" and come to where she belonged. His home.

Their home.

But he needed a way to speed up the process. He needed a way to light a fire underneath her. She was working quickly, but without urgency. She did not feel the frantic desperation that burned in him as he waited. The illusion he had created for her, the lie he was telling, was enjoyable, but enough was enough. He wanted her *now.* He needed her *now.* He wanted to hear her cry out his name. He wanted her to whisper her devotion to him in the early hours of the morning like she did to "Charles."

She had given him a wicked, terrible idea. She had placed the seed of a plot in his mind. The poor beautiful girl had not even realized what she had done. He grinned to himself as he schemed. It would be a terrible ploy, but it certainly would speed the process.

She would have to find him immediately. She would not rest until she did.

The real tragedy was that it came from her own mouth.

"He might hurt you because he's jealous."

Oh, the irony. The sweet irony.

He was sometimes amazed at the depths of his own capacity for cruelty.

SHE WAS SO CLOSE.

So close.

She only had one more book to go through to find the rest of the coordinates. She wanted to wait until she had them all before she tried to figure out what they meant. She knew that without the whole picture, it wouldn't do her any good.

Julian was too good to write a puzzle where she could jump to the end. He would have made sure she needed to find every last scrap of information before she could go on to the next part of it. She wondered if this was the end of the line, but she didn't want to get her hopes up. The man was a devious mastermind, and she was beginning to wonder if it was ever going to end.

One more book. One more hour of searching for notes, and then she'd be on to the next thing.

It was on one of her nightly walk-throughs of the house that she stopped to stare at the bookcase that hid the entrance to Julian's fourth-floor apartment. She picked up her phone to call Charles. He was asleep in the carriage house, but he usually answered the phone. No answer. She sighed. He was probably passed out.

It'll only be one book. One book. That's all. It shouldn't even take her that long. She walked up to the bookcase and pulled the trick switch that opened it.

"I'm coming up to find those last symbols, Julian. That's all. This isn't an invitation, you got it?"

Silence.

It didn't mean he wasn't listening. It certainly didn't mean he wasn't there. She flicked on the lights. The corridor to the stairs had been dusted and cleaned, and the lightbulbs replaced. Julian was hellbent on making his home presentable, and she couldn't fathom why.

The last time she had been upstairs with Charles, it looked like he had even laundered his bedding. *Because he wants to fuck you in his bed, that's why.* She shuddered and chewed her lip. There was an odd mix of emotions that came along with Julian every time she thought of him. Fear, fascination, dread, and...a tiny bit of attraction. It was hard not to find him alluring. There was something dark and deadly about him, and it drew her in.

But she was engaged.

She loved Charles.

Julian was a *ghost,* for fuck's sake. It wouldn't work out between them even if Charles wasn't around.

Climbing the stairs to the apartment wasn't nearly as harrowing as it used to be. Like anything in life, she was getting used to it as she climbed them again and again. Flicking on the lights, she scanned the place quickly for anything out of the ordinary. Any ghastly, shadowy figures looming in the corners.

Nothing.

She let out a sigh of relief and went to the bookcase. She pulled the last tome off the shelf, a copy of the fourth book of Agrippa's works on occult philosophy. From what she could Google, it was suspected that the last book was bunk and was probably written several hundred years later. It was attributed to Agrippa to make it sound more official.

Pseudepigraphal. That was when somebody wrote a thing and pretended to be someone else. She hadn't known it was even a thing until she had looked it up. It was amazing how much there was to know in the world. She set the book on the coffee table and, sitting on the edge of the sofa, opened it to begin searching for the last few clues.

The apartment was silent. The whole house was silent. It creeped her out, even more than when she could hear music drifting from places in the home. Julian loved to play, and she often heard him pounding away on an organ or a piano this late at night.

But there was nothing. It was more unsettling to feel like the place was empty than when she knew he was nearby.

She focused on the task at hand. After about forty-five minutes, she finished. She had six more coordinates, and she smiled. She was positive she had them all. Now she could try to figure out their meaning. There were too many to be the key to opening the player piano in the basement. There was something else in between.

Closing the book, she stood to put it back on the shelf.

The lights flicked off and plunged her into complete darkness. It was a new moon, and the sky was dark outside, and her eyes tried to adjust to the sudden nothingness. "Julian. Knock it off."

"My patience has worn thin."

The whisper in her ear made her skin crawl. She felt his breath against her neck. Arms snaked around her, pinning her own to her sides.

"I've given you so much. What will you give me in return?"

"Julian—I—"

He shoved her down to the sofa, and she grunted as her face hit the cushions. She tried to push herself up on her hands, but his fist tangled in her hair, pressing her down hard. She let out a muffled shout against the fabric.

"Shush."

He was over her, on top of her. She felt him pressed against her legs and her back. His breath was pooling hot against her throat as he kissed her skin. His other hand trailed down her side, slipping underneath her to cup her breast and knead it in his grasp.

"Mmhff—"

"I love you, Alice. I love you, and I will have you. You belong to me. Give in. You know you want this."

He threw her onto her back, and she went to scream at him. He kissed her roughly, silencing her cry by muffling it against him. She couldn't see in the darkness. She tried to punch and swat at him, but he snatched her wrists and pinned them over her head. Trapping them there with one hand, he let his other wander down her again.

His tongue entered her mouth, devouring her, possessing her. He was like a force of nature over her, and she felt bowled over by him. When he nudged her legs apart to lie between them, she gasped against him and struggled. Weakly. But she did.

What the fuck is wrong with me?

When his hand drifted to her core and she felt him touch her *through* her clothing, her face exploded in heat. She was so damn embarrassed by what he found. Her body had no qualms about telling the ghost that yes, he was right. And yes, she did want this.

But it was very, very wrong.

On so many levels.

He chuckled against her lips but didn't give her a chance to tell him to stop. She bucked her hips against him, trying to shake him off, but he was intent on his goal of stroking her slowly, gently, coaxing her body into forcing her mind into giving in to him.

No, no, no—

She bit down on him. He snarled in pain—ghosts felt pain, that was a nice surprise—and yanked his head back from her. *"You little—"*

"Get off me. Get the *fuck* off me, Julian!" She kicked at him. "Let go of me this instant and stop touching me!"

A dark laugh echoed in the darkness before that breathy whisper returned to her ear. *"Why should I? This is my home. I am god in this place."*

"Because if you don't, I'll get in my car and never come back. I'll take Charles with me. Stop touching me, or I swear to Christ you'll never see me again!"

That made him pause. He pulled back from her. When he released her hands, she scooted away from him frantically. She kicked at him a few more times, but they met empty air.

"Y'know what?" She was nearly crying now. She felt tears start to run down her cheeks. "Screw you, anyway. I'm done. I'm done with this game, Julian. Fuck you. Fuck your mystery. I don't care. I'm done with this puzzle of yours. You can rot in the walls for the rest of time!"

"Mind what you say." That time, his voice wasn't a whisper. That time, it was a full-volume snarl. She felt the anger in the air around her, thick and vivid. It felt palpable, like if she reached out, she could touch the fury that crackled in the darkness around her. "Choose your next words very, very carefully."

She took a deep breath, held it for a moment, then let it out. No. It was true. He was a monster. "I never want anything to do with you ever again."

"Very well, pretty little rabbit...very well. We shall see how long that lasts. Know that what comes next is *your* fault." There was something familiar in his voice, but it was too bound up in anger for her to fathom what it was.

When the lights flicked back on, she jolted in surprise. There was no one there. Silence. The anger in the air was gone. Julian was...gone.

She swallowed thickly. That was it. That was the end of it. She was going to pack her bags and go. She'd marry Charles, but she'd never set foot in this place again. He'd understand. She took her notebook and left the apartment, not even bothering to turn the lights off behind her.

Slamming the bookcase in her fury, she headed back to the carriage house. It was after midnight. Charles would be annoyed being woken up at this hour, but she didn't care. She needed to tell him what had happened. She needed to quit her job and start packing this instant.

They'd spend the night in a hotel in town or at his house an hour away. Messy place or not, no matter his excuses, they were leaving.

Sinking onto the edge of the bed, she reached out to touch Charles in the darkness, to gently wake him. Her hand touched nothing. Only empty sheets. She searched for him for a second before flicking the lights on.

He wasn't there.

She checked the bathroom. Nothing.

"Charles?" she called. No answer. "Charles!" Silence.

Racing around the house, she searched everywhere. But it was too small for him to hide for long. Maybe he had gone into the house after her. Racing back into the estate, she searched everywhere for him. She ran through the halls calling his name for hours. She called his home and got no answer.

He was nowhere to be found.

Now she really was crying. Screw that. She was weeping.

She collapsed onto the foot of her bed and saw the light of the sun slipping up over the horizon. Something crinkled as she shifted. Looking down, there was a note placed there. Picking it up, she let out a wail of dismay at what she read and sank to the floor, holding her head in her hands.

"You know where to find him. –J.S."

Julian had taken Charles.

God help me, what have I done?

IF THERE WAS a hell and his soul ever left this place, he knew he was doomed to burn there for all eternity. He really was a right and sorry bastard. Julian sat on the ground next to her. He wanted to hold her as she wept. This was a terrible game, and seeing her so distraught, he regretted playing it.

But it was too late now.

He thought it would be fun to twist her around his finger, to watch her frantically search for "Charles," not knowing the secret. She would know soon enough, and she might truly despise him for what he had done.

He might well despise himself for it.

When he had pinned her down and tasted her, he hoped she would surrender to her desire for him. But her love for his false identity—oh, the irony—was too strong. When she vowed to leave this place and never return, he knew he had to find a way to keep her here.

He had planned to "threaten Charles" to urge her forward. He had wanted to whisper to her that if she wished to keep him safe, she had better solve his mystery double-time. But when she pledged to quit her role as caretaker and leave the grounds, never to return...he had to act fast.

It was desperation that made him do this.

I cannot lose you. I cannot. I don't think my mind or my soul would survive it. He wanted to reach out to her. To stroke her hair and soothe her, to tell her it was all a foolish prank. He wanted to bring her to the upright piano and play the keys that would unlock the chamber. He wanted to show it all to her.

But he had come too far to turn back now. They both had. She had to do this herself.

He looked down at the carpet by where he sat and noticed a few small dots of moisture had gathered in the strands. He, too, was crying.

For her.

For her love of him.

For the hatred that very well might replace it when she discovered what he had done.

He stayed there beside her while she wept. He would not spare himself the agony of watching her. This was his burden to carry too.

I love you, Alice. Now I only hope you can forgive me.

7

Charles was missing.

When he failed to show up to work the next day, she knew it. He never missed a shift without telling her. She kept calling his house, but no one answered. When the staff asked her where he was, she played dumb. She didn't have to hide being worried—she wasn't that good an actress—but she didn't tell them what she really knew.

He was missing, and Julian was to blame.

She had finally crawled into bed at some point and fallen asleep clutching his pillow to her. She had been too tired to cry, and too tired of weeping to do anything else. She didn't so much as sleep as she stopped being awake for a while.

When she woke up, she prayed she'd find him there with her and it would all have been a twisted nightmare. But no. This nightmare was real. Julian had done something awful with him, and the only way she could save him was to solve this stupid puzzle and find Julian's corpse.

She just prayed she would only find one corpse and not two.

Oh, Charles...

She wanted to call the cops. But what the hell could she say? *A jealous and psychopathic ghost abducted my fiancé.* They wouldn't issue a missing person's report for another day, anyway. And by then, it might be too late.

What if he was being tortured?

What if he was injured?

She was shaking and had to try very hard not to throw up several times in fear. She had to focus. The sad and terrible truth was Charles had one chance—her. She had to find Julian and finish this sick puzzle to save him.

She had to believe there was hope. She had to believe he was going to be okay. It was the only option she had. To believe otherwise, to think it was too late to save him, would destroy her. And so she set about solving the mystery once and for all.

After plugging in the last coordinates Julian had scattered in his books, she laid the plot over the floorplan of the home. It still made little sense to her. The points on the map seemed random. She picked up her laptop and started walking around the house, trying to find anything in the rooms that lined up with the points to see if there was anything there.

Nothing. Nothing she could see, anyway.

There had to be something else. Another layer to the mystery. She was still missing something. She sat back down in one of the rooms kept off the path of the tourists and tapped away at her computer, trying to think.

But she was drawing blanks. She was too tired. Too dredged out. She needed sleep. Charles was missing, but she wasn't going to be able to solve this without being able to think straight. She crawled into bed and passed out. It felt like she had been hit by a car. Her dreams were empty of anything, and she was glad for it. She got a few hours in before her mind insisted she needed to be awake to worry and fret.

The next day was a Friday, and still no sign of Charles. *Of course not. He's Julian's prisoner. Or victim.*

The staff was worried. Not only because there was no sign of their boss, but because the evening's show was sold out.

"Do you think we're going to have to cancel the performances?" Greta asked her, looking down at the RSVP sheet. "I can start now."

Alice nodded. It was better to be safe than sorry. The odds that she could find Charles before the evening, or that he was even in any condition to perform, were slim at best. "I—"

"Um. Alice?" One of the other guides, Jim, caught her attention. "Uh. I. Um. Charles is here."

"What?" She exclaimed, whirling to face him. "Where?"

"He's. He's up in the organ room. But he's...um...not okay."

"Is he hurt? We can call an—"

"No, he's um...you'll see. You should go see him. I tried to talk to him, and he threw a glass at my head." Jim shied away and rubbed the back of neck nervously. "He's insisting he'll perform tonight. He said, 'Julian Strande never misses a performance.'"

Oh, no. Julian, what did you do to him? She shuddered and, nodding, left to find Charles. The organ room was deafeningly loud as she approached. Machines sat stacked every which way. It was named such because, well, Julian had owned a lot of organs. Pipes ran up all four walls, soaring overhead in a dizzying and countless array of tubes. They all seemed to resonate with the tune being played on one of the larger instruments.

A man was sitting with his back to her. The extreme lighting in the room kept it such that she couldn't see his face. He had his head bowed, and he was bashing away at the keys, playing some grandiose and melodramatic piece that sounded like it should have accompanied a silent film.

Slowly creeping forward, she stopped a foot or two behind the man. It was Charles—but wearing Julian's costume. His hair was slicked back, and the suit was dated. If he turned to look at her, she knew he would be wearing the contacts that colored his eyes blue and brown.

Reaching out, she put her hand on his shoulder. He was warm beneath her palm. She wanted to feel relieved, but all she felt was dread.

The music stopped. He turned his head to keep it hidden from her.

"Charles...?"

"No."

"What?" She blinked, not understanding. "I—"

He cut her off. "How I've wanted you to touch me...how I've wanted to feel you."

She yanked her hand away from him. Dismay and panic welled in her stomach, thick and threatening to mix with her bile and send it up her throat. "Oh, god, please...no. Charles..."

"I am *not Charles.*" The man vanished. Disappeared before her eyes.

She jumped back in surprise. "Julian! What've you done to him? Let him go!"

"Come and see," the voice whispered in her ear. *"Find me and see what has become of your Charles."* The voice chuckled darkly then switched sides. She struggled to stay standing

still but couldn't stop herself from shivering uncontrollably. *"Poor thing...so tired. So worn out. Get some rest. Charles can wait another day. You will need a clear mind to find me. Stay away from my performance tonight. Or else."*

The threat was clear. He was going to take the stage tonight, and he didn't want her to see. She nodded weakly. She couldn't watch either. She ran from the room, feeling tears stinging her eyes again.

She locked herself in the carriage house, poured herself a tall drink, and drank it probably a little too quickly. Crawling into bed, she buried her head beneath the pillow and forced herself to get some rest.

She was too wrung out. Sleep finally came for her hard, and when it did, she slept the rest of the afternoon and well into the night. Still feeling like trash, she knew she couldn't wait any longer. It was midnight, and the performance was over.

She *had* to solve this mystery. And she had to do it now. Taking all her notes, she laid them out on the floor of the living room and sat in the center of them with her laptop.

And she thought.

What did she have?

Points on a map. A grid of coordinates.

The house was a spell to keep Julian's soul here. The zero point on the graph lined up with the gap in the center of the house. That thirty-foot mystery shaft that ran all the way from the basement to the third floor. Looking at the satellite view of Google maps didn't help. She could see there was something there that was odd, that there was something weird about the roof, but she couldn't pick out enough details to give her anything.

She put her head in her hands and tried to think. She traced through everything she had learned.

The house was a giant magic spell.

What did she know about spells?

They took precision, and work, and—oh. *Oh.*

Circles and symbols. Every spell she'd seen had something to go along with it. Weird geometrical shapes with writing in them. The array of dots on the map didn't create a circle. There were too many, and they were clustered oddly.

But that was if the circle was trying to be *flat.*

The symbol he had built around the shaft in the center of the hole wasn't *flat,* it was in three-dimensions like he had warned in the foreword of his journal. She had to stop thinking about it like ink on paper!

She looked up and began to work frantically, laying the information over the three-dimensional model of the house. She tried to find lines that connected, things that made sense. It took her all damn day. She forgot to eat, and only when she felt kind of faint did she manage to take the time to make herself something.

She had to stop herself from making food for two. Or rather, food for four. Charles ate enough for three people. Tall, skinny bastard. She was jealous of his metabolism. She tried not to cry at the thought of him and forced herself to focus.

Once she didn't feel so shaky, she went back to work. She sat there for hours, chipping away at it. The clocks struck one in the morning just as she thought she might have solved it.

She sat back and stared at the screen in awe. There it was. Laid out *through* the house. A magic shape that used its bizarre architecture. The whole house wasn't a collection of random stairwells and infuriatingly complex pathways built for fun. It was laid out that way to create the magic that kept Julian's soul as part of the building.

All the secret pathways. All the corridors that connected the first floor to the third but skipped the second, all the seemingly bizarre and nonsensical room shapes suddenly had meaning. Every ounce of the sprawling, hundred-and-ninety-two-room building served a purpose.

The shape it drew in three dimensions was an eight-pointed star. She had watched a Netflix special at one point about hypercubes, and she wondered if it wasn't actually trying to be a three-dimensional representation of a fourth-dimensional shape.

Fuck you, Julian. But this is impressive.

Picking up her laptop, she headed into the house itself. She walked to the closest room that was one of the points of the shape. She scoured the room. There *had* to be something there; she knew it.

There, hidden in the detail of the room, scratched on a piece of faded paper tucked into a display of old bottles and medical equipment on display...was a musical note.

The first part of the key!

She wrote it down frantically and went to the next room. And then the next. Stashed away in each one was a note. She collected seven, and she looked at her three-dimensional model to try to find the last point.

She groaned loudly and put her head in her hands. "No, no, no!"

The last point wasn't simply anywhere.

It was in the tower.

So close, my love. You are so close.

Come. Come and see.

He watched her eagerly. The poor thing was so tired.

She was emotionally dragged thin. She had barely slept, and what she had managed to eke out had been fitful and restless. It had taken every ounce of his self-control not to make her a sandwich and slip it onto the table next to her without her noticing.

No. She had asked to be left alone and to never see him again, and he needed her to think the ball was fully in her court. When she solved the clues of the coordinate map, he had nearly cheered. He was so very proud of her.

He had to leave the room to go to the gardens and take in the fresh air. He would have been unable to resist touching her if he had stayed. To hug her, kiss her, and tell her how proud he was.

He sat amongst the flowers, invisible and intangible, and let himself enjoy the early summer air and the breeze. The scent of the roses wafted to him, and he chuckled. He couldn't help it. He gathered a handful of them and went to secret them off.

Soon, she would lay eyes on his body. With the rate she was working and discovering the notes he had hidden around his home, she would find him at the break of dawn. It would be the perfect time, when the lighting was just so.

And the game would be over.

And a new one would begin.

He bent his nose to the crimson petals and breathed deeply.

Come and see, my love.

Alice stood at the unopened door in the fourth-floor apartment. It was painted solid black. It was narrow, like it might lead to an attic stairwell. But she knew where it went. It was the stairs to the tower no one had ever been in, save Julian—not even Charles.

She stared at it. She was shaking. She was exhausted. She had barely slept, barely eaten, and she didn't have any plans to rest until she found her fiancé. Until she knew what Julian had done to him.

It was barely past dawn, and the sun was rising on the horizon. Beams of light cut soft angles across the floor as the dawn shone on the newly polished furniture. It would have been almost friendly, almost serene, if it weren't for the fact that she didn't think her heart had stopped pounding since Julian had taken the man she loved.

Please be alive, Charles. Please.

She kept glaring at the door. The last note to the key to the piano was hidden up in that tower. From her years of playing piano, she could tell the notes had a definite order to them. But she was missing one. An important one. "Julian. I need to go up there. You can either unlock the door for me, or I'm going to fucking break it down."

A pause, and then the lock clicked. The handle turned and swung open. As she expected, a narrow set of stairs turned quickly to the left and out of sight. Julian hadn't cleaned this room. It was still a disaster of cobwebs and dust. She didn't care. Climbing the steep stairs, she half expected to hear the door slam behind her.

But Julian wanted this over with, and in that they were agreed. She wanted to find him and save Charles, and then promptly leave with him. She didn't know how she'd convince him to move, but she'd find a way. Maybe being abducted by his psychotic dead uncle would be enough to do the deed.

Finally coming up from the floor, she looked around, fighting her fascination with what she was seeing. It was built a little like an attic, the stairs coming up into an open space. Windows covered the walls on all four sides. The room was square and fifteen feet wide or so.

The ceiling was pitched upward at a steep angle, matching the climb of the roof on the outside. A single chandelier hung overhead, old Edison bulbs doing their best to march on through the passing of time and carry on their duty to stay glowing. That was the source of the light she had seen from the tower the few times it had been mysteriously lit.

Turning her attention to the floor, she pulled her foot back from what she saw. She had nearly stepped on it. In it. Whatever it was.

A large white circle was drawn around the room. Nine feet in diameter. She knew it was exactly that because of the books she had read. It would be nine feet in diameter and facing true north. The symbol was archaic and strange, and the writing around the edges was in a language she didn't understand.

Lining the white paint was something dark, rusty, and brown, standing out against the worn and faded floorboards. If Julian's rooms had been neglected, this room had been abandoned.

She knew what the stains were, tracing the white paint line for line. Blood. Julian's blood, probably. This was where he must have finished the spell. He knew he was going to die because he had killed himself.

Sort of.

This was where he had died; she knew it. She shuddered. She didn't need him to confirm it. She could feel it in her bones like an ache.

The whole room made every nerve in her body feel like they hurt. Like everything was on edge. She felt uneasy, and she didn't want to stay here any longer than she needed to. There was a musical note hidden up here somewhere. Scanning the walls, she searched for a few minutes before she finally found it, etched onto the jamb of a window. Scratched there in a crude fashion, as if Julian had put it there in a rush.

It was the view from that window that stopped her. It overlooked the roof of the house, with all its pointed gables and spires that seemed to make no sense at all with the way they were attached. There, in the center of the house, was what she couldn't see from the satellite map.

A dome. A glass dome, some thirty feet in diameter, and it looked like it was made entirely from stained-glass artwork. Whatever was beneath it...was the answer to the riddle.

Julian.

And Charles.

She wrote the note down in her book and looked at the page. Eight notes. It would be a single phrase played in 4/4 time. It was the key. The answer to that damn piano. She carefully made her way down the stairs to the tower.

The last thing she needed was to fall and hurt herself. She was unimaginably tired, and if she wasn't careful, that was going to be how she broke her neck. Not because Julian killed her—oh, no, that'd be too dignified. She was going to bite it from exhaustion and a missed step.

Once she was on level ground, she half-ran to the basement. Reaching the piano, she placed her notebook on the grooves of the stand and her hand on the keys.

This was it.

This was the moment.

This was the end to the mystery. She had asked Julian for a surprise the day she found the answer. She had hoped she'd solve it with Charles standing at her side. This was the last way she had expected or wanted this to go.

She hesitated.

What if Charles was already dead...?

No. Don't think like that. He might be bleeding. He might be injured. You can save him. She played the notes in slow succession in silence.

Clunk.

She jumped back, startled to the point that she nearly fell over, as organ music blasted loudly from the player piano. The light on the inside of the cabinet sputtered to life then glowed a bright amber as the machine roared into action.

It was playing a dirge. The notes she had played were the first portion of the melody. The sound echoed through the house and seemed to fill the very stones themselves. She could hear it rumbling in the foundation. Everything in the house was playing at once. It seemed like the house itself was shouting to the heavens, *"Come and see."* She had to cover her ears it was so loud.

The whole house is a calliope.

The piano lurched then jolted back on a track that hadn't been used in a very, very long time. It slid into the wall and then to the side, disappearing from view.

Then the music stopped. The silence was deafening, and her ears were thrumming from the aftermath of the music. Light streamed down on stone stairs that climbed up and away from her.

This was it.

Julian Strande was waiting for her.

One foot in front of the other, she stepped into the chamber.

8

STEPPING CAUTIOUSLY INTO THE SPACE, Alice looked up. Steps wound up around the edge of the space. They were carved out of solid stone. This must have been built first, and the rest of the house put up around it in wood. Above, three stories overhead, she could see the underside of a platform. The stone steps climbed to it and out of sight.

She had come this far. She had to see. She had to know.

She didn't hear anything coming from up the stairs. Only the dim morning light drifting down greeted her. No sobbing, no cries for help. *Please be okay, Charles. Please.* One step after another, she made her way up the stone stairs and to the platform overhead. One wrong step, and she'd fall to her death. She pressed close to the wall, keeping her hand along it for balance, and forced herself not to look down. Instead, she looked at the step ahead of her, or at the glass dome high overhead.

Finally, she made it to the top.

Stepping onto the stone platform, she pulled in a sharp breath through her nose.

On the center of the platform was a wide dais, carved in

stone and etched on all sides with the J.S. monogram that decorated the house, twined up in vines like the carving had tried to consume the words themselves.

It was what was on the large dais that had made her gasp.

What was I expecting?

It was a glass coffin. Rectangular in shape, with a tapered top. On the lid, she could see another stained-glass emblem, bearing his initials. Save for the symbol and some other embellishments, the coffin was clear.

She could see a figure lying inside in repose, hands folded across his chest. There was only one body there. One. She had expected to find Julian and hopefully a hog-tied, but otherwise fine, Charles.

At worst, she had expected to find two corpses.

Creeping closer, she approached the edge of the dais. It was bigger than it needed to be, and it meant she had to lean close to see. The man inside was blond, his hair swept back from his face. The suit he wore was a dated hound-stooth. She had seen that outfit many times before. It was the one Charles wore when he pretended to be...

Her heart hitched.

The man's face wasn't decayed at all. It was as though he had died only minutes ago. The skin was perfect and untouched by rot. The only thing that betrayed the fact that he was dead was that he was pale, and his lips were tinged blue.

The face.

It...it was Charles.

But it couldn't be. There was only one body here, and —and she was meant to find Julian. She was shivering. Her hands were shaking when she placed them on the edge of the dais. When she did, she looked down in surprise. There were photos spread out along the edge of the stone.

Old photos. She flipped them over, one by one. She knew instantly they were the images that were missing from the frames in his home. She *knew* she had seen them the first time she had been up there. Julian must have pulled them out to hide them from her. But why?

And then she knew why.

Cold rushed over her like ice water had been poured down her shirt. Her knees almost went out from underneath her. She felt her breath shorten and shallow, coming in quick and desperate gaps.

"No...no. Please, no."

The man in the images...was Charles. Any chance that they only looked alike was dashed when she turned over the man's headshot. Written along the bottom, an acid etch process used to write onto the negative, read *"The Impossible Julian Strande."* The image was dated June 1904.

They were *identical.*

Too identical.

Swallowing the rock lodged in her throat, she tried to hold back the bile that threatened to come up to replace it. She looked up at the body in the coffin and realized it was holding something.

A little plastic octopus. A stupid little toy.

"I've named him Inky, and I'm going to keep it forever." That was what Charles had said to her when she had given it to him.

It seemed he meant it when he said forever.

Charles and Julian.

They weren't relatives.

They were the same man.

When a voice came from behind her, she froze.

"Alice."

She turned slowly, leaning back against the stone dais. She needed it for support. If she didn't hold on to the edge of it, she'd collapse. She was shaking, and she felt sick. Standing there, a foot or two away...was Charles, dressed as Julian. He held a bouquet of roses in his hand.

Just as she had seen him a hundred times performing on stage.

Those mismatched eyes watched her with a darkness shining in the depths. One she had always known was there and had enjoyed toying with. One she had enjoyed letting toy with her.

But it wasn't Charles. It had never *been* Charles, had it?

He held out his hands at his sides, presenting himself. That familiar and fiendish expression spread across his perfect face as he held the roses out to her. "Surprise."

Alice screamed.

And went for his face.

He had expected the terror. He had expected the scream. Next, he expected her to sink to the ground and cry. What he hadn't expected was for her to *punch him in his goddamn face.* Her fist clocked him clean across the jaw and knocked him back a step.

He grunted in pain and grabbed his cheek. She was already running down the stairs.

All he could think of to do was to laugh. *Good girl. There's fight in you yet!* He cackled in joy as he heard her nearly trip down the stone stairs as she fled his mausoleum. He vanished and followed her by passing through the walls. He knew where she would go, and he wouldn't let it happen.

You're mine, Alice. You'll come to understand this in time.

You'll forgive me. I know you will.

You have to.

Or I'll go insane.

OUT. She had to get out.

She ran for the door and flew into the parking lot, skipping several steps on the way down off the porch. She was going to get in her car and drive as far away from this place as she could.

"Where do you think you're going?"

The voice came from behind her, taunting and playful. She didn't turn around to see him. She knew who it was by the voice alone.

Julian.

It had always been him. The whole time. Charles had been a lie!

I'm such a fool! She could barely see through her tears, and she scrambled for her car keys as she half-staggered into the side of her beaten up old Toyota.

Her car keys.

They were gone.

"Do you think I'd let that happen?"

Alice yelped and fell back, nearly landing on the ground as he appeared standing next to her. Simply...appeared. His body formed out of smoke that seemed to come from nowhere until he was standing there, looking at her with that same predatory smile.

She had always thought it was sexy. Now it carried new meaning. "Stay away from me!"

"No." He sighed. "Calm down, please." He reached for her. "You're going to pass out if you—"

"Don't come near me!" She ran. She didn't know where to go. She was panicking. She wasn't thinking straight. She ran to the carriage house and slammed the door behind her, throwing the bolt. She knew it was stupid.

She didn't care. She needed to hide. Hide, escape, and get away.

"That's pointless. You know that, right?" he said from next to her. He had stepped straight through the front door.

Alice screamed and ran up the stairs, tripping on the way up, scraping her hand as she fell. Ignoring the burn, she raced to the bedroom and slammed the door behind her, locking it. She stood and stared at it.

And waited.

She heard a heavy sigh from the other side. "Let me in, Alice. We need to talk."

"No! Go away."

"Sorry, I can't do that. We need to sort this out."

"And why should we do that?"

"Because I love you, and you love me."

"I loved Charles!"

A groan of annoyance. "I'm not doing this through the door. Open up, Alice."

"No."

"Don't make me do this."

"I'm not opening that fucking door!"

"All right, fine, suit yourself. Do this the hard way."

She gasped and recoiled as he stepped through the closed door into the bedroom like it wasn't there. She took another step back until her legs hit the end of the bed. Julian stood there, mismatched eyes watching her with a sad, beleaguered expression. With pity.

"Alice."

She sank to the ground, pulling her knees up to her chest, and buried her head against them. She curled into a ball, hugging her knees, and wept.

She heard him approach and felt him kneel close to her. When a hand carefully rested atop her head, she twitched. She didn't know what to expect. Was he going to hurt her? Slowly, he began to stroke her hair.

"Alice, look at me."

"Go away, please..."

"You don't mean that."

"You lied to me!" She finally lifted her head, pulling away from his hand. "You lied the whole time."

He was kneeling in front of her, sitting on his ankles, watching her with an expression she could only describe as heartbroken. "I did. But how was I supposed to explain it to you? I've been Charles for ten years. I was Eli for another twenty before that. And William before that. I did not wear the mask for you. It was simply who you met first."

She was shivering still, watching him in horror. "You... you were messing with me. Making me think you were two separate people."

His jaw ticked, and he nodded.

"Why?"

"I needed you to find me. I needed you to find the truth for yourself. You wouldn't believe it otherwise."

"Walking through a door would've summed it all up pretty fucking nicely, ass-clown." She glared at him.

He smiled, seeming to prefer her anger over her misery. He reached out and rested his hands on her knees. She twitched again but didn't pull away. There was nowhere she could go. He inched closer to her. "Would it have? Would it have really convinced you?"

"Yeah. I'm goddamn sure it would."

"You knew, deep inside, what was going on. You could sense something was wrong. All the excuses...and all the similarities. Think about it. You rejected it because you didn't want to accept what you knew was true." He reached out for her, and she flinched away.

"Are you going to hurt me, Julian?"

"No...never. Never in a million years." He reached out again and ran his hand over her hair, edging a little bit closer to her. "I will never hurt you. I *love* you, Alice. More than anything else in this world. Even more than I love myself, and that's a trick, I promise you."

She refused to let his smile cheer her up. She refused to let his joke comfort her like Charles's comments always did. *They were always the same man.*

Slowly, she felt her heart stop pounding in her ears. Panic wasn't sustainable. It petered out like an engine running out of gas, and she had already been running well past empty and only on fumes by the time this all came crashing down on her.

Charles claimed he had agoraphobia. *He couldn't leave the grounds.*

Charles claimed his house was a hot mess. *There was no house at all.* She furrowed her brow at him. "If I called you on the phone, where would it ring?"

"Nowhere. Tricking phonelines is an easy stunt when you can speak through the wires. I mastered it early on. I have to play a lot of games to keep up the act, after all. The excuses all come easier as time goes on."

The similarities between the two men. Their voices sounded the same. The way they felt. Their kisses. Their touch. Their smell. Anger suddenly crashed over her, and she slapped him. Hard. His head rocked to the side.

"Ow."

"You son of a bitch!"

"You remembered the sexual encounters we've had, I take it?"

"You cock-sucking, donkey-fucking, giant piece of trash!" She tackled him to the ground, pinning him there, and poised her fist over her head, ready to pound him into a pulp.

Except he was laughing. He was lying there looking up at her, cackling with glee in his eyes. His hands were resting on her thighs, and he was squeezing them. He made no move to stop her.

"What's so funny?"

"Nothing. I'm not laughing at you. I'm delighted."

"Why? Nothing about this is okay!"

"I know. Go ahead. Punch me. Hit me all you want. I deserve it. I want it. Make me pay."

No. That'd be too easy. That meant he'd be getting away with it. She snarled and climbed off him, moving to sit with her back against the bed again. "I thought—I was so worried about—you *monster.*"

"I know. You were resisting me so beautifully." He sat up and shrugged out of his coat. He tossed it aside, and she watched it melt into smoke. His vest and tie followed. He began rolling up his shirt above his elbows. "I dislike being so formal. The suit is nice. I look good in it and all, but it's stuffy."

Now he almost resembled the man she had fallen in love with. The man she had...agreed to marry. She looked down at the ring on her finger in horror and sadness. "Char—" She stopped herself. She cringed and felt tears prick her eyes. "Julian. You...why did you do this to me? What did I ever do to make you so angry?"

"No, no, Alice. It's not like that at all..." He moved toward her and reached out to touch her. She flinched, but she let him trace his fingers over her cheek. They were so familiar. So identical to the man she adored. "I love you. I proposed to you because I want to marry you. Nothing has changed. You simply know the truth now."

"But you're...y..."

"Dead. I know. It's all right." He cradled her cheek in his hand and traced his thumb slowly over her skin. "I feel real, don't I? I feel alive. Here, in this place, I'm as good as the same thing. Only better."

Soon, he was kneeling with her legs tucked between his, and he shifted to sit against her side. She was shivering, feeling cold and tired. Overwrought. She shook her head dumbly. "I thought...when you were touching me, as—as the ghost—I thought I was a terrible person for..."

"Your body knew what your mind refused to accept. Deep inside, you knew something was wrong, but you were happy, and you wanted to ignore it. People are so eager to look the other way when it leaves their lives simple and safe. But when I touched you, you knew. You weren't cheating on me, sweetheart. You were still in my arms the entire time."

"Mrow," Loki shouted from the other side of the door. He had missed dinner, and he was clearly annoyed by that.

She ignored the cat. She had other things to worry about. "You did this all because you enjoyed watching me struggle. The puzzle. Pretending to be two people. All of it."

"No." His hand was combing through her hair. She shot him a look. He cringed. "A little. Okay, fine. Yes." He pouted. Literally pouted. "I did. I'm sorry. You were so sweet, solving my puzzle, and watching you fight how much you wanted me to strap you into one of my props and f—"

"Mrow!" The sound of claws scratching at the door interrupted the ghost of Julian Strande.

Julian Strande.

She had screwed him already. So many times. She had kissed him. She had—her face went warm. That night in the prop box had been otherworldly, and she had felt so guilty, and now—

"Mroooooooooooooowl!"

"Okay! Okay." Julian pushed to his feet. "I'm coming, you fat ball of fur. I'm coming." He walked to the door and opened it, looking down at the gray Maine Coon who was rubbing up against the jamb like he had no idea what the problem was. "Yes. Fine. I'll feed you."

Loki meowed happily and stood on his haunches to put a paw on Julian's calf and claw up toward him with the other. Julian chuckled and crouched to pick him up, slinging the large, loudly purring animal against his shoulder to walk down the stairs.

She heard him descend then rustle around in the kitchen. He knew where she kept the cat food. He'd fed Loki before. He'd taken care of her cat while she had gone to visit her family in San Jose over Christmas.

She thought it had been Charles. It had been Julian.

The dead ghost of the world's most impossible magician had cat-sat for her.

Standing, she crept to the door then to the top of the stairs. She looked down to the kitchen and saw *Julian fucking Strande* feeding her cat. He had a can open and was scraping out the food into the empty dish, much to the purring animal's delight.

This was insanity. This was the definition of insanity.

He threw the can into the trash, popped the spoon into the dishwasher, and walked over to the armchair by the sofa.

He sat in it, crossed his ankle onto his knee, and only then did mismatched eyes meet hers.

"I'll be here when you're ready to talk. When you're *really* ready to talk."

She shuddered. She knew she couldn't escape this. Whatever was going to happen next...she couldn't run away. It wasn't that she wasn't sorely tempted to try to hotwire her car and race off for the horizon, but she suspected that chance was long gone.

And something in her heart ached at the idea.

"Are you really the same man? Are you really Charles? You didn't throw him in a creek and are playing pretend?"

He chuckled. "I promise. I am Charles, and he is me. It wasn't even a character or a persona. It was only a change of eye color and new clothes. That's all. I am the man you love." He tilted his head to the side slightly. "Or loved. Get some sleep, Alice...you're so tired. When you wake, I'll try not to burn the coffee again, and we'll talk."

Swallowing, she nodded. What else could she say? She turned and went to do exactly that when she heard him call after her.

"I promise I won't sneak in to join you this time."

She shut her eyes and resisted the urge to scream at him. Or throw something at him. He was a ghost; it'd probably pass right through, anyway. With a disgruntled sound that might have been a groan or a sigh, she wasn't quite sure, she shut the door behind her.

Sleep first.

Beat the shit out of a dead man later.

She could get on board with that plan.

9

No dreams came for her that night. She couldn't have been happier. She was exhausted, and her mind was too run thin to even conjure nightmares for her. She awoke and felt cold. Empty. Lonely. She missed the feeling of someone there beside her. It was amazing how quickly she adapted to good things and how much they were missed when they were gone, despite the fact that she had slept alone for her entire life.

The sheets smelled like cloves. Charles always carried that smell even though he didn't smoke, and even after a shower it still clung to him. And now she knew why. Charles didn't smoke—but Julian had.

One more thing she had shoved into the back of her head. One more thing she could see in hindsight as an obvious clue, but at the time she didn't want to think about. It was so obvious now that she could see how the trick was done.

Charles had been Julian the entire time, and now that she knew it, it was all clicking into place. All the excuses. All his weird eccentricities. He didn't own a computer. He didn't have friends or family to whom he ever talked. He was always around. He could seemingly come out of nowhere.

Pushing herself out of bed, she ran her hands through her hair and glanced at the clock. It was one in the afternoon. It had been around five in the morning when she had gone to bed. She'd worry about her sleep schedule, but something told her she wasn't going to have any problems being tired later. It felt like something had gone into her chest and hollowed her out.

Picking up the clock on her nightstand, she stared at it. It was the carved wooden rabbit—the white rabbit—that Julian had made for her the day she arrived. It was his first gift to her. The two carved purple roses were on her dresser. She was tempted to throw the clock to the ground and smash it.

She should.

She should destroy it, and everything he had ever given her. She should toss the engagement ring in the trash. She should grab her things and head to the horizon and never look back.

But she loved the clock. The idea of wrecking it hurt her. She couldn't do it. She simply couldn't. Setting it back down, she let out a beleaguered sigh.

She threw on a hoodie and walked out of the bedroom. Standing at the top of the stairs, she found *Julian* lying on the sofa, with Loki sprawled out on his chest. It was going to take a long time to reprogram herself to think of him as the ghost of the magician and not Charles—not the man she had fallen in love with and agreed to marry.

Mismatched eyes opened to look at her, and he smiled sadly. "Did you sleep well?"

"No. Did you stay here the whole time?" She walked down the stairs. She needed coffee viciously, and she was starving, but she opted not to make breakfast. Not yet. She wouldn't be able to resist the urge to make them both food, and she wasn't going to cook sausages and toast for Julian in her current state of mind. Coffee would have to do.

"I did. I stayed out of your room."

"Have you been in there every night?" She couldn't help but keep glancing over at the ghost, waiting for him to leap at her or terrorize her. But he looked...normal. In fact, he looked ridiculous. The first few buttons of his shirt undone, the sleeves rolled up, sprawled out on her sofa underneath twenty pounds of purring fur.

Loki clearly adored Julian. The cat had probably never seen, nor cared, about any difference between the ghost and the man. Loki had adored "Charles," and it was obvious nothing had changed.

Julian seemed unwilling to answer her question. He glanced away.

She pressed again. "Have you been in my bed the whole time?" It would explain why it always felt so warm. So cozy. *Stop it.*

"Since the day you came to stay here. This was the first time you've slept alone since you moved in."

She sighed and shut her eyes. That was more than a little creepy. The ghost had been stalking her, even before she had invited Charles to stay with her every night. *Julian. You invited Julian. You just didn't know it.* Her mind couldn't stop tripping over itself, tangling itself up in that thought over and over again. It made it hard to pay attention to what she was doing. "Do you sleep at all?"

"Not like living people do. I rest. It's hard to describe. It's like part of me shuts off for a while. I'm aware, but not focused. I read something once about dolphins being able to turn off one half of their brains at a time. I think it's something like that."

"You laid there all night, every night...what...staring at me?"

"Well, when you say it like that, it sounds perverted." He chuckled. He was petting the cat. He was one of the few people Loki allowed to pet his side or stomach, and the cat stretched out even longer, basking in it. "Yes. I suppose."

"The whole thing was a lie. All of it."

"No, Alice." He sat up. Loki meowed in annoyance and jumped onto the back of the sofa to clean himself, swishing his tail irritably at being disturbed. Julian stood from the sofa and approached her.

She backed up against the counter, her heart instantly beating faster. He was a ghost. *The* ghost. None of it had resolved itself in her head, and she found herself afraid of what he might do to her.

He clearly saw her fear. His shoulders drooped. He paused a few feet away and ran his hand down over his mouth. Sighing, he leaned against the counter as well, crossing his feet at the ankles, trying to show her that he wasn't going to come any closer. But he could *basically* teleport, so she wasn't sure it was as comforting as he thought it was. "You're afraid."

"No shit."

"I'm not going to hurt you. I love you, Alice."

"You keep saying that. But how do I know you're not lying again? How many of me have there been?"

He looked up at her in shock. "What?"

"How many *brides*"—she couldn't believe she had to say that—"have you had, Julian?"

He laughed. He actually laughed. That made her furious. She stormed up to him, her anger pushing through her fear, and she slapped him hard on the chest. She went to hit him again, but he caught her wrists.

"Stop making fun of me!" She yanked away from him, and he let her go.

He forced himself to stop laughing, but the smile plastered on his sharp features betrayed that he really wanted to keep going. "I'm not laughing at you. You really think I've done this before? You really think I'm capable of that?"

"I'm not sure of anything anymore. How many dead women are lying in a hole somewhere in that house?"

He let go of her to run both his hands over his face. "I've fucked this up."

"No shit." Tears were stinging her eyes again. She turned away from him, not wanting to let him see her cry. Again. She didn't know why she bothered. Coffee. She should focus on the coffee. It was still brewing, but she glared at the pot and tried to will the tears away.

"I've never been in love before, Alice. Not until you. I haven't been interested in a woman since I've been dead. I didn't even think it was possible. And when I was a living man, I...didn't make time for things like that. One-night stands, fine. Dalliances. But never anything substantial. Never anything that mattered to me."

His hand fell on her shoulder, and she twitched in surprise. But she didn't pull away. She either didn't want to, or she didn't know how to. Her anger and her grief were warring with each other. It hurt. Everything hurt.

"I'm sorry." He stepped into her. She felt him there at her back, and he wrapped his arms around her in a gentle embrace. It felt so warm. So soothing. So familiar. He really *was* Charles. "I'm sorry I lied. I...I'm a bastard. I play stupid games. It was harmless fun for me. It wasn't harmless fun for you."

She was locked tight, her muscles tense, even if she wanted to lean back against his chest and let herself melt into his arms. No. She wouldn't give in. Not that easily. She tried to stay angry. She tried. She really, really did.

He kissed her shoulder. "I don't expect you to forgive me. Not yet. But please, don't shut me out. And don't...make good on your threat. Not until I've had a chance to make amends."

"What threat?"

"To leave here. To leave...me." He sighed heavily and bowed his head to rest it on her shoulder where he had kissed her. "I can't follow. Please, please don't go."

"You stole my keys."

"You have feet. You could walk."

"You could stop me from leaving. Trap me in the house. Tie me up. I don't know."

He turned her around to face him and cupped her cheek in his hand. She tried to look away, but he turned her back to him. "Look at me, Alice."

She didn't want to.

"Please."

With a heavy breath, she finally gave in. She met those beautiful, dangerous, amazing, mismatched eyes. And she saw so much love in them that it made her ache. So much love, and loneliness, and hope, and hurt.

"I could trap you here. I could do as you say. But I don't want to make you hate me. I want you to love me, as I know you do. I want you to *want* to stay with me. I could have pretended to be Charles around you for years, but I knew it would only make it worse for you. I play my own great-grandnephew so I can walk my home and run my own affairs without needing to hire some kind of patsy. You met me as Charles. I hired a caretaker to keep me company, someone to watch and amuse myself. But I never thought...I never thought I'd fall in love. By then, it was too late to tell you."

"It wasn't too late. You could've said something. Anything. You made me solve that whole puzzle of yours. Why?"

"You loved it. You were so happy. And, fine, I was being selfish. I loved the attention. You were so deep in the game I created. It was beautiful, watching you unravel me. The way you would light up when you discovered a new clue or found a new lead was stunning. I couldn't ruin it for you. You deserved to solve it."

He took her hand in his and placed her palm over his heart. It was beating beneath her hand. How? He was dead. She had so many questions. There were so many physics issues she wanted to bring up. How could he eat food? Where did it go when he was done with it? *Or how can he have sex with me?*

His insatiable appetites. It all made sense. He could recover with seemingly inhuman speed. If it hadn't been for her limitations in bed, she had always been sure he could have gone for days.

Maybe she'd ask him later. Maybe. If she didn't run for the hills first.

"Let me make it up to you. Let me try. Give me some time to win you back to me. You'll see that I'm the same. Only better." He grinned cheekily. "Think of all the fun we can have now. Do you know how hard it's been not to show you what I'm really capable of?"

Her face went warm, and she looked away.

"If you think that night in the box was impressive..." he purred, leaning into her. He brushed his lips across her ear, and she shivered. She couldn't help it. He did things to her.

He always had. And now that she knew Julian *was* Charles, it seemed her body finally gave up trying to fight what she had already deeply wanted. "Wait until you let me do more."

She pushed him back a step. "Knock it off."

"Okay, okay, fine. I mean, I could really make it up to you, y'know. I couldn't think of a better way to make you forgive me than to make you unravel again and again, all over my—" When she glared at him, he stopped himself. "Sorry. I'm a flirt, remember."

His hands rested on her hips, toying with the hem of her hoodie, twisting it in his fingers. He looked down, and his playful expression faded into a serious one. "Let me try, Alice. Let me try. Don't leave me. I think that would end me."

"What do you mean?"

"The idea of going on without you for eternity...I don't know how I could do it. Now that I know what I would be missing...I might snap and go insane. Or I'd resort to burning my house down and letting the void finally take me."

She looked at him in shock. "You wouldn't."

"Do you care?" He lifted a hand to wipe at his cheeks. He was crying. That hurt her more than it should have.

She instinctually went to answer *yes.* She stopped herself. She did care. She cared about him a great deal. She loved him, but he had lied to her. Toyed with her. Messed with her head and danced her around on his puppet strings. The idea of him harming himself, of destroying himself, hurt her deeply. It cut her to the quick.

But.

Damnit, she was so confused. It was all too much for her to process at once. His stupid comment had made her realize she was hurting because she loved him. Julian

Strande. The idea of it made her shut her eyes and lower her head.

She tried to picture herself getting in her car and driving away, never coming back again. She had threatened to do it before, but that was when she thought Charles would be in the passenger seat. When she thought they'd move away from Julian and the house and all his terrifying antics. But now, everything had changed.

The image of herself in that car, heading for the horizon, felt hollow. Empty. Painful. Lonely beyond words. The idea of him alone in the house, crying...it was worse.

She didn't know how she could forgive him.

But she also didn't know how to leave him.

Pulling in a deep breath, she held it then let it out in a long rush of air. "Fine. I'll stay for now. Don't ever, *ever* pull any shit like that on me again."

He cackled in laughter, and suddenly her feet weren't touching the ground as he hugged her and lifted her. When she glared at him, he set her down and coughed, stepping back. "Sorry. Overexcited. I'll make it up to you, Alice. I will. I'll show you that you love me. I promise."

She turned to pour herself a cup of coffee. Cringing, unable to slight him that badly, she pulled out a second mug and made him one as well. When she handed it to him, he was smiling like an idiot. He headed back to the sofa and sat, reaching up to pet Loki who was still perched there. "I'm sure you have questions."

She watched him for a moment. "Why the fuck do you even eat? Where does it go? Do you need it?"

"Because I like the flavor, it disappears, and no, in that order." He chuckled. "I think I just kind of absorb it, for lack of a better word. I can dissolve matter. I can also create it, like my clothing. I could swallow that spoon and do the same thing, but that'd just be...weird." He wrinkled his nose at the idea. "It's complicated."

"I...see." She didn't. She shook her head. "What the hell do we do now?"

"Sadly, I will have to resume the role of Charles during the day. You can explain to the staff that I had a mental break, but I'm fine now. Everything will go on as usual. You will help fix all my broken toys, and I will resume running my museum like I always have."

She took her coffee and walked to the armchair and sat. She ignored the empty pit in her stomach, but it was growing in insistence. She'd make food later. And she'd do it for both of them. It was inevitable. "How is it that you're...so real?"

"It's easy to remember how to be alive. It's strange for me to not have a body at all, to be honest. I spend most of my time like this. I can do all the things a living man can do, as you are quite well aware." He smiled wryly, unable to help himself. "And more." He clearly forced himself to stop flirting and be serious. "I can even bleed because I remember how."

"Why did you do it? Not the selling your life for power, but why did you trap yourself here?"

"I'm not trapped. I love being like this. I have my own domain. My own kingdom. And people come in droves to see my masterpiece. I perform to sold-out crowds. It's a joy, not a curse."

She remembered "Charles's" bizarre hatred of the other magicians who would come to see his show. Now his zealous opinion of them made more sense. One more piece of the puzzle clicked into her head.

Christ, it had been so obvious the whole time, and she had refused to see it.

I sucked a dead man's cock. A lot. And I liked it. She looked away, trying not to laugh. She failed. Once the first chuckle broke free, she let it come. She laughed. It was a tired-sounding thing, and maybe a little overwrought, but it felt cathartic. It certainly felt better than crying.

"What?" He was smiling at her, confused, but clearly hopeful.

"This is ridiculous. This whole thing." She paused. She looked down into her coffee, her laughter fading. "I thought you had hurt Charles. I was so afraid. I was terrified."

"I know...I am so sorry for that. I didn't know what else to do. I was desperate. When you said you were going to leave, I acted rashly, and then it was too late. That is what I regret more than anything." He reached out to take her hand, and she let him. He wove his fingers between hers and squeezed. "Fear has a fine line. There is a palpable barrier to be found between terror that is delightful, and that which is miserable. I crossed that line when I made you believe I was in danger. When I saw you weep, I did too. I couldn't handle the thought of never seeing you again."

"Don't ever, *ever* do anything like that to me again." She implied for a second time that she was staying more permanently. It was too late to take it back, and she discovered she fully meant it. She still didn't want to leave, even with his lies.

"I promise." He lifted her hand to his lips and kissed her fingers. "I have been exceedingly cruel. I'm sorry. Let me make it up to you."

"I don't know how you can."

"But I'm really looking forward to the attempt." He winked at her, and his teeth grazed her pointer finger.

She shook her head with a faint smile and pulled gently out of his grasp. He was incorrigible, even when she was mad at him. But he was already winning her over. She wasn't screaming, crying, or throwing things at him. She was letting him touch her. She was letting him make her smile.

Now that she could see it, he really was the same man. The ghost on her sofa, petting her cat, drinking her coffee, was the man she had fallen in love with. She looked down at the ring on her finger. "How the hell did you get an engagement ring if you can't leave here?"

"The internet is wonderfully useful, even if computers make my fingers itch. Prior to that, Sears catalogs were my method of procuring whatever I needed."

"What's up with that, anyway? Your issue with electronics?"

"I think I'm made entirely out of electromagnetic wavelengths." He shrugged. "I can use computers and phones and the like, but they're uncomfortable. I manage when I need to, but I would hardly spend hours staring at them like a zombie like you do."

"I don't stare at it like a zombie."

"Mmhmm." He smirked. "Sure, you don't. The whole human race is slowly being corrupted into screen-staring junkies." He made an exaggerated zombie groan and lifted his arm to claw at her. "Feed me. Feed me your *braaaaain*..."

She smacked his arm away from her, and she was smiling, even if it was still a little against her will. She looked away from him again. Damn him. He really *was* Charles.

Her stomach growled loudly. Something else was demanding to be fed.

The hopeful shimmer in his eyes was impossible to miss.

"Yes. Fine. I'll make food."

He grinned. And she resisted the urge to smack him.

Barely.

10

Alice took the rest of the day off. She couldn't fathom walking up to the house and trying to go through the motions. Charles—*Julian, you shithead*—had gone to see to business. It really was going to take a long time to reprogram his name in her head.

She stacked up all the notes she had gathered while trying to solve Julian's riddle. She kept out her translation of his journal. She'd give him back the original one later. She didn't need it anymore.

She paused, looking down at the translation. There was a spell there, meant to trap spirits. She stared at it for a long time before shaking her head and putting the pages down on her desk. There was also one to summon fire. Now that she knew magic was real, she was a little tempted to try one and see what happened. But she also knew the cost—she'd be spending a piece of her life in exchange.

She tucked everything away and wondered if she should shred it. She'd ask Julian what he wanted her to do with it all. She didn't imagine he wanted to leave it lying around for other people to find.

She cleaned the carriage house, for lack of anything else to do. When she was done, she lay down on the sofa and shut her eyes. It smelled a little like him. That rich and tangy scent of cloves that she had come to love so much. She sighed.

She was still confused. Distraught.

And exhausted.

She hadn't realized she had fallen asleep.

It was then that the nightmares started. Running. Screaming. Something chasing her. She was running through places that didn't make any sense. Summoned from the dredges of her mind in the way that dreams could manage. Stitching together places she had been before into corridors of nonsense that rivaled Julian's estate.

Her childhood home. Her aunt and uncle's home. Her school. Her college. The funeral parlor where the wake for her family had been. Then Julian's estate finally bled into the nonsense.

She was screaming. Crying. Begging for it to stop.

But the fear wouldn't let her go.

JULIAN COULD FEEL her distress from where he was at his desk in the estate. He had plenty of bills and paperwork to deal that piled up during his absence. Funny thing—he was dead yet still caught in the trappings of life all the same. *Death and taxes, isn't that the old joke?*

But something in him lit like a bulb, and he knew she needed him. He was all at once himself, and a part of the grounds as a whole. He could feel every window, every door, every nail and plank of wood. He could feel the mice in the walls and the ants in the dirt, even as he could feel the hairs on his arms. It had been jarring at first, but he had adapted. Most people never caught his attention. He learned to ignore it.

But he could feel her fear. He vanished and flew through the walls and across the parking lot, then through the wall of the carriage house.

She was whimpering, tossing about on the sofa. She was dreaming, but her body was caught in a cold sweat. A nightmare. Loki was sitting on the coffee table near her, tail swishing, concerned for his mistress.

I'm to blame for this. This is my fault.

He materialized next to the sofa and sat beside her. He couldn't let this continue. He reached out and took her shoulders and shook her gently. "Alice. Alice, wake up."

She tossed her head, crying out.

He shook her again. "Alice!"

Her eyes flew open, and she sat up and threw herself into him. He clutched her to his chest, holding her tightly. She was shivering, her arms clasped around his neck, her head buried against him.

Although he knew she hadn't meant to do it, it felt like bliss to have her there. He stroked her back, shushing her, holding her. "It's all right, Alice. It was only a dream. I'm here. I'm here now. I will always be here for you."

Even if I'm the monster in your dream.

He knew the precise moment that she woke up enough to realize where she was and who was holding her. He knew because she twitched and went stiff.

That hurt him more than he could have expected.

I need to fix this.

Someone was holding her. Her nightmare had shattered, but she was panting, and her heart was racing. Something had been chasing her in her dreams, and now she realized she was in the arms of the very same thing that had been the source of her fear.

But she didn't want him to let go. He was warm, and strong, and *safe.* But that was a lie, wasn't it? He wasn't safe. He was a ghost. A ghost who was whispering words of love and promises of security and telling her that he would never let anything hurt her.

He tilted her head to look at him. His breath was warm against her, and full of life. He was a ghost, but he certainly never felt like one. His lips hovered over hers. "I want to kiss you, Alice. May I?"

I shouldn't. I shouldn't. I shouldn't. "Yes."

The word had come out as a whisper, and her whole body shuddered as she said it. She wanted to not be afraid anymore. She wanted the terror she had felt over the past few days to go away. It was all an illusion—it was smoke and mirrors. The danger had never been real, and she wanted the source of it to leave her alone.

And as his lips pressed against hers, she felt it melt away. He kissed her slowly but insistently. It felt like their first kiss all over again. And in some ways, it was. He was kissing her now for the first time with all the curtains drawn back.

And, oh, it felt like heaven.

He laid her back down on the sofa, following her, until he was leaning over her, his weight on his elbow by her head. His arm was beneath her neck, cradling her, as the fingers of his other hand drew slow circles on her cheek.

And the kiss. It felt like it seared into her soul. It lit her from the inside. It was possessive, but not forceful. Firm, but not harsh. He kissed her again and again, breaking now and then to look at her as if he wondered if she would tell him to stop. But she never did.

Her hands were tangled in his button-down shirt. Each time he broke from her, she pulled him back. All the fear, all the terror, seemed to vanish like ice in the summer sun. Oh, she was still *mad* at him, but his embrace gave her the thing she needed. The promise that the phantoms that had threatened her were all a lie.

His lie.

But she would deal with that another time.

He finally broke away and feathered kisses along her cheek to her ear. "I would keep going…but I'm already in a sorry state, and I don't know as you're ready to forgive me *that* much yet." He paused. "Are you?"

She didn't miss the hopeful tone to his voice, and she chuckled. "No."

"Damn." He leaned up and kissed her forehead. "Go to bed. It's late. You should get some rest."

"Don't I need to walk the house tonight?" She narrowed her eyes. "Or was that all an excuse to give you a chance to haunt me?"

"A little of column A, a little of column B," he admitted sheepishly. "Don't worry about it tonight. Go to bed. Sleep." He straightened and, taking her hands, pulled her to her feet. Kissing her forehead, he urged her toward the stairs. "Go on. I don't like seeing you like this. I want my Alice back."

She felt rather like she did after Billy died. Hollowed out and out of charge like a used battery. She nodded and found herself agreeing with him. She didn't like feeling like this either. She walked toward the stairs then stopped.

The idea of a cold, lonely bed didn't sound inviting to her. She knew the nightmares would come back. She shut her eyes, swore at herself for being a lovesick fool, then turned to look back at him. She held out her hand to him silently.

The smile he gave her broke her heart. It was so full of love and happiness that she didn't know what to do. He walked to her, slipped his hand into hers, and followed her up the stairs. Without really looking at him, afraid of what she might do if she saw those mismatched eyes—she really shouldn't want him as badly as she did right now—she climbed into bed. She felt him slip under the sheets behind her.

She shut her eyes as he took her into his arms, holding her against his chest. This was why she had slept so well in the carriage house every night since she had moved in. She had always thought it was simply the nice bed, the coziness of the house, or some combination of it all.

No.

It had been him.

It had always been him.

He held her while she slept. He would never tire of it. The feeling of her against him, her breathing smooth and slow. He would keep away the nightmares if he could. Nuzzling into her hair that smelled so wonderfully of lavender, he let his eyes drift shut.

This could never end. He wouldn't let it. She would forgive him. He could sense her fighting against her desire to welcome him back into her arms. He was always pulling her down the street faster and faster. How often she had squawked at him about how he moved too quickly for her tastes.

Now was no different. He wanted her forgiveness, and he wanted it *now.* But some things weren't that simple. He knew she would take a little time before he could really make it up to her. Before he could *really* show her how much she loved him.

Wicked ideas ran through his head, and he forced them away. *Stop it. As she says so frequently, "Knock it off." Let the girl sleep. Tuck your metal rod away and deal with it later. At least wait until tomorrow night.* He smiled. Tomorrow night. Yes, that would be plenty of time. He'd give her an amazing day, and a night, and then well into the night.

She was always helpless to resist him. It was so beautiful to watch her struggle against what she wanted, only to give in. Ideas tumbled around each other and began to form into a scheme. He would sweep her off her feet.

And then make sure she stayed on her back for the rest of the night.

Or on her front. Either way. He wasn't picky.

Or both.

Both would be nice.

I really am the worst, aren't I? He forced himself not to laugh and wake her up. But if she knew what was running through his head, she'd slap him. He'd invite her wrath. She could hit him as much as she wanted to.

Anything if it meant she wouldn't leave him.

She couldn't ever leave him.

He'd see to that. He already had a plan in place. It would take a little time. Not as much time as she'd want, though. He really was an impatient man.

Soon, they'd be wed, and then she would never, ever leave him.

She wouldn't be able to.

THE FOLLOWING DAY, Alice did her best to pretend everything was fine. She was allowed to act a little shaken up around the staff, she figured. The excuse that "Charles" was going through some rough times was enough to keep them from thinking something else was wrong.

Part of her wanted to tell them what was really going on. But how the hell was that supposed to go? *Hi, guys. Charles isn't real. He's actually the super-powerful ghost of Julian Strande. Has been this entire time. I'm engaged to and in love with a ghost. What's wrong? Why're you calling the loony bin? I'm fine, I promise!*

Yeah. That'd go over great.

So, she kept it to herself. She had been neglecting her repair duties while trying to solve the mystery of the house, and she needed to take stock of where she was and what she had been doing. She...tried to get on with life.

She had woken up with Julian in her bed, snuggled up against her. It had felt good. Screw that. It had felt amazing. She had made them breakfast, and he donned the appearance of Charles before her eyes.

"Like Clark Kent and Superman," he had said as she watched his eyes shift to hazel like a magic trick.

She had teased him for reading comic books. But he reminded her that being dead meant he had plenty of free time, and simply because he wasn't alive didn't mean he couldn't keep up with the times. He was shockingly modern in his language and his references, she had to give him that.

Part of keeping up appearances, she supposed.

Down in the workshop, she looked down at the printed pieces of the house she had been working on. Even after everything, she wanted to finish it. She was certain Julian knew what she was building, but she was going to do it for herself, even if he had spoiled the surprise.

She started the printer on the next set of pieces and went about walking the house to see how some of her more recent fixes were holding up. The house was filled with people. It was the start of the summer season, and the tourists had descended in full force.

It made the day feel normal. It made life feel...like it was going to go on. Like this could be okay. Routine. She didn't run into "Charles" until lunch. He was talking to a group about one of the big stage props from his collection. She leaned against the wall and watched him explain how it worked. It was an older trick, and he seemed not to mind revealing a little bit of his magic. Because the building was so busy, he had to pitch in to give tours.

He really knew how to hold the attention of a crowd. Everyone hung on his every word. Including her, if she were honest. He was charismatic, and when he reached the very end of the explanation he revealed the mechanism he was showing the entire time—a series of gears and pulleys he said was operating the trick—was actually a flat poster that only looked real because of a forced perspective trick. His demonstration of the workings of the illusion had been another illusion.

A trick within a trick within a trick.

The crowd gasped and applauded, and he took a proud bow. The group moved on, and he leaned against the prop and smiled over at her. "Want to climb in?"

Her cheeks went warm even as she glared at him. *Kind of.*

"Maybe later." He chuckled. "I know how you hate it when I hit on you during the workday." Before her very eyes, he vanished into smoke. Simply disappeared as if he hadn't ever been there. A voice whispered in her ear, one she now recognized. *"You really would make the best assistant."*

His hand pressed against her ass, grabbing it, and she whirled. No one was there. Not that she could see, anyway. She glared into empty space and swiped her hand through where she assumed he would be. Nothing. She didn't even feel a tingle.

A hand pressed against her stomach, fingers splayed, and she gasped. She went to brush him off, but it was like there was nothing there. And yet she could feel his warm skin on her under her clothes.

"I've been such a good boy not showing you what I'm really capable of. Oh, Alice, you have no idea what I can do to you."

She backed up, and the sensation of his touch left her. "Knock it off."

"You love to say that." He appeared in front of her, gathering out of nothingness. Hazel eyes were watching her but carried the wickedness she usually saw only when he was "dressed" as Julian.

No, he had always been that devilish thing. He was simply toning it down when he was pretending to be Charles.

She was still working on getting it straight.

"Maybe I wouldn't have to if you weren't so impossible."

"It really is the perfect moniker for me, isn't it?" He shrugged. "All right, fine. I'll stop." He looked down and nudged her foot with his. It was what he liked to do when he wanted to ask for something that mattered a great deal to him, but he was trying to pretend it didn't. "Dinner tonight?"

No. Yes. No. Yes. God damnit all. She admitted to herself that she wanted to have dinner with him. When he had touched her, fire had pooled dangerously in her stomach. She wanted him. She loved him. She wanted to beat the shit out of him. She was furious with him. She wanted him to kiss her everywhere and make it up to her.

It was going to give her a headache. Julian was looking at her, eagerly waiting for her response. Both hopeful and looking as though he was expecting a rejection at the same time.

He really was such a puppy dog sometimes.

She gave in with a heavy sigh. "What do you want me to make?"

"Nothing. My treat. Come up to my place at seven-thirty when you're off the clock." He smiled.

Oh. Oh, you shithead. "That's why you've been cleaning upstairs."

"What? I couldn't very well expect you to want to spend time in my place looking the way it did. The carriage house is nice and all, but I lived up there for a reason." He was still beaming, knowing he had won a little bit of a victory in her agreeing to have dinner with him. "I'll wait to ask you to move in." He paused. "Want to move in? Loki will love it up there."

She shook her head and walked away. "I'll see you later, *Charles.*"

She heard him laugh behind her.

Tucking her hands into her pockets, she shut her eyes.

He always moves so fast for me, but it's never anything I don't already want.

I know I should be mad at him. And I still am.

But the idea of leaving him hurts worse than forgiveness.

She looked down at the ring on her finger and found the answer was already staring at her in the face. She hadn't taken it off. She was mad. He had hurt her with his lies. He had terrified her. But...she still loved him.

One thing was painfully clear, though.

I'm an idiot.

11

It was seven o'clock when she heard the fire alarm go off. The panel was screaming loudly, and she ran to it to see where the alarm was coming from. The fourth floor.

Julian, you moron. What did you do?

She turned off the panel and was already halfway up to the fourth floor when her phone rang. She answered it and was greeted by the alarm company. "Hello, Ms. Monroe. We have a fire alarm coming from the estate."

"I know, I was in the house when it went off. I'm heading up there now. I think I know what it is, and I suspect it's probably smoke from a stove." She pulled the book that released the hidden door and found the lights were already on. She shut it behind her and walked up the stairwell.

Sure enough, Julian was standing in his kitchen, his sleeves rolled up past his elbows. The room was filled with smoke, and he had all the windows open. He was cussing up a storm, holding a dish towel and trying desperately to fan the smoke out the window.

She laughed. "It's fine, it's burnt food. Unintentional flambé, that's all."

"I wasn't aware there was a kitchen on the fourth floor," the guy from the alarm company said. "I'll have to put it in the notes."

"It doesn't get used much. Have a good night."

"You too, miss."

She hung up and put her phone into her pocket. She couldn't help but smile at how *angry* Julian was. He was red in the neck and was still swearing like a sailor. A very burnt whole chicken was sitting on a rack on the counter. It looked like something out of *National Lampoon.*

It wasn't until he threw the rag across the room and went to send a bottle of wine after it that she stepped in to intervene. "Hey, hey. Don't make a mess. It's not the wine's fault." She put her hands on his chest, and it stopped him from hurling the bottle. He seemed far more upset than a ruined chicken should warrant. Something else was up. "What's wrong? It's just a chicken. We'll—"

"I ruined it!" he snarled. He put the bottle of wine down hard enough that she was impressed neither the countertop nor the bottle cracked. "I ruined everything!" He paced the kitchen, fuming.

Oh. That would do it. She walked up to him and caught his elbow as he went past. He turned to her, his jaw ticking. The poor bastard. He had tried so hard to do something nice, and it hadn't exactly gone the way he had hoped, not even a little. She could sympathize. Wrapping her arms around his waist, she looked up at him with a smile. "It's okay."

"It isn't."

"It's just a chicken."

"It's more than that."

"And I'm telling you it's okay." She stood on her toes to kiss his cheek. "It's the gesture that counts."

He hung his head, the lines of his face smoothing as she kissed him. When she kissed his cheek again, she watched his shoulders slowly loosen. She knew she was the reason he was upset. He wanted her to forgive him, and he was trying to make it right with a nice dinner.

It was a sweet thought, even if the scale was a little off. She laughed.

"What?"

"'Sorry I terrorized you and made you think I had murdered your fiancé, who, in secret, has been me the whole time. Here's a chicken dinner. We good?'"

He smiled. "And? Is it working?"

Putting her head against his chest, she sighed. It was, but like hell she was going to let him know that. "Let's order something. Chinese?"

"I'll never turn down fried rice."

"Let's go sit on the porch and wait for it to show up. It's a beautiful night out, and it'll give this place a chance to air out."

He agreed, and they walked down there together as she placed the order on the phone. He sat next to her on the front steps. He had shed the illusion of Charles—really, it was only the eye color, some newer clothes, and that his hair wasn't slicked back like he wore it as Julian—and was looking out at the parking lot with his arms folded on his knees. He looked troubled.

"What?"

"I love you, Alice. I really do. And I don't know how to make up for what I did, but...I hope I will." He shut his mismatched eyes. "I'm not a good man. I never have been. I do terrible things. I don't know if my love is enough for you."

"Have you killed people before? Really?"

"Yes."

"In self-defense?"

"No, Alice."

She thought of Billy. "Recently?"

"No."

Small favors. She nudged herself closer to him until her arm was touching his. All of this made her a terrible person. She had never thought of herself as someone morally questionable. She'd never broken the law, she tried to be nice, to do good things, but...accepting that she loved someone like Julian was the same as condoning everything he'd ever done.

He was a murderer. An evil ghost. He had built a house to capture his soul. He had played games with her that transcended anything she had ever heard of someone pulling on anyone else. But when she pictured his smile and his laugh, it made her happy. When she remembered the feel of his kiss, it touched something in her that was profound.

Oddly enough, it wasn't the fact that he had pretended to be Charles that she was upset about. When she thought about it, she could see it from his point of view. How else *exactly* was he supposed to explain it to her? *Hi, honey. So, yeah, um, about everything. I'm dead! Ta-da. You don't have to worry about life insurance for me. Where're you going? Come back!*

It hadn't been the most graceful way to reveal the truth, and it was a little deranged to make the woman you love solve a puzzle to find your corpse, but he was a melodramatic man. Now that she could see the truth, it was clear that Charles and Julian didn't simply share a familial flair for the dramatic. It had been the same sick sense of humor the whole time.

It was when he had made her believe that Charles was

hurt that she was more upset about. And he had apologized profusely. He had acted rashly because she threatened to leave. It had been a desperate act to hold himself hostage. She was upset about it, but, again, in some stupid way, she could understand *why* he had done it.

"Julian?"

He turned to her, and those mismatched eyes of his seemed to cut to her soul. They were so beautiful.

"I'm going to stay. I don't know if I forgive you, but I—"

She didn't get the rest out. He had captured her words with his lips and pulled her into his lap.

The poor Chinese food delivery man had to clear his throat to interrupt them.

SHE MADE sure to feed Loki before heading up to the fourth-floor apartments to eat dinner. Julian had commented that red wine and Chinese food was an odd combination, but that he wouldn't complain.

They ate, drank, and it was like everything was normal. It was as if nothing had happened. He cracked jokes, played cards, and was still the same silly, over-the-top man she had fallen for. He was only Julian Strande instead of Charles Mensonge, was all. The apartment was well-lit and oddly comfortable now that it was cleaned up and cared for. He had spectacularly overdramatic tastes, but she wasn't shocked in the slightest when she thought about it.

Two bottles of wine later, and she felt comfortably a little drunk. It felt nice, letting all her concerns dissolve into a warm hum. "Can you even get drunk?"

"Uhm. No, sadly. It doesn't do anything to me anymore. I like the taste. But like food, or water, or sex, the aftermath doesn't keep." He shrugged and sipped his glass regardless. "I do really love the flavor."

"You're sitting there watch me slowly get toasted, then. That's not fair."

"I love watching you give in to your needs." He smiled sinfully. "Especially when they're wicked desires. Or when it's me. Even better is when I'm that salacious thing you want."

She felt her face explode in heat. He could always do that to her. She put down her glass and started to argue, but he vanished. Simply disappeared into thin air. She squeaked in surprise. "I wish you wouldn't do that."

"No, you don't. You love it. I see the way your eyes go wide. And it isn't in fear, is it? Not really..." he whispered, hot breath against her skin, and she felt his hands trace down her arms underneath her shirt. *"I warned you what would happen if you came up here, didn't I? And now, you've answered my invitation."*

Something picked her up. She would say it was hands, but it wasn't. It was a *force* that scooped her up from the sofa. She shrieked and flailed, but she couldn't touch anything. "Put me down!"

"No."

She was moving then. She didn't need to ask where. Suddenly, she was being tossed, and she fell onto a plush surface. His bed. As she hit, the lights flicked off and sent the room into darkness. "Julian, I—"

Lips sealed to hers, and she felt hands on her shoulders press her down onto the bed. She felt hands running up her legs. She felt fingers curling under her shirt, pulling it up.

Too many hands!

She struggled, but there were too many of them. They pinned her down even as more started to strip her of her clothing. Her shirt was pulled off over her head without ever stopping the kiss that seemed intent on devouring her.

She moaned against the lips pressed to hers. She couldn't help it. She heard him chuckle, and it was only then that he broke the kiss and let her breathe. She gasped. "Julian, I—"

"Ssh...It's okay. I have you. It's only me."

"But—"

"This is only the start of what I can do," he purred as he ran his tongue slowly along her lower lip. "Give in."

She gasped as the hands wandering up her legs reached her waist, undoing the fly of her pants and sliding them down slowly. Soon, she was lying there in her underwear, feeling like her body was on fire. She felt him everywhere, touching her in too many places at once.

The noises she made weren't ones of protest. She was writhing against the cover of his bed, pressing into the fingers that trailed all over her. They were holding her down and worshipping her all at once. Her hands were put over her head, pinned there by a tight grasp around her wrists. He was strong and gentle.

And he was *everywhere.*

"Look at you," he breathed in awe from somewhere above her. Her eyes were adjusting to the darkness, the only light the moon and the stars outside. But she could see well enough that there was nothing over her. He was invisible. But he was very much there all the same.

Hands wandered her and caressed her. She cried out and arched her back into his grasp.

"So beautiful. Such a perfect, wonderful, pretty, *naughty* girl. And you're all mine...Oh, Alice. Yes. Feel me. The *real* me."

An arm slung behind her back while she was arched up

into him, and deft fingers undid the clasp of her bra. He slid it up over her head, and once more, the pressure on her wrists didn't shift as the straps of her underwear passed through the presence there like it wasn't real.

But it very much was.

Lips captured one of her already hard nipples, pulling it into a hot, wet, hungry mouth. He only seemed to have one of those for now. She didn't know if she could handle more than that. He moaned as she watched in morbid fascination as her skin bent to his embrace, even though he couldn't be seen.

Her other breast twisted in invisible fingers as he pinched her other pert bud. She gasped and whined, tossing her head and squirming beneath him. "Fuck—oh, god—"

"I plan to, and yes, here in this place, I am," he murmured against her before nipping at her skin with his teeth. The rest of the hands that roamed her never stopped stroking, trailing along every part of her, yet skipping the place that was screaming for attention.

This wasn't simply turning her on—it was turning her into a raging inferno. It was official. She had problems. Serious, messed up problems.

On and on it went, more and more he teased and tormented her. It seemed like he was going to take his sweet time with her. When fingers traced over her parted lips, she opened her mouth to them willingly. She heard him groan as he slipped them into her mouth, pressing against her tongue, exploring her. She sucked on them eagerly. But she wanted more.

"Christ, I'm starting to wonder if you aren't as twisted as I am. Look at you. Oh, Alice, beautiful Alice." He pulled his fingers away from her. She lay there panting, her head spinning. "Open wide for me."

Her chest heaving, she whimpered. But she did as he asked. She wanted it just as much as he did. It wasn't long before she felt something press against her lips. Something she couldn't see. Something hot, hard, and throbbing. It slipped into her mouth, and she heard him moan obscenely from above her as he rocked forward. *"Shit,"* he snarled. "I will never, *ever* get sick of this."

She wondered if her pleasure was going to peak just from this. She was close. Her body felt like it was crawling with lightning.

"Brace yourself, pretty girl."

He began to pump himself inside her. He wasn't rough. Tonight clearly wasn't about that. The tempo he set was gentle as he filled her and relented, passing back and forth through her with a sinful and wonderful friction.

When a finger traced up her underwear, brushing against the place that felt like it was melting, she unraveled. Ecstasy exploded through her without warning, and she cried out, seeking more of the single finger that had barely even touched her. She squeezed her eyes shut tightly, careful not to clamp her teeth down around the invading invisible force in her mouth.

Julian laughed. A dark, vicious, and victorious sound. "Enjoying this, are you?"

Fingers stroked her through her underwear, before one parted her and slipped inside. For a second time, she was sent reeling over that cliff. She nearly screamed. She would have, if her mouth hadn't been more than a little full. She would have bucked and twisted away from him if it weren't for all the hands holding her down.

He left her then, and she filled her lungs with much-needed air. She felt dizzy.

"God*damn,* Alice." He sounded out of breath. That was a

stunt, seeing as he didn't currently have lungs. She didn't have the presence of mind to ask how that worked.

Her underwear was peeled away from her, and she watched in fascination as her legs were split by unseen hands, parting them wide and pressing her knees to the sheets. It put her on full display, and she felt her face grow warm, despite everything they had done.

When she felt a tongue slip up her body, she whimpered.

"Your turn," he murmured.

Hands grasped her breasts firmly and never left her. Never stopped twisting and playing with her as he lavished her. She couldn't take it. She unraveled again, and again, but he never slowed. Never stopped. He only chuckled at her as she gasped and wailed.

Every thought seemed to be dissolving into white noise. All she knew was his touch. His presence. Him. *Julian.*

It threatened to unravel her again. "Please—no more—"

"Oh?" The hands all vanished. They left her. She was lying there, panting, feeling her body covered in sweat. She was shaking. Lowering her hands from over her head, she grasped the pillow instead, overwrought.

"Julian..."

"Hm?"

He was still there, hovering somewhere near her, his face close to hers. She felt wrung out. She squirmed. She had felt his touch everywhere—literally everywhere—and now it was gone. It felt like such a disappointment. "Please..."

"You said to stop."

He sounded so goddamn pleased with himself. She didn't need to see him to know he was wearing that shit-eating grin on his face. She glared up at the source of his voice, and it drew a dark chuckle out of him.

"Do you want more?"

She parted her legs again for him, bending her knees. As she did, he took shape over her. The moonlight caught his blond hair, and she saw his naked form between her legs. He was warm, solid, and firm. And real. She reached up and let her hands run slowly through his hair, stroking over his neck and shoulders.

Blue and brown eyes were watching her, shining in hunger, in lust, and in love. He was so beautiful.

Her voice was a whisper when she broke the silence. She was honestly surprised she could speak at all. "Julian, I want you."

His lips descended on hers, and she felt his hands catch her knee and hook it over his shoulder. His tongue stole into her mouth as he pressed his body into her, filling the part of her that had been so desperate for him.

She wanted the ghost.

And he was eager to give himself to her.

JULIAN WATCHED her twist in the sheets of his bed beneath him as he slowly took her. It felt different this time. All of it felt somehow...more vivid. More visceral. As though now that the lie was gone, something had changed. When she whispered her desire for him—using his real name—he had nearly finished right there.

How perfect she had been only moments before, lying in his bed, crying out her release again and again as he tormented her body. Being a ghost certainly *did* have serious advantages. And oh, how eager he was to show her all of them. But he would teach her slowly, little by little. No point in rushing everything.

He rocked himself in her like a lover. She gasped with each thrust. He met her small sounds with his own. She felt like a volcano around him, and it was bliss. He wished they never had to stop.

Alice held on to him, her arms around his shoulder and back. *Him,* not Charles. She was embracing *him.* It almost sent him into a frenzy, but he held himself at bay. She had been to the edge of her limits, and if he pummeled her like he wanted to, it would be too much. He'd ravage her soon. Tonight was about her.

"Julian," she gasped. His heart danced at the sound of his name. It sounded so good passing those beautiful lips that were a little swollen from his attention. He kissed her cheek as he watched her fight another release that was trying to claim her.

"Go on. Let go. I have you."

She unraveled on him again, and he nearly spent himself in her depths. It felt *so good.* But he didn't slow, didn't stop, and in fact, sped up. It kept her there on that edge. She whimpered and mewled, tossing her head, desperate to be left off the knife's edge. No. He chuckled at her dismay, at what she must be feeling.

"Please, please—" The poor girl was at her breaking point.

He kept up this new pace, torturing her, not letting her come down from her high. "Please what?"

"I can't—" she gasped.

"Tell me you love me, Alice. Tell me the truth."

"Oh—oh, god, Julian—"

"If you love me, say it." Now he was pounding into her with the force he had wanted to use the whole time. She jolted with the impact against the sheets, and her eyes almost rolled into the back of her head. She clung to him in hopeless need. He really was a cruel bastard.

"I love you—I love you, Julian—I—"

He rammed himself into her then, pinning against her end. He couldn't help it. He tossed his head back as he felt pleasure consume him. A roar left his lungs as he felt it wash over him, threatening to empty everything else out of his mind in the process. As he did, she wailed, her own pleasure cascading to meet his.

When they were finally done, they were both gasping for air. He kissed her cheek slowly, again and again. If he could fall to his knees and worship the creature before him, he would do it in a second. "I love you, Alice."

Her arms tightened around him slightly. "I love you, Julian." She paused. "Even if you are a massive shithead."

He chuckled. She'd have no argument from him about that.

She fell asleep cradled in his arms. Naked, spent, and the most beautiful thing he had ever laid eyes on.

12

ALICE WOKE up feeling like she had been run over by a train. She had been. And the train had been named Julian Strande. But if given the opportunity, she'd lie down on those tracks again and again. Holy *shit.* What had happened last night wasn't just good, it had been...damn.

She had figured being with a ghost was going to be wild, but she hadn't expected that. She hadn't expected to have a nearly out-of-body experience at the hands—an impossible number of hands, and incredibly skilled ones at that—of a dead man.

She was nuzzled into his chest, her head lying in the crook of his shoulder, and she couldn't think of anywhere else she'd rather be. One of his hands was lying on her lower back, and the other was on her upper arm, tracing the colorful swirls of her tattoo. He loved them and found them fascinating. He had said as much several times.

Stretching, she let out a small grunt. Their bout might not have been as rough as previous times, but it had still worn her out. Muscles had clenched that she didn't know she owned.

"Good morning."

She grunted again in response. She didn't want to get up. She didn't want to move. He chuckled, and the arm around her squeezed her against him. They were both still very naked, although now she was lying under the covers and not on top of them. She was glad he had laundered. The last thing she wanted was dust caking into places it had no business being.

"Do you forgive me yet?"

"A little. Not all of it." She draped her arm over him and pulled herself the rest of the way against him. She loved the feeling of his lithe body against hers. "Not yet."

"Hm. I'll have to try harder, then."

"There's a harder?"

He snickered. "You have no idea."

She lifted her head and ran her hand through her hair, smoothing what felt like a tangled mess. When she finally opened her eyes, she found him looking at her, blue and brown, with such affection that it made her cheeks warm a little bit. "Stop it."

"Stop what?" He lowered one eyebrow quizzically.

"Looking at me like that."

"Like what?"

"Like I'm your whole world."

"But...you are." Without warning, he flipped them over, and she squeaked as he found herself on her back on the sheets, him over her, caging her in with his arms on either side of her. "So why shouldn't I?"

"Julian—"

"Keep saying my name. I love hearing it." He leaned his head down to her neck and kissed her throat. "To be fair, I've always loved hearing my name, but hearing you *scream* it transcends anything else I've ever known."

"I can't. Not again. Not yet. Give me a few more hours." She laughed and pushed his shoulders gently, trying to dissuade him before he started at it again. "Or at least let me take a damn shower."

"How about a sponge bath? How about I scrub every inch of your perfect"—he began kissing her between each word—"wonderful, amazing, beautiful, awe-inspiring, phenomenal—"

"Julian!" She slapped his shoulder. Not hard, but hard enough.

He sighed and lifted his head. "You're no fun." He fell down onto his elbows and smiled. "Breakfast?"

"If it isn't one hunger with you it's another, huh?"

"You're such a fast learner."

Shutting her eyes, she resisted the urge to slap him across the face. "Waffles?"

"Waffles!" And with that, he climbed out of bed.

Putting on her clothes was an adventure in "I didn't know that thing could be sore," but when she was dressed well enough and didn't look like she had been rolled down a hill in a trash can, they made their way downstairs and to the carriage house. Loki was both grumpy and excited to see them in a way only cats could manage.

"Oh, I know," Julian crooned to the cat as he picked up the ball of fur and hugged him to his shoulder. Loki mewed and did his favorite thing, which was to plant a paw flat against Julian's cheek. "Poor pooky. We left you alone all night, didn't we? Pretty soon, you and mom'll move in, and then we won't have to worry about it anymore."

"I never said I was moving in." She shot him a half-hearted glare as she went about making breakfast.

"No, but this back-and-forth game is going to get silly."

It was. He was right. It was clear he wanted to spend time in his apartments where he felt he most at home, but moving up there felt...too significant. It might be nonsense, but it would represent that she had fully accepted him, forgiven him, and she and Julian were officially together. She and a ghost.

She didn't know if she was ready for that. She still couldn't wrap her head around it. She loved him, and she loved being with him. Last night had been incredible. All of it including before, during, and after the Chinese food. But committing to a life together?

Life.

What the hell kind of life could they have, anyway?

She looked down at the ring on her finger. She was still wearing it. She had already committed to a life with him. *With Charles, who I thought was a breathing man. I thought we would grow old together. Now I'll grow old, and he'll stay the same. I'll die, and...he won't.*

"What's wrong?"

"Nothing. Thinking."

"Dangerous thing, thinking." He put the cat down on the dinette table and walked up behind her, slinging his arms around her. "I'll ask again. What's wrong?"

She shut her eyes and ran her hand through her hair, scratching her scalp. It was so hard to put into words she didn't know where to start. "You're dead."

"I've noticed."

"I'm engaged to...to a dead man."

"Mmhm." He kissed her shoulder over her hoodie. "And?"

"It makes things complicated."

"I went five months fooling you into thinking I was alive. And you had a front-row seat the entire time. If I can pull it off with you, I'll pull it off with everyone else. We can make this work."

"For a little while. I'll age. I'll die. You...you won't."

"We'll cross that bridge when we get to it." He turned her to face him but kept his arms around her. "I've lived too long. I've been alone for so long. I'm not going to turn away from happiness only because it's fleeting. I'll take what I can get. And I'm happy with you." He paused and lowered his head, his mismatched eyes still on her. "Are you happy with me?"

"Yes, but..."

He winced. "But?"

"I'm still adjusting. I'm willing to give this a shot, but it's all so strange." She sighed. "And I'm not sure I should even be trying to forgive you for what you did."

Julian nodded and leaned in to kiss her forehead. "I've been thinking."

"Uh-oh."

He chuckled. "No, no. Nothing bad. I want to teach you how to be my assistant on stage."

"Um...I'm not sure if that's the best idea."

"It's a great idea. Once you get over your stage fright, you'll love it. You're certainly flexible enough." He winked at her with that trademark smile of his. "You'll be fantastic. I have an eye for talent." With that, he pushed away to lean against the counter near her. "I'll teach you to be my assistant, and you teach me how to cook."

"Those are both impossible tasks."

"That's why they call me the Impossible Julian Strande, isn't it?"

"You're going to burn the house down, and I'm going to make an abject fool of myself." She turned back to the counter and began gathering all the ingredients she needed for waffles. She paused as she put the box of mix down. "You're doing this to give me another project, aren't you?"

"No."

She glared.

"Yes." He always looked grumpy when she called him out on his easy-to-spot lies. "You're happiest with a project."

"And you're happiest when I'm giving you attention." She folded her arms across her chest. "You're sad I solved your puzzle."

"You're right on the first count. The second, it's not sad so much as it's…I spent my life, literally and figuratively, setting that up. It's strange to think someone's solved it. I'm not sad. I'm elated it was you. But it's new territory for me as well." He picked up the box of waffle mix. "So, how do you use this shit, anyway?"

"The instructions are on the back."

He turned it over and made a face. "Instructions are boring."

"And that's why you can't cook." She laughed and pulled out the waffle iron. "You need to follow directions. More importantly, you need to pay attention."

"Two things I hate doing."

"Consider this lesson one, then." She pulled out the mixing bowl, the eggs, and the measuring cups. She took a step back and gestured at him.

"What? Now?"

"No time like the present."

"This was a terrible idea." But despite his complaint, he looked at the back of the box, and with a beleaguered grunt, began mixing the waffle mix. He kept looking back at the instructions, double- and triple-checking, before going on to the next step. She plugged in the waffle iron for him. "Does this mean you'll be my assistant now?"

"I'm going to be terrible."

"No. You'll shine. I promise. I have an eye for these things." He was mixing everything up now, looking down at the goop with a vaguely disgusted expression on his face. More than once, he picked up the whisk to watch the batter dribble off in sick fascination.

She shook her head. He was both a monster and adorable at the same time. This whole being his assistant thing was a terrible idea, but the only way to convince him of that was to show him. "Fine. I'll be your assistant. But as soon as you realize how bad I am, we stop."

"Deal." Glaring at the box again in annoyance, he poured the right amount of mix into the waffle iron, shut it, and flipped it over. "Now what?"

"We wait for it to beep, and then we take the waffle out *before* it's burnt to a cinder."

"How long will that take?"

"Two minutes, maybe."

He groaned and looked up at the ceiling. "I have to wait two minutes?"

"You have to listen for the beep, you impatient weirdo." She laughed. He turned to her, and there was a wicked gleam in his eyes. "What?"

"I know what we can do for two minutes."

He stalked toward her, and she took a step back reflexively. When her eyes went wide, his smile bloomed into a fiendish one.

"Julian, no."

"Mmmh, I don't believe you." He lunged at her, and she ducked under his arm to try to run around him. This was a game they had played a few times. Catch-me-if-you-can. He always could, and the end was always the same. Her stomach twisted in excitement. But she could make it past the sofa before he—

Something snagged her. Something wrapped around her waist and pinned her arms to her sides. Looking down... nothing was there. She gasped and couldn't think about it for very long before she was suddenly on the sofa, on her back. Well, mostly. She was hovering several inches off the surface but felt like she had hit something solid. *God this is weird!* Julian appeared beneath her, chuckling.

"Not fair."

"I'm a ghost. You'll learn exactly how unfair I can be."

She struggled, but whatever was holding her arms to her sides was still invisible and hadn't loosened its grip. "How're you doing this?"

"Magic." He snickered.

He tilted her head to him and kissed her. Cupping her cheek, he deepened the embrace, growling in his throat in need. She could feel his desire pressing against her rear from where she was lying on top of him. When he flicked his tongue against her lips, demanding entry, she granted it with a breathy sigh.

He slipped his knees between hers and split them, spreading her legs as he did. His hand slipped down her stomach slowly, his destination clear.

Beep.

His tongue tangled with hers, exploring and conquering every part of her as he slid his fingers against her body *through* her pants as if they weren't there. She arched against the force that was keeping her trapped.

Beep.

"Mmfh—" she mumbled against him, trying to pull her head back. The hand on her cheek went to her hair to grip it tight, keeping her still. "Mmf!"

"What?" He glared at her irritably as he broke the kiss.

Beep.

"The waffle."

He threw his head back and let out the world's most defeated groan. He disappeared out from under her, and she squeaked as she fell the eight-or-so inches to land on the sofa. Julian reappeared in the kitchen, opened the top of the waffle machine, and was glowering at it like it was the enemy.

She couldn't help but laugh and climbed off the sofa to join him in the kitchen. "You're ridiculous. You wanted to learn how to cook."

"I'm rethinking my decision." He reached for the waffle with his bare hand, and she tried to warn him before it was too late. But he plucked it out of the machine, his fingers grazing the hot iron, and he didn't make a sound.

"Julian—"

"Hm?" He looked over at her and plopped a waffle onto a plate and went about getting another cup of mix to make a second. "What?"

"The hot plate."

"Oh. Ah." He looked at it and shrugged. Putting his hand flat on the hot iron, he closed it down on himself. When she gasped, he shrugged one shoulder. "I can choose to feel pain or not." He lifted the lid and showed her his hand. No marks, no burns, nothing. There was no smell or hissing sound from the iron, either. "I'm real and not at the same time."

"Huh." She shook her head. "Why would you ever choose to feel pain, then?"

"Because it's a human thing to feel. I expect I'd go insane if I didn't." He poured the mix into the machine, splashing a little with a mumble, and shut the lid, repeating the process.

He cleaned up the drips with a paper towel. "I get dressed in the morning even though I can apparate clothing at will. I drink, I eat, I lie in bed at night. I yawn, I will my heart to beat. I can cry, I can bleed, and I can feel pain." He gestured her over to him.

Walking up, he folded her in his arms, her back against his chest, and he nuzzled into her hair. "Why? If you can be superhuman, why bother with all the silly stuff?"

"It isn't silly. It's what keeps me, well, me. I think other ghosts—weaker ones, things not like me—forget how to do them. Or choose to forget because they can't accept what they are. What a miserable way to exist. I'm human, and I always have been, and I never want to be anything else."

"Is that partially why you play Charles?"

"I like to be in charge of my own affairs, for one. And two, yes. I like to be alive. And I can be, so why would I choose to be dead?"

He had a good point. She snuggled into him, resting her hands on his.

"Besides. This means I get to fuck. And you can see how much I *love* to do that." He snickered. "Although that's been a new development of late."

"What do you mean?"

"I haven't been with anyone since I died. I'm...incredibly excited to see what other benefits my slightly-askew existence might give me." He grinned against her cheek before kissing it slowly. "You're going to be a very sore girl, Alice."

His hand wandered down her stomach again, and she gasped as he slipped his fingers against her, and into her, without even batting an eye about her clothing. She had to grab on to the counter for support as he delved into her. "Julian—"

"Oh, I love hearing you whimper my name." His other

hand twisted in her hair again, and he pushed her forward, bending her over at the waist. Running his hand around her, he had a much better angle of approach now. He moaned as he slipped two fingers inside her, slowly sinking them as deep as they could go.

Shutting her eyes, she couldn't help it. She surrendered to it. It felt too good. He was very, *very* skilled with his fingers. When a third one joined the fray, she let out a small cry, trying to arch out of his grasp. But he pressed her head down harder, keeping her still, as he slowly worked himself inside of her.

"I'm never going to get sick of this. Ever. I could keep you in bed for months. Well, maybe not only the bed. The sofa, the floor, the walls, the ceiling..."

"What?" she exclaimed, turning her head as far as she could.

He laughed darkly. "You think I'm joking? I think I'll fuck you on the ceiling next, then. You aren't afraid of falling, are you?"

"Julian! You wouldn't dare, you—" She was choked off in a cry as he rammed his fingers hard into her, jolting her body forward. The sound ended in a moan as she shuddered at what it did to her.

Beep.

Julian snarled. *"God damnit!"*

13

ALICE WAS SINCERELY REGRETTING her decision.

Agreeing to be Julian's assistant was an experience in trying not to run and hide. It wasn't that he was an impatient teacher. It wasn't that he was a bad teacher. He was neither of those things. He walked her through every moment of each trick with all the gentleness she could ever imagine. Even when she was convinced she was screwing it up.

No, it was the idea of standing on stage and having to *do* the things he was teaching her that scared her.

Julian had a very different opinion. He thought it was all going wonderfully.

"This is miserable." She looked down at the box she was standing on. It was a famous trick—called Metamorphosis—but he had created a special twist on it. One he couldn't perform since he had died because it required two people. "I suck at this."

"You do not, under any circumstances, suck at this." He took her arm and spun her to face him. For one of the few times since she'd known him, she was taller than he was.

She rested her arms on his shoulders. "That isn't to say you aren't very good at sucking, but this—"

"Julian."

He smiled, revealing his mischief, and leaned his head to kiss her forearm. "You are doing wonderfully."

"I don't think I can do this."

"You don't think you can get over your stage fright, is what you mean. You can perform the trick, no problem. You've done it flawlessly ten times in a row out of eleven attempts. You're perfect."

"I..." Okay, he was right. She was shy. She didn't want to be on stage in front of three hundred plus people. "I don't know if I'll be able to do it with so many people watching."

"Voyeurism not your thing, check." He hooked his arms around her waist and held her casually. "But you'll be fine. I promise. You'll freak out until the lights hit you, and then instinct and adrenaline will take over. You'll know what marks to hit, you'll know where you need to be, and you'll smile for the crowd. I promise."

"I think you're lying."

"When have I ever lied to you?"

She glared.

"Okay, okay, yes." He kissed her arm again. "Don't answer that." He flashed her that award-winning, trademark, perfect expression that was halfway between being sweet and evil. It was a little bit of both. It was both utterly punch-able, yet she wanted to kiss him anyway. He was such an egotistical bastard she wanted to push him down the stairs sometimes. But now she knew how little good that would do in the short or long run.

"You're a jerk."

"You've said. All right. One more time from the top? You're ready to perform tomorrow night."

"No. No, I'm not."

"Yes, you are. You're scared. You've got to rip the Band-Aid off, pretty rabbit. You—"

"What did you call me?"

Julian looked sheepish and lowered his arms from her waist and tried to turn away from her. She didn't let him. Grasping his shoulders, she forced him to stay facing her. "Nothing," he finally muttered.

"No. Seriously. What did you call me?"

He mumbled something under his breath. When she slapped him lightly upside the head, he grunted and repeated himself louder, like a kid caught with his hand in the cookie jar. "Pretty rabbit."

"I've never heard that one before."

"I…It generally doesn't come out as the loud part." Julian shrugged and looked down toward her feet, his fingers twisting into the fabric of her pants. "You always struck me as a rabbit."

"Why's that?" She wasn't sure if she was offended or not. She reserved her judgement until she heard his explanation.

"Beautiful, graceful, easily startled. Big eyes."

"And prey," she added to the list. "Your prey."

"No." He leaned his head in and rested it against her stomach. "That's not what I mean at all. I've always loved rabbits. I've kept several of them as pets before—" He groaned loudly. "That's not what I meant! I meant I think they're shockingly intelligent, resourceful, and underappreciated. They certainly don't get the credit they should and—shit, damnit all, I'm still not helping."

She laughed and pulled him up to her, hugging him. "You're an idiot."

"I am." He hugged her back, nestling himself closer. "No

arguments there. With you, I'm an abject fool. I'm certainly the dumbest smart person I've ever met."

Running her hand over his hair, she was glad it wasn't the kind of jelled hair that felt chunky or crunchy. It was smoothed back, but still felt soft under her fingers. It felt like Charles's hair. The more time she spent with him, the more she came to accept they were really the same man.

She had fallen in love with a ghost who had been pretending to be alive for various and sundry reasons. The most concerning still lingered in her mind. He had done it for fun. Because he enjoyed toying with her.

What else was he doing to toy with her?

"Julian?"

"Hmm?" He seemed utterly content where he was, nuzzled up against her.

"What else are you hiding from me?"

When he looked up at her, blue and light-brown eyes concerned and confused, he didn't need to speak to express that he didn't understand what she was asking.

"Tell me there isn't any more. Tell me there aren't any more lies, secrets, or stupid games. Your whole 'I'm Charles, psych, I'm Julian,' was the big reveal. No secondary round of applause. Right?"

In the past few days learning to be his assistant, she had been taught that some tricks carried two beats. The first reveal, and then the second, which would always one-up the first. Showing people one conclusion then pulling the rug out from under them with another, more spectacular punchline.

"There's nothing else." He shook his head. "No other lies or secrets."

"You promise."

"I promise."

She held up her pinky finger to him, and he took it with his. It felt childish to pinky swear with a grown-ass adult—ghost—who was older than two or three lifetimes, but she did it anyway. Pinky swears were law.

End of story.

"Great. Now that we have that settled..." Julian patted her on the thigh. She rolled her eyes. "Let's get back to the trick. You premiere tomorrow night, after all!"

"I'm not—"

"You are."

"I'm not."

"Oh, but you are." He chuckled. "And there's nothing you can do to dissuade me. When I get something in my head, I don't stop until it's reality. I bent the laws of physics and the universe to enact my will. Your stage fright is nothing in comparison."

She narrowed one eye at him. "Are you going to work dark magic to get me to perform on stage with you?"

"If I have to. Or I'll plug you full of a few shots of whiskey. I figure it'll do about the same thing." He patted her on the ass that time.

She tried not to smack him. "Once more, and then we're calling it for the night."

"Deal."

"And I'm not going on stage with you."

SHE WENT on stage with him.

Why does that asshole always get to be right? And he was. She had stood behind the curtain, terrified and shaking, until it parted, and she had no other option but to go out on stage with him. The outfit he had her wearing was ridiculous, but not nearly as skimpy as he had tried to get her to wear.

Once the lights hit her, once the music started, it all became reflexive. She hit her marks, she gestured when she was supposed to, and—damn him—she even smiled at the audience.

When he shackled her arms behind her back and tucked her into the wooden box, she knew how to get out of the restraints. It turned out, quite to her surprise and Julian's, that she had a knack for escape artistry. It was simply another kind of puzzle. She had never tried picking locks before or anything of the sort, but it came naturally to her.

She didn't think she had a single skill in anything. It was nice to be able to do *something* right for once.

Slipping out of the shackles, she pulled the pin that allowed her to roll out of the box on cue. Julian was standing atop the box, supposedly preventing her escape. He was pulling the sheet up and over his face to show he was still there. One more time, and it would drop away. She climbed onto the box to take his place.

In the real trick, he was supposed to climb into the box for the reveal. But most magicians couldn't literally vanish into thin air. As he let go of the sheet, he did exactly that, revealing only her. The crowd applauded.

Two reveals. It was always about the second beat. She bowed then hopped off the box. Opening the lid, she tipped the box onto its face, revealing it to be completely empty.

Julian walked in from the back of the theater, the follow-spots swiveling to illuminate him. She could barely see him from the glare of the stage lights, but she heard the crowd's cheering double in effort. It had only been a second, maybe a second and a half between when he had disappeared from the stage and reappeared in the aisle.

Alice took a step back as Julian jumped back up onto the stage, clearing the lip with easy grace. He took her hand in his and brought her to the front for a bow.

"Not so bad after all, huh." He had his microphone turned off. She appreciated not being taunted over the speakers.

"I hate you sometimes."

"I know."

After the show, she met him backstage. She had only been in two of the tricks, thankfully. She was exhausted and didn't know how he could handle an hour going full tilt like that. No wonder he was always jacked up after the end of a show. Ghost or not, she knew he must have been exactly the same as a living man.

Julian was beaming. When he saw her, he made a beeline straight for her. She squeaked as he scooped her up off her feet and twirled her around. "You were astonishing! Amazing. Oh—oh that'll be your moniker. The Amazing Alice Strande!"

"Whoa—whoa, now, settle down." She laughed and clung to him.

"You were so fast with those cuffs I almost didn't make it to my mark in time. You are a natural with escaping restraints. Maybe it's because of how much you like being *in* them. I don't know, but—"

"Julian!" She was still laughing.

He was rambling a thousand miles an hour and showed no signs of stopping. "I'll teach you all of Houdini's famous tricks. We can make you a new part of the act. The crowd *loves* you. You're such a perfect foil for me. So innocent looking, so beautiful. The angel to my devil. We have to do this again. No arguments!"

He finally stopped to breathe—although she realized he didn't honestly have to if he didn't want to—and collapsed onto the sofa, with her still in his arms. She wound up on his lap. He leaned his head back and let out a long and contented rush of air from his lungs.

To say he looked happy was to put it mildly.

"I figured you wouldn't like to share the stage," she teased.

"Maybe with anyone else, that's true. But with you? Oh, I haven't had this much fun in forever. I've felt—pardon the pun—like my act was starting to lose its spirit. Its life. You bring such a new energy to it." He picked his head up to kiss her, catching her cheek in his palm as he did.

For once, he was kissing her without the clear and burning desire to throw her over a piece of furniture and hump her for hours. Not that she usually minded that. But this kiss felt different. It was elated and full of love. The tenderness in it took her breath away, and she returned the gesture.

When he finally broke away, mismatched eyes were gazing at her once more like she was his sun, moon, and stars. She had never had anyone look at her like that. She had never meant that much to anyone before. She knew he loved her, and she loved him—but to see it so clearly reflected in him was another thing entirely.

She couldn't even muster the strength to be annoyed that he assumed she'd take his last name. Or that she was really going to marry him at all. She didn't even know if she wanted to make the argument, for starters. He had a better last name than she did. And...she was still wearing the engagement ring he gave her for a reason.

"Julian?"

"Hm?"

"I love you."

Something sparkled in his eyes again, and she realized he was tearing up. She furrowed her brow in concern. "What's wrong?"

"Nothing. Absolutely nothing. Everything is great." He shook his head and wiped his eyes with a sleeve. "I never pictured myself for a crier. I never really did my whole life. I suppose now I have something worth all the emotion."

"I should probably call my aunt and uncle and finally tell them we're engaged." She sighed. "How're we going to handle this? With you being, well, unable to travel and all."

"Use the agoraphobia excuse. Tell them I have a crippling issue where I suffer mental breakdowns when I travel. It always works. People are too polite to ask questions. Ask them to come here. I would love to meet them."

She smiled. "You're saying that to be nice."

"Well, of course. But that's what you do, isn't it? Meet the in-laws. I have a large house with things to gawk at to take the brunt of the time. That should diffuse most of the awkward conversation."

"I suppose the wedding will have to be here too. Unless you want me to video stream you in. We could put you on a tablet on a stand."

He laughed and shut his eyes, leaning his head back against the sofa again. He looked no less pleased and cozy than he did a few seconds ago. "Yes, we'll have a ceremony here. As amusing as that would be otherwise." He opened one eye to peer at her curiously. "I take it, then, you've forgiven me?"

"Mostly. I'll hold a grudge for a while. I'm really good at it." She fiddled with the edge of his vest, needing something to focus on that wasn't the way he was looking at her. She was in love with him. She was happiest when she was around him. Heading off to the horizon sounded like a miserable and empty existence.

It seemed like a sad and terrible thing to admit, but considering all that, it didn't really matter if she forgave him or not. If she couldn't leave him, if she wanted to be with him anyway, what he had done wasn't awful enough to outweigh it.

"Did you have fun tonight?"

The question snapped her out of her thoughts, and she blinked as she tried to figure out an answer. It was an answer she hadn't expected. She had wanted to answer no and say that was the most miserable and harrowing experience of her life, but she found...that wasn't true. That would be a lie. But admitting that to him was also annoying. She hated letting him win things. He won all the time, and he always looked so smug when he did.

"I suppose I did, a little bit." She shrugged, trying to downplay it. "It wasn't the worst thing ever, I guess."

Her ruse didn't work. He cackled and squeezed her to him in a hug. "You did enjoy it! I thought so. I saw that glimmer in your eye. You're a terrible liar. You were smiling for real. That's why you were so radiant."

"Don't rub it in."

"Oh, I'm going to. When have you known me to let anything go? I'm never going to let you live this down. We're going to start practicing more elaborate escape acts with you starting on Sunday."

"It's my day off." Any port in a storm.

"This isn't part of your day job." He poked her in the side, making her jump. "This is your new hobby."

"So, you're saying I'm not getting paid for this?" She scoffed. "Bullshit. I demand half the take."

He looked shocked at first, and then realized she was joking. She yelped as he tossed her onto her back on the sofa and caged her in with his arms on either side of her head. "Ridiculous. You're in two tricks. It hardly deserves such a steep cut."

"Well, see, you've already made it clear you need me to save your failing act, so I think it's worth it to you."

"Failing! Pah." He laughed, his blue and light-brown eyes catching the light, giving him a wicked and devilish appearance. She really did love him like this. She adored the puppy-dog, teddy-bear aspects to his personality, but it was when the demon came out to play that she had the most fun. "Fine. Half. You drive a hard bargain, and I showed my hand before negotiations were over. My fault, I suppose. But I'm not going to pay you in money, dear Alice. Oh, no. I'm going to pay you in something far more valuable."

He leaned down, sinking onto his elbows. He bent his head to kiss along her jawline, and she tilted her head away to give him more room. He feathered his way up to her ear. It was only when he rolled his tongue slowly along the sensitive hollow beneath it that she remembered they were having a conversation.

"Oh? What's that?"

He nipped at her earlobe. "Me."

14

JULIAN WINCED at the scream that came from the computer speakers from the older woman on the other side of the video chat. Technology was certainly becoming impressive. It felt to him like this kind of thing wasn't possible as of yesterday. Everything in the world seemed to be moving at an exponential speed.

He was sitting beside Alice, his eyes hazel, his clothing carefully tailored to be modern. He was "Charles" for the duration of the call. As much as Alice had bemoaned having to lie to her family, she finally conceded trying to explain to them that she was engaged to the ghost of a man who had been dead since 1912 was an exceptionally bad idea. It wasn't going to go well, and the lie was unfortunately the better option.

The older woman on the call—Aunt Beth, he thought he remembered, but he hadn't really been paying attention—was clearly ecstatic and over the moon with excitement. The older man, Alice's uncle, was looking at Julian with far more scrutiny.

Julian smiled at him, probably with more of a layer of

taunting smugness than he was supposed to, but he didn't care enough to try to stop it from happening. *Disapprove all you want. There's not a damn thing you can do about it.*

Apparently, his expression was easy to read, as Alice elbowed him out of view of the camera. He turned his head to cough. Mostly, he did it to hide his amusement.

"Isn't this kind of fast?" Alice's uncle asked. "And isn't he your boss?"

Julian glanced to Alice. "I see where you get it now."

She elbowed him harder.

"John, be nice!" Aunt Beth smacked John in the chest. "Be happy for her."

"I am. I'm plenty happy." The man's tone said otherwise, but he figured that was likely his standard mode of expression.

Julian had the man pegged instantly. He was the grumpy, stern, overbearing type. His own father had been very similar. Or...he imagined he had been. Julian had honestly never known his father. Edgar had only been a violent specter of his youth. He had always been rather happy for the man's absence. Being in Edgar's presence never ended well. Instantly, Julian did not like her Uncle John. The aunt seemed all right, if utterly uninteresting.

They were also quite old. From the looks of things, the couple was in their early or mid-seventies. There must have been an age gap between Beth and Alice's mother.

It meant they would not be around for long.

Good.

Excuses only went so far and so long. "Why don't you two come and visit us soon?" He wrapped his arm around Alice and shifted in closer to her. "I would love to show you the museum."

"That sounds lovely." Aunt Beth was beaming. "Oh,

Alice, I'm so happy for you! I was so worried you would spend your life alone. I'm glad he was smart enough to do something about it, since I'm sure you were too shy to say anything."

There was a twitch in the corner of Alice's eye, but she kept her annoyance from showing up anywhere else on her face.

He had deeply disliked his own parents, and now he was adding his in-laws to that list. *They have five years, ten at most. They won't be an annoyance for long.* He would suffer a great deal of irritation for her sake. Far more than a few insipid phone calls and awkward conversations with an aged couple.

"That's fairly accurate," Julian interjected. "Well, this has been wonderful meeting you both, but *we* both have to get back to *work.*" It was a lie, it was Sunday, and he had started taking the day off to enjoy it with Alice. But he already enjoyed needling her uncle, whose disapproving glower had deepened at his words.

"We'll check the calendar and see when we can come by for a visit!" Beth was still beaming, clearly ecstatic. They said their goodbyes, and Alice ended the video call.

She sighed. "I'm shocked she didn't ask me if I've gained weight. Or get accused that you knocked me up and that's why we're getting married."

"Lovely people," he said dryly. "I can't wait to meet them."

"They're really not that bad. I promise. Uncle John'll warm up to you."

"I can make him warm up to me." He grinned darkly. "Maybe I'll possess him and make him dance around on a table with his shirt off."

Alice blinked. "Wait, what?"

Oops.

"Hm?" He tried to brush it off.

But his astute little puzzle-solver was too quick for that. "You can...*possess* people?"

"I'm a ghost. Of course, I can." He shrugged. "I can take control of any living thing for a short period of time."

"That's...creepy."

"I'm a ghost. What else would I be?"

"Fine, but it's still weird."

He stood from the chair and stretched, cracking his back. He had always had a crick in his spine that had come from many years of working over a bench. If it weren't for his stage performance requiring him to look dignified, he expected he would have terrible posture. While his body was a lie, it was also a memory. And he always remembered having to pop his back after sitting for too long. The human mind was an astonishing thing. Human needs defined so much of it.

Speaking of. "When you go grocery shopping today, I have some things I'd like you to pick up." He handed her a note from his pocket.

She looked down at the list curiously and shrugged. "Sure."

They had been continuing their "exchange program." She was teaching him to cook, and she was learning to be his assistant on stage. Honestly, she had a far more natural talent at her assignment than he did his. She was wonderfully quick with lockpicking. He was an abysmal cook, no matter how patient and careful she was in showing him what to do.

But it was a wonderful game, and he was happy to keep

playing it. Especially because he was slowly getting his way. He had no real interest in preparing food, but he did have a great deal of investment in getting her on stage with him.

Alice headed out an hour later to pick up the groceries he had requested. He took the opportunity to whisk off into one of his secret workshops beneath the house to stand and gaze at the wedding present he was going to give her very soon.

The gift was complete, but the preparations around it were still in the works. It would take him more time to set everything up before he could begin.

Magic was such a complicated thing. The illusions he performed on stage paled in comparison. Laying his hand on the glass surface of his sculpture, he smiled. But it was all going to be very much worth it.

He would wait until Alice's irritating family came and went. He would entertain them, he would be charming, and he would even win over Uncle John. Without the aid of possessing him, even.

Then he would marry her.

Maybe not in the way she expected.

Maybe not in the way she would hope.

There would be no ceremony. No service. No reception. It would be a very private...very intimate moment between the two of them.

Stroking his hand over the surface of his masterpiece, he let his fingers trace over the monogram he had laid into the lid in emerald stained-glass. A.S. Alice Strande. He picked up a cloth and polished off a bit of solder on a piece of copper he had missed earlier.

While they had been intimate many, *many* times before, and he expected to continue to repeat that pattern, their wedding would be certainly something special. One act was repeatable, and the other was not.

He took a step back and examined his work. It was perfect. The spell was still in process, but this part was truly magnificent.

I'll only be able to kill you once, pretty rabbit.

Alice's coffin was complete.

A BAGUETTE, some crabmeat, some mayonnaise, a whole bunch of random things, and two bottles of white wine. She looked down at Julian's shopping list and shook her head with a smile. It wasn't hard to figure out what he was doing. He was trying to make a dinner for them. One that wouldn't require turning the stove on.

He could follow instructions well enough when he focused, but recipes that required paying attention for longer than sixty seconds generally did not end well. The only reason the carriage house hadn't been burned to cinders was because she was there to keep an eye on him.

She hated to say he didn't stand a chance, but he was pretty damn hopeless.

When she got back home after grocery shopping, she shouted for him. He appeared a few moments later—literally out of thin air—and she jumped in surprise. "Stop doing that!"

"Nope. Never." He began digging through the bags of groceries, shoving a few grapes he found into his mouth as he rooted around. He was pulling out all the things he had asked for and setting them into one of the now-empty paper bags.

"What're you planning?" She was pretty sure she knew, but she liked needling him over it anyway.

"Nothing."

"Julian."

"What? Why can't I have a few surprises? Geez, pretend to be a living man once, and now you don't trust me."

"I can't imagine why."

"Let me have my surprises, you have yours. You've got that model you've been printing in the basement for months now, and—" He looked at her, cringed, realizing what he'd done, and his shoulders slumped comically. "I mean...I'm sorry."

She laughed. He looked so concerned she was going to be upset that he knew that it was hard to feel disappointment. She pulled him into a hug, draping her arms behind his neck to stand close to him. His hands rested on her hips casually, even if he did still look sheepish and ashamed. "I figured you knew."

"It's hard not to. I mean, the house is kind of me, after all."

"Huh?"

He shrugged. "I'll explain later over my surprise. Which is a picnic out in the gardens by the pond." He kissed her forehead. "I ruined yours, I'll ruin mine. It's only fair."

The grounds of the estate were as big and winding as the house itself. The gardens were beautiful when they were in full bloom. She hadn't known what to expect, since she had begun working in the fall and through the winter. Now, at the beginning of summer, everything was ablaze in color. She hadn't even known there were koi fish in the pond until a few weeks ago.

A picnic sounded fun. Julian had the yard sprayed for mosquitos fairly regularly to benefit the tourists, and it meant they could go out and enjoy the weather when it was nice. Wisconsin had such a small window of nice weather. But then again, she was from San Jose, and it was always nice there.

After piling everything into the paper bag, he picked it up in his arms. He could take objects with him when he vanished, which was bizarre at best.

Apparently, he could do it with living things as well. He had walked Loki through a door once as a demonstration, and the cat had seemed utterly nonplussed by the whole ordeal. He had offered to show her too, but she politely declined. He'd pull that kind of stunt with her eventually, she was sure. She didn't need to volunteer for it early.

"I'll see you out by the pond in an hour?" He was adorable when he was excited, and it was clear he was itching with impatience like a kid on Christmas morning. It was only three in the afternoon, but she wasn't going to shoot down his early dinner.

"Sounds great. Try not to burn the house down."

He looked down into the paper back thoughtfully. "Nothing in here requires turning the stove on."

"You'll still manage to burn something, impossible or not."

Chuckling, he vanished, taking the bag of groceries with him. His voice came from nowhere in particular. "That is my moniker, after all."

And with that, he was gone. She was starting to get a sense for when he was near, even if she couldn't see him. It was a strange little buzz in her head. It was subtle, but it was that inkling of a sensation like someone was watching her.

She flopped down on the sofa, reaching out to pet Loki, who was loafing on the arm. He purred and shut his eyes happily before stretching and wandering down to plunk himself into her lap. She set an alarm on her phone in case she nodded off.

Sure enough, as soon as her head hit the pillow, she dozed. There was something about a warm purring ball of fur in her lap that did it. She grunted in surprise as the alarm chimed. She had given herself fifteen minutes of warning to get up, change into nicer underwear—she knew how tonight was going to go without question—and put on something that was a little prettier than whatever she shlubbed around the house in on her day off.

After feeding the cat early and patting him on the head, she slipped her phone into her pocket and went to find Julian out in the garden. It wasn't hard. He had set up the blanket by the shore of the pond and was arranging the food on a serving tray. He was wearing slacks and a white button-down that was rolled up at the sleeves with the first few buttons undone. He somehow managed to look both nice and casual at the same time.

"Right on time." Julian smiled as she walked up to him. He had cheese and crackers, some crudité, and it looked like he had made crab salad sandwiches. Spreading his arms, he gestured dramatically at the picnic spread. "Ta-da!"

Lordy, he was adorable sometimes. She was smiling like the smitten idiot she was as she walked up to him to kiss him. "You're sweet. This is wonderful."

"I might not be able to cook you a dinner without adult supervision, but I can make a good sandwich." He wrapped his arms around her and kissed her back, slower that time.

"Baby steps." She chuckled. "I'd ask you if you cut your hand open making the food, but you're already dead."

"There are definite benefits to my state of being." He took her hand and led her to the center of the blanket, sitting down and patting the ground next to him. She took a spot next to him and only around then did she realize she was hungry.

She snagged a few pieces of cheese as he poured her a glass of wine. He handed her one and lifted his in a toast. "To us."

"To us." She tinked her glass against his and took a sip. "What's the occasion?"

"A beautiful day and a beautiful girl. That's all. Why do I need an excuse?" He picked up some prosciutto and a piece of melon from another plate and began wrapping the meat around it. She hadn't ever seen that before, and now she had to try it.

"Fair point."

They ate in comfortable silence for a little while. The sandwiches were fantastic, and she told him as much. He had made it from scratch, otherwise she would have thought it had come out of a can that way. He might be terrible at making anything that needed to be heated up, but seasoning was apparently his strong suit. She'd have to figure out how to work with that.

"Alice?"

"Hm?"

"Move into the fourth-floor apartment with me." He paused. "Please?"

"Why is it so important to you?"

He took in a breath, held it, and seemed to think over his answer before exhaling. As he let it out, the first few words came out as a rush. "I know it's silly." He shook his head. "But the carriage house has become your space. It's more modern, it's smaller, it's...separate. I want you to be in my home, *with* me." He laid back on the blanket, tucking an arm behind his head, looking up at the blue sky dotted with the occasional white cloud. "I know I'm a lot to deal with. Even if I weren't dead, I'd be more than a handful."

She chuckled but didn't interrupt.

His lips twinged upward as he fought a smile at her quiet laugh. "And as I'm a ghost, I know this is so much to take in. I'm asking a lot of you. I have since the day we met. I push you too hard, maybe. But my apartment is...me. It's my home. I knew when I built it, it's where I would spend a thousand years if I was lucky. Does that make sense?"

"It does." She looked off thoughtfully. "You said you were the house. What do you mean by that?"

"I put my soul into a body, even if it isn't flesh and bone. I meant it literally. Its walls, its wiring, its plumbing and paint, it's all me." He shut his eyes as he basked in the sunlight. "I feel every open window and every door. Right now, if I focus, I can tell you which bulbs are on and which ones aren't."

"Now I feel really gross about going to the bathroom."

He howled in laughter. "No, no, it's not like that." He cackled still and opened his eyes to watch her with a joyful smile. "It's like feeling your fingernails or your hair. I have to touch it to really know it's there. That's one kink I'm not into, so don't worry. Yet."

She laughed and slapped his side.

"Please move in with me, Alice. You can say no. But I'm going to keep asking."

"You won't mind having me constantly underfoot? Poking through your things, adding my stuff to your shelves?"

"I could think of nothing that would make me happier. Loki can even smash a few glass candlesticks by shoving them off the mantel if he wants. Alice, I love you. Want you to be with me for as long as possible, as much as possible."

For as long as possible. She repeated the words to herself silently and looked off into the pond. She didn't want to ask him what he would do when she was gone. It was like the thought of Loki dying. She knew it would crush her. She loved that cat more than she loved most people. He was her little fluffy soulmate. When she died and left Julian here alone, she knew he might snap. He might go insane. At the very least, she knew he'd be destroyed for a very long time.

"Okay."

He sat up so fast he nearly knocked over his wine. "Really?"

"Sure. It's going to get stupid bouncing back and forth between the two places. Loki will love all the windows and all the nooks and crannies. We can't let him wander out into the rest of the house. He'd wedge himself somewhere stupid, and we wouldn't find him for weeks. And—"

She didn't get out the rest of what she was saying. He was hugging her too tightly. And then he was kissing her, stopping any other chance she had of getting a word out.

When she finally broke off, he was grinning like a pumpkin on Halloween, and she was laughing. He really was adorable when he was excited.

"Oh! Oh. Watch this!" He vanished in a swirl of what looked like incense or smoke. She jumped and growled in frustration. Damn him and his constant "ghosting" in and out of conversations.

She looked around, unsure of what it was she was supposed to be watching. She couldn't see anything. A few seconds later, she saw movement in a bush nearby. Out from under it came hopping a little brown rabbit. It was adorable.

Even if it was moving a little weirdly. At first, she wondered if it was hurt. It wasn't using its limbs right. But after a few feet, it seemed to get the hang of it. It hopped over to her, and she looked down at it in surprise.

"Hey, there, little buddy, what's up?"

The rabbit bounced up to her and put its front paws on her leg. She chuckled, unsure of what was happening, and reached down to gently pet it. It was soft, and it nuzzled into her fingers, apparently loving it.

When the rabbit looked up to her, she gasped.

Its eyes were mismatched.

One bright blue. The other light brown.

Julian.

He had possessed the rabbit, as he said he could. Her mouth fell open, stunned. She didn't know what to do.

And just like that, the rabbit blinked a few times, and its eyes went back to large dark circles. It looked around, clearly confused and disoriented, before it sniffed the air, then her, and then decided it wanted to be back in the bushes and very far away from the strange monster that she was. It hopped away and went back into the underbrush.

"Being a rabbit is strange."

She shrieked at the sudden voice. Julian was sitting next to her on the other side, right where he had been before he disappeared.

"Sorry," he chuckled. "Right. Try to startle you less. I'll get there."

"That...that was you."

"Mmhm."

"You can...possess people. And animals."

"I promise I've never haunted your cat as an excuse to climb into your lap." He picked up his wine glass and sipped it. "Promise."

She glared. She didn't believe him.

"Oh, I've snuck into your bed *plenty* of times. I didn't need the cat to do it."

"You're a jackass." She drank the rest of her glass of wine in one go and refilled it. She'd need some more. "An absolute jackass, and the fact that you can do that is creepy and weird. Someone like you shouldn't be able to do that kind of thing."

He laughed. "There's the motto for my life. Julian Strande: What Happens When A Jackass Gets Too Much Power." The moment she set down her wine, he snaked an arm around her waist and pulled her into him then down onto the blanket. "Don't pretend you don't like it."

She looked down at him and shook her head. "I shouldn't like it."

"But you do. Not only that, you love it."

"Which is even worse."

He leaned up and kissed her. His hand tangled in her hair, and as he rested his head back against the blanket, he took her with him without ever parting. She shifted to move closer to him, bracing her weight against his chest. She knew if she wasn't careful, he'd want to screw her on the blanket in broad daylight on a day the museum was open.

It was the thought of onlookers that made her pull away from him. He didn't seem to mind. He was lying there, a blissful smile on his features. His eyes were shut, and all the lines of his face were smoothed. He couldn't look any happier.

"I love you, Julian." She knew it had been true, but seeing him like this solidified it in her mind. Come what may, she couldn't imagine anything that could drive her away from him. "And I forgive you."

She had thought he couldn't look happier. Now she knew he could. He squeezed her to him, hooking one of his legs over hers as he hugged her. She leaned her head down to rest her cheek against him. She could hear his heartbeat, and it was comforting, even if it was an illusion.

"I love you so much, Alice...more than you may ever really know. But I promise I'm going to try to show you."

She smiled wistfully and shut her eyes, letting herself enjoy his presence and the smell of cloves that always clung to him.

Life was good. Strange. But good.

15

SHE WAS SETTING her last box of stuff in Julian's apartment when her phone rang. Loki was prowling around, sniffing at everything. But as Julian had predicted, the cat already seemed to love the larger, more sprawling place to live. It also smelled like someone he was already fond of, so that helped.

Looking down at her phone, she narrowed an eye. Her phone still read "Charles," and it was that dorky picture of him and her cat. She would have to fix the name as soon as she hung up. He had gone off to take care of some things.

Answering the phone, she lifted it to her ear. "I still don't know how you can do this."

"I'm in the house, and I am the house. I can feel everything in here, and I can control every wire in every wall like they were bits and pieces of me. Wireless electronics may not plug into my walls, but they're still in my domain. So, I can call you when you're inside the footprint of my property. Have I ever called you when you've been off-site?"

She thought about it. "No, you haven't." She sighed. Another thing she hadn't noticed. The more he pointed out how obvious it was that something fishy had been going on, the dumber she felt. "So, why're you calling me if you can ghost your ass up here?"

"Easier than going all the way up there. I'm down in the theater, and I've decided it's time to teach you a new trick. A real one. A big one. Come down and meet me on the stage." He paused. "And I do not *ghost* my ass anywhere. That isn't a verb."

"It is now."

It was Tuesday, and ten in the evening, so the staff was long gone. He often wandered off to take care of random tasks without warning. Either he said he had paperwork to do, or other mysterious excuses. Much to his chagrin, she had dubbed it "ghosty things" or "dead guy stuff." But she didn't pry. He had his right to some alone time.

Most of the time, he was somewhere in the house working on one trick or another, she guessed. And this time it had proved right.

"Okay, sure. I'll be down in a few minutes."

"Great!" And with that, he hung up. It was still very, very strange that he could spontaneously call her phone from anywhere. *How is that different than if he had a cell phone? This way, he can't text random dick pics.* She knew he was *definitely* that kind of guy.

She chuckled at the idea and, patting Loki on the head, she headed down to the stage. It was weird, thinking she was living in the big museum, but she would get used to it. The staff had already been informed, and they all seemed fine with it. The carriage house would go back to its role as a guest house for weddings or a private event space.

When she walked into the theater, Julian was on stage, humming and polishing a...giant wall of metal spikes.

Well, okay, then.

There were two walls of spikes, to be precise, to the left and right of a truss structure that was built in the shape of an upside-down U. The top of the upside-down U had two holes in it, roughly wrist sized.

A folding table nearby had an arrangement of handcuffs. Several of them, about five or six, all laid out.

She could see where this might be going.

It looked like the walls of spikes were meant to fit around the truss, and...squish whoever it was strapped into the terrible device. It'd be a horrifying way to die. She'd seen other things in the museum like this, like a riff on Houdini's famous water escape, and so on. But never anything like two giant lever-arm walls of metal spikes.

Luckily, they weren't attached to anything. They looked lowered off of whatever mechanism was meant to drop them. She followed the cables that were meant to draw them upward and saw they led to a large mechanical clock that was the backdrop for the whole thing. Both hands were set at zero. It looked as though it was a sixty-second timer.

Julian was watching her, leaning against the frame of the spikes. He had a knowing smile plastered across pleased, wicked features. He was up to no good. "Have you figured out what it's for yet?"

"I think so. I don't think I'm quite ready for this, unless your plan is to make an Alice-kabob for dinner tonight."

"No, no. We'll take it one step at a time." He fished into his pocket and pulled out her little white plastic kitchen timer. "Thirty minutes on the clock, and no spikes. Eventually, you'll need to be able to do it in thirty seconds. You'll have sixty for the real trick, but I want to make sure you can beat it by half before we try it for real."

She walked up the stairs to the right of the stage and stepped up to the enormous, vicious-looking thing. It looked old. "I've never seen this one in the collection before."

"It's been in my private warehouse." He touched one of the spikes almost lovingly. "I made it for Houdini himself, but he decided it too dangerous. Said he finally had proof I was trying to kill him. So, off into storage it went."

"Private warehouse?" She narrowed an eye at him. "Where's that?"

"There's a level beneath the basement you haven't even found yet."

"But there aren't any doors or stairs."

"There isn't. You're correct."

"So, there's no way to get in or out unless—" She almost smacked her forehead. The answer was so obvious. She was thinking about the house from a living person's perspective. "Unless you can walk through walls." She shook her head. "Clever bastard."

"Thank you." He set the timer on the table next to the handcuffs. "Here's the game. You stand in the center, slip your wrists through the holes over your head. I lock each of these cuffs around your wrists. Six in total. I give you a hair pin and nothing else. You have to get them all off and free yourself before the spikes end your life. But, like I said, I'll set the timer for a thirty-minute goal."

"What's your record?"

"Thirty-seven."

"Seconds?"

"Minutes."

"What? No. What do you mean, you can't get it in under a half an hour?" She shook her head. "I can't do it if you can't."

"You're a better escape artist than I am. I get frustrated with locks. You don't." Scooping up the pile of handcuffs, he went to stand in the center of the upside-down U that was meant to string her up. He waved her over. When she hesitated, he waved again. "Come on, Alice. Let's see how you do. What's the worst that could happen?"

"You're seriously asking me that?"

He thought it over then smiled as innocently as he could. It was a pretty lousy attempt at best. "Please?"

Groaning, she finally gave in. She walked to stand underneath the center of the truss and looked up to the plate of steel over her head. It was flat, maybe ten inches wide, and a quarter-inch thick, with two holes clearly meant for her hands.

He nudged her gently. "The spikes aren't attached to anything. Look, they're sitting there. I haven't even rigged them to the wires. Trust me."

"But..."

"I'm not going to hurt you." He kissed the back of her head. "I won't let anything bad happen to you."

With another grumble, she fed her wrists through the plate over her head. He quickly set to attaching the cuffs to her wrists, one and then the other. He placed them on top of each other until all six were stacked in order.

"I'll warn you that all these cuffs are real. None of them are rigged with any kind of quick release." He fished through his pocket and, producing a bobby pin, slipped it into her fingers. "That's all you get."

"I..." She was getting pretty good with locks, but this was ridiculous. "I don't know if I can do this."

"Alice, you don't know if you can do a lot of things. But from what I've seen, you always pulled it off. You've met every challenge I've put in front of you." He kissed her cheek slowly then walked around to the table where he had put the kitchen timer. "And, if after a half an hour, you're still hanging there like an idiot? I'll let you down and try something else."

"Great." She looked up at the plate but realized she couldn't even see the locks. The slab of metal blocked her view. This was going to end incredibly poorly.

Less poorly than the day he hooked up the spikes for the first time, but hey. Details.

"You ready?" Julian wound up the timer past the thirty-minute mark then eased it back down to the right point. "Go."

And so, she started trying to pick the locks. It took a few seconds to even find the hole to stick the bobby pin into, let alone to start fiddling with the lock itself. Seconds she wouldn't have if there was a giant ticking death-machine going off behind her.

Fifteen seconds in, she hadn't made any leeway. It was then that Julian walked up to her, humming a little tune to himself. She watched him warily, curious as to what he was doing, as he bent down and started unlacing her shoes. "Julian?"

"Keep going. Pretend I'm not here."

He took off one of her shoes and then the other, tossing them aside. When he peeled off her socks and did the same, she pulled her feet away from him. "What're you doing?"

"Distracting you. And it's working. You need to be able to focus. I want you to be able to pick these locks in a burning building surrounded by screaming banshees. You need to do this trick like you can breathe air. Nothing can get in your way."

He stood slowly, sliding his hands up her body. It was, as he pointed out, incredibly distracting. When his fingers slid into the waistband of her jeans and began to meander their way to the fly, she jolted. "Knock it off!"

"Free yourself and stop me, then." He had that predatory, fiendish, dark expression that seemed to come over him as reflexively as a fish might be able to swim. Not only was he planning on doing something terrible, he was going to enjoy every second of it.

She swallowed thickly. "Julian..."

"Keep going. One minute off the clock already."

Growling loudly, she squirmed and struggled as he flicked the button of her fly. She shut her eyes and tried to focus on the handcuffs over her head. She had found the mechanism for the first handcuff, and that meant she might stand a chance of getting them off.

The handcuffs weren't the only thing intending on coming off. He unzipped her fly and began to slide her jeans down her legs. He followed them down, kissing the exposed skin of her thighs, and then her calves, until he slipped them off her.

"You're a bastard." The invective came through gritted teeth. He was trying to keep her from focusing, and now all she could think about was how on fire she felt. She couldn't even swat him away. She tried to nudge him with her knees, but he caught her legs in his hands and was standing too close for her to do much. If she tried to punt him, she'd put her weight on the handcuffs, and that meant she wouldn't be picking the locks, and he would win.

The last thing she wanted was for him to win. Again.

His hands slid up her legs slowly once more, fingers pressing into her as he kissed her thighs. She shuddered despite herself. Chewing on her lip, she tried to focus on what she felt. Or rather, what she felt of the lock above her. Not his fingers twisting the waistband of her thong and lowering them inch by inch.

Her body was a traitor, plain and simple. She was trembling now as he pulled her panties free of her feet. She tried to focus. She could do this. She could ignore him, and—

He put one of her legs over his shoulder, and she gasped as she felt his tongue stroke up her thigh, hot, wet, and sensual. And with one clear goal in mind. When he reached it, she cried out, her efforts at lockpicking forgotten.

"Focus, Alice..." he murmured, even as he gripped her exposed ass cheeks and dragged her closer to him, angling her body to his face as he began to lap at her, exploring her. Goddamn, he was good.

And doing a very good job of making sure she couldn't, under any circumstances, focus.

"Shit—" she gasped. He was amazing with his hands. He was phenomenal with his tongue, as well. "Julian—I—"

He chuckled without lifting his head. His tongue delved into her, pressing deep. Pleasure arced through her body like lightning. Whimpering, she twitched in his grasp, but he held her firm. No matter how she struggled and bucked, he kept her still. With her weight balanced between his shoulder and her foot, she already felt off-kilter without him adding to her sense of imbalance.

When he began to nip and torment her oversensitive nub of nerves, it didn't take long before she was tossed headlong over the cliff into ecstasy. She swallowed her shout but couldn't help but let out a strangled sound as everything in her body clenched tight in release.

Julian pulled away from her, kissing her thighs, before traveling up her body, kissing her over her clothing until he was standing. He was smiling victoriously, and it made her want to deck him.

"I hate you sometimes."

"But you love what I can do." He glanced over his

shoulder at the clock. "Six minutes. How far have you made it?"

She silently glared at him in response.

Shrugging, he began to gather the fabric of her shirt in his hands. "I'm going to show you a trick. I love this trick. Ever see the stunt when people pull a tablecloth out from under a vase?" He now had the fabric of the front of her shirt in the palm of his hand, from neckline to her waist. He pulled the center of her bra into his fingers as well, until he was holding both articles of clothing in his fist.

"What're you—" Her protest broke off in a yelp.

Julian yanked his hand back sharply, and she expected to go with it. But she watched, astonished, as her clothing passed harmlessly through her. He had "ghosted" it straight through her—she didn't care what he said, it was a great verb—and rematerialized her clothing on the other side of her.

She was now utterly naked.

And he was holding her bra—still clasped together in the back—and her shirt in his palm. "Ta-da!"

"I really, really hate you." She glowered at him.

He shrugged. "It's worth it." Dropping her clothes to the stage, he began to wander his hands over her body, leisurely exploring her. He cupped her breasts and began to casually caress and stroke them as if he were in no rush. "Tick tock, Alice."

"I'd be doing much better if you weren't—"

He pinched her nipples and pulled, and she had to stop talking to keep from shouting. Her head was spinning. Christ, if this wasn't turning her on. And judging by the massive bulge in his pants, she wasn't alone.

"I love having you like this. Tied up. At my mercy. And you like it too. I do love playing rough with you, but sometimes it's nice to take it slow. Enjoy the *ride.* And oh, I plan to ride you tonight in a brand-new way." There was something dark—well, darker, anyway—in his smile.

He wandered behind her, circling like a shark, but his hands never left her. They stroked her up and down, playing her like a piano, touching every nerve and square inch of flesh that cried out for attention. She leaned her head back against him as he bowed his in to kiss her shoulder.

"The locks, Alice. Remember...this is about you focusing."

"You're ruining my motivation."

"Oh, you want a threat? All right. If you don't get out of those locks in thirty minutes, I'll leave you here butt-ass naked for the staff to find when they come in tomorrow morning."

"You wouldn't!"

"I would." He grinned against her cheek. "Oh, I very much would. Because listening to you whine and complain about it all night would be wonderful. I will sit in that chair, right there, with some popcorn,"—he pointed at the front row center spot—"and I will laugh, and laugh, and laugh..."

"Fine! I'm focusing."

"Good. Because I am going to do everything I can to make sure you're not." He reached into his pocket, and she watched as he held out a bottle in front of her face. It was some kind of body oil, said the label. She furrowed her brow, not understanding what he was doing. He flipped the top and poured a copious amount into his palm before flicking the lid shut.

"What are you doing?"

"I told you."

"Specifically. I want details."

His oil-slicked hands were already stroking all over her,

covering her in the substance. It felt wonderful and strange at the same time. His hands smoothed over her breasts, toying and kneading them before drifting lower and sliding to grasp her ass again. He began to caress them much harder than he had the rest of her. "Details? Are you sure? You might not like what I tell you."

She swallowed the rock in her throat. She was helpless like this. "Julian," she scolded. She sounded *mostly* firm about it.

He chuckled and nuzzled close to her, his hot breath pooling against her ear as he whispered, "I'm going to pound this beautiful, tight ass of yours, Alice. I'm going to claim a part of you nobody else ever has. I'm going to make you scream my name and beg me to fuck it harder. There. Happy now?"

"Julian!" She bucked and squirmed, trying to swivel away from him. "Don't you dare! Don't you goddamn dare!"

"I said you weren't going to like it." He turned to stand slightly to her side, one hand pressed against her abdomen, the other now wandering to the place he was threatening to torment.

"W—wait—"

"Why? Are you afraid you won't like it?" His finger circled her, oiling her, teasing the sensitive skin.

She went silent. She hated when she couldn't answer his questions the way she wanted to.

Sensing another victory, he continued. "Are you afraid I'm going to hurt you?"

She gritted her teeth and refused to respond.

"Then is it because it's too fast for you? When have I ever listened to that?" He turned her head to him, kissing her slowly, both reassuring and passionate, gentle and possessive, bruising and sweet. He was such a strange dichotomy all at once. And with the kiss, he pressed his finger into her. It slipped inside, and she gasped at the sensation, breaking the kiss. He was watching her with lidded eyes that had gone dark with lust. "Oh, Alice...You are so beautiful...look at you."

Slowly, carefully, he worked his finger inside her. A little bit in, half the distance out. Again and again. All she could do was gasp and whimper.

Soon, he had worked his finger into her up to the knuckle, and he began to languidly stroke it inside her. Bit by bit, she felt the tension in her muscles began to ease as she adjusted to the still-foreign sensation. It felt...raw. Like touching a live wire. It felt so brutally sexual, so unusually erotic, she couldn't do anything but gasp each time he reached the end of his path and began again.

"Good. That's it. Don't forget the locks, Alice."

"Fuck you."

"Mmh, someday, maybe. Not tonight. Tonight, I'm fucking you." He chuckled at her vicious glare and kissed her again. This time, he teased her lips with his tongue, asking permission to enter. She parted her lips and let him in as a second finger joined the first. She twitched and struggled as the invasion grew, stretching her, and she tensed, waiting for the pain to start.

But it didn't. Either because of the oil, or the fact that he was a ghost, or his skill, or all three. He moaned low as he stepped into her, pressing the considerable proof of his desire against her thigh, clearly seeking any friction against the part of him that was so desperate for attention.

The pattern repeated in a perfectly deliberate, masterful tempo. He would creep his fingers slowly deeper, then retract a little, then go a little farther in, then back, then a bit more, until he was once more up to his knuckles. She mentally braced herself for what was going to follow.

When he pulled his fingers back, he broke the kiss, but his face hovered near hers. He wanted to watch her expression. And she knew why as he pressed a third finger into her.

She wailed. She arched her back, her eyes rolling into her head and slipping shut as he filled her. Gasping, she hung off the handcuffs, unable to support them with her legs for a brief moment. "Oh, oh, god, Julian—"

"That's it...just like that. Let go. I have you. I'll always catch you. Trust me, pretty rabbit. My beautiful girl." He murmured praises to her as he moved to stand behind her, kissing her shoulder, working his fingers into her with the same leisurely, meticulous pace as before.

Each movement sent sparks racing through her, lighting a fire she couldn't deny was very real and more visceral than anything else she had ever experienced.

But she knew it was going to only get more intense.

Julian was an impatient man. But he treated her with all the care of a porcelain doll, even fetching more of the oil to ensure nothing was going to go awry. Several times, he asked if she was in pain, and she shook her head each time.

When he pulled his fingers away, she heard the rustle of fabric, and she hung her head and took a deep breath. She wouldn't tense up. She wouldn't. This was going to happen. She...wanted this to happen.

Christ, she was messed up.

He took the globes of her ass in his hands and kneaded them slowly, groaning. "You are utterly perfect." When something larger, hot, and throbbing pressed against her, she couldn't help but twitch in his grasp. "Stay still, sweet girl. Stay still. It's all right. Let me do this."

She took a deep breath, held it, and forced herself to ease her muscles as she exhaled. She shut her eyes and nodded.

He pressed. At first, she thought he was insane. She thought he wouldn't ever fit. It was nonsense to think he could cram himself up her—

She let out a loud cry as he did exactly that. It was only a little, and it was only the beginning, but he was inside her. The noise she made was a sound of shock, horror, terror, and excruciating, deep-seated pleasure at the same time. It was white-hot, searing, and felt nothing at all like pain. But every nerve in her body was still on fire, all the same.

It ached—but there was no ripping, stinging agony like she had expected. Only an impossible, erotic *fullness.*

He pressed a little farther, and her breathless, aimless sounds choked off. They were replaced by a growl from behind her. It was guttural, explicit, and filled with abject bliss. She didn't need to ask if he was enjoying it. Julian retracted himself half the distance he had gone then slowly slipped a bit more than before.

Each time he moved, he repeated the pattern. Out half, in a little more. Out half, in a little more. Working his way into her, filling her in a way she couldn't have even fathomed.

She was dizzy from lack of air, her breathing fast and shallow, as he crept his way into her. He lifted her thigh with one hand, using the extra room to press his body to her all the way. With his other hand, he took her hip and pulled her back, pressing that last bit into her until he was as far as he could possibly go.

Her cry tangled with his moan as he did. She could feel him, every inch of him, throbbing inside her. She squeezed her eyes tight and tried to focus on breathing. She was going to pass out if she didn't.

When she felt like she wasn't going to tank it, she let her eyes slip back open. It was only then that she realized Julian was kissing her shoulder and up her arm, and anything of her that he could reach. He hadn't move at all, still seated in her to the hilt, waiting for her. She could feel him twitch occasionally, eager for more. Desperate. But waiting.

"Julian..."

"Ready?"

She didn't know if she was. But she knew she was going to find out. She nodded weakly.

He withdrew, slowly, almost all the way, before sliding back into her with the same gentle stroke. He was easing her into this, and she couldn't have been more grateful for it.

Each time he pressed forward, she thought she might be undone in that moment alone. It felt impossible. It felt incredible. And she wanted more.

But she couldn't tell him that. She couldn't let him win.

"How're those locks coming?" He snickered from behind her as he worked himself into her with all the patience of a saint. "I'm making great progress back here."

She snarled and glared over her shoulder at him, drawing a loud laugh from him in response. "Shut the hell up, Julian."

"Mmmh, nope." He groaned as he pressed into her again. "Ah...damn, Alice...this is better than I could have dreamed, and I've dreamed about this since I saw you. Bending you over, stuffing your tight little body every way possible." He wandered his hand from her hip to her front, delving lower, slipping three eager fingers deep into her core. "All at once."

She cried out and tossed her head, pressing into his

thrust and his fingers, trying to find more of both. "Oh—Oh, god—"

"Hm? What's this?" He was gloating. Teasing her as he nipped at the skin of her arm. "Do you want more? Do you want me to be harder with you? Hm? Say yes, pretty girl. Please say yes."

The bobby pin slipped from her fingers and fell to the floor, skittering across the stage.

"Oops. Well, now you're doomed, aren't you?" He chuckled, his voice thick with his own pleasure.

She gasped as he pumped his fingers with the same maddeningly slow pace that he was pressing himself into the other part of her. She had never felt so frustrated and so good at the same time.

It went on for what seemed like hours. It had probably only been seconds.

Finally, she caved. He won. Again. "Yes. Julian, please, yes!"

The sound he made wasn't a word, and it wasn't quite describable. His fingers left her to grip her hip hard.

And then she felt what he had *really* wanted to be doing to her the whole time. All thoughts left her. All she knew was him and his presence. That driving force that seemed to want to turn her body into the piston chamber of an engine the way it was coring her out.

Her pleasure crested, and she made a breathless, gasping sound as everything in her tensed around him. But he wasn't done. He wasn't near done. He was going to use her, rut her, and make sure he hollowed out a part of her that only he could ever fill.

And she leaned into each impact as he did it.

Again and again, she pitched headlong into ecstasy. Her thoughts dissolved into white noise, and she figured she might forget her own name by the end of it. It seemed to stretch on into eternity, and she decided that if this was how she died, she'd go happy.

Eventually, right when she thought she might cry for mercy, when the pleasure became too much, he roared. His thrusts became erratic and needy. He yanked her back against him roughly, keeping her pliant and still as he took what he needed from her. Once, twice, three, four times he impacted her like that, before he buried himself in as far as he could go and wrapped both his arms around her like a vise.

He was twitching, shuddering, moaning against her back and into her hair as he spent himself deep inside her. She felt him throbbing, felt the heat pool inside her as he did. It was enough to undo her one last time, and she joined him in his release.

They were both sweating, chests heaving for air. Slowly but surely, they both seemed to come down from their respective and joined clouds. He pulled in a long breath and let it out with a sated, contented sigh. As he removed himself from her, he kissed her hair. "We're doing that again. And again. And again."

She wouldn't complain, as long as he didn't mean tonight.

"Your half hour was up a while ago." He kissed her arm. "I suppose I wasn't playing fair. I guess we should let you out of those cuffs now."

"No need." She pulled her wrists out of the holes overhead and reached over to hand him the pile of cuffs.

Julian looked down at them in his palms, his eyes wide. His mouth fell open. He stared at them as if she had just pulled them out of her—"Wh...huh?"

"Minute and a half. Still not fast enough." This time it

was her turn to grin like she had eaten the canary for once. She walked over to her clothes and began to piece them on well enough to walk upstairs. Lordy, she needed a shower now.

"You got out in a minute and a half." He was still standing there, buck naked, staring at the pile of cuffs in his hands as if he couldn't fathom what had happened. "You were faking being stuck...?"

Leaning up, she kissed his cheek. "Ta-da."

16

After a week or two, she settled into Julian's home. It was no longer eerie or frightening to her. So much had changed in so relatively little time, it was astonishing. He made her print out a few of the photos they had taken together so he could swap them into the frames along the walls among the more dated photos of when he had been alive.

It was weird to be on the wall next to people like Kellar and Thurston, or even a picture of Julian posing with freaking *Teddy Roosevelt.* That photo had garnered a double-take from her. Yup. TR and her fiancé. Hangin' out like bros.

Life was weird.

Her aunt and uncle had come to visit, staying in the carriage house for a few days. Her aunt had instantly adored "Charles," and thanked him more than once for "saving Alice from a life of solitude" and "keeping my niece from becoming a spinster."

She tried not to take it personally.

Tried. Failed. Moved on.

Her uncle had taken a little bit longer, but when he talked shop with Julian about all the mechanics that ran the room-sized calliopes, he had finally given in. One of the prize machines in Julian's collection was a steam engine—a real train, not a prop—that was meant to pull an enormous pipe organ adorned with drums, hammers that would strike glass bottles to make notes, or even ones that blew air across large clay pots to act as wind instruments. It had little four-foot-tall wooden figures of men who were automated to strike triangles or shake tambourines.

When "Charles" let her uncle climb into the cabin to poke at all the levers and knobs, and even flip up the panels protecting the engine, her uncle had finally smiled. After that, they were friends.

Most of the conversations with her aunt had centered around when they were planning on getting married, who was going to be invited, how big was it going to be, who was "Charles" inviting, and so on. Julian lied flawlessly, his story seamless as he made excuse after excuse for why the wedding would be here, why they were taking their time picking a date, why his family was going to be absent from the planning, and so on.

Her aunt and uncle fell for every word of it. It was amazing to watch the illusion from the other side. To see a trick from behind the curtain, and not the audience. He really was a master. Every doubt in their mind was soothed, every question smoothed over by the time they left.

It wasn't that she didn't love her family, but there was something harrowing about having them there. She was a tiny bit relieved when they left. Relieved, and exhausted. The moment their car pulled out of sight on the winding driveway leading back to the road, Julian had let out a long, exaggerated groan and pledged they were never putting up with that again.

But family was family. There was no getting around it.

She resumed her work in the museum. She missed repairing things. She was starting to make serious progress in fixing all the broken oddities. Every week, she made a routine of going around to all the calliopes to tune the instruments.

Player violins, for instance, weren't ever supposed to be a thing. They were a nightmare, a catastrophe, and they always sounded like they were trying to summon Satan himself. She was convinced if she ever flipped the cam wheel upside down for them and played the song backward, she could open the gate to the abyss right there.

Julian laughed at her theory, and then asked her not to try it, just to be safe.

Loki adored the fourth-floor apartment. He had so many more sunbeams to bask in, so many more ledges to perch on, and so many shelves to climb. His new favorite place was atop one of the bookshelves in the parlor, hiding behind the wooden detailed molding. His new favorite game was swiping at Julian's head as he walked by.

He was also enjoying hunting mice. When they had woken up with a carcass of a mouse in the bed, she had laughed and praised her cat for his gift and hard work. Julian had been less amused. It was funny to see him grossed out by a dead mouse.

The more days went by waking up in his arms, living beside a ghost, the less strange it became. She stopped freaking out every time he vanished into thin air or skipped the task of opening a door for simply walking through it.

Every other night, she practiced with Julian on stage. She was getting much faster at picking locks. She wasn't quite ready to start trying the more life-threatening and dangerous tricks without a bit more practice first, though.

That would take many more months of work before she was even willing to think about doing them for real.

There were quite a few of his props and tricks she couldn't look at without blushing. Julian had a penchant for taking advantage of a situation and doing terrible things to her. Terrible things she never did tell him to stop doing. He was incorrigible, unstoppable, and had a fiendish imagination.

And she loved it. Every second of it. She welcomed each new progression in their love life. He had yet to try something she hadn't come to adore. She trusted him. Even when she was shackled into some bizarre stage trick, utterly at his mercy, she knew he wouldn't hurt her.

There was no question in her mind that he loved her.

Performing with him on Friday and Saturday nights stopped being horrifying. They transitioned from being her waking nightmare, to routine and not so terrifying, to actually enjoyable.

The crowd seemed to love her. They were still there to see Julian, but when she performed her first trick on her own, with Julian being the assistant and her being the main attraction, she had felt something in her light up that she didn't know had ever been there.

The trick had been one where she was trussed up by her ankles, hanging from a beam, her arms shackled behind her back. That wouldn't have been so spectacular of an escape if she hadn't also been submerged in a tank of water at the same time. She had to pick the locks behind her back and then her ankles and get out before she ran out of air.

She could do it in thirty seconds. He had taught her how to make it look like more of a struggle than it was, to drag it out until the very last possible second. "Escape artistry isn't about getting out in time, it's about making it look like you won't," he had said.

And he was right.

There was something thrilling about pushing herself to the last half-second on the clock. The more dramatic she made it seem, the more the crowd cheered.

Standing on the stage, she took a bow and laughed at the size of the puddle she was leaving on the wood surface. A stagehand would come out and mop it up before the next act.

"I bet most men would kill to get their fiancée this wet," Julian had muttered to her with the microphone off.

She had resisted the urge to elbow him, but barely.

Weeks turned into a month, and one month turned into two. Two turned into three, and she was shocked that the summer was almost over. It was September, and the air was turning crisp and sharp. She missed the warmer days already. She liked the fall as much as anybody, but it meant winter was around the corner.

It also meant she had been at the museum for nearly a year. Ten months had passed since she had set foot inside the foyer and looked up into the infinity tower illusion overhead. She still never got sick of staring at it.

She had finished the model of the house a few weeks prior. It had taken her months of work to assemble it, smooth all the little ridges the 3D printer always left behind, and paint it.

She had given it to Julian for his birthday, which had been in August. He hadn't celebrated it since the day he had died, but she insisted. Even if he wasn't getting older, it was still a reason to be happy about something, and there was no harm in that. There was never a bad excuse for cake.

Not to mention the crazy birthday sex.

He had instantly built a display stand for the model and put it right at the beginning of the tour. The guides learned how to carefully take parts of it off to show the inner workings of the house.

She had been curious to see if Julian would enjoy revealing some of the workings of his home, or if he would try to keep it all a secret. But the model was missing key things—the interior of the tower, and the contents of the thirty-foot gap in the center. Those would forever remain a mystery only two people knew the answer to.

The notes she had taken over the course of her efforts in solving the puzzle of Julian Strande were tucked away in his mausoleum. Hiding the key in a room behind the lock was a good way to keep anyone from ever getting in.

Life was good.

Right up until the point that it wasn't.

The trouble began seemingly out of nowhere. She was sitting on the floor behind the railing of one of the huge calliopes. She was trying to fix one of the actuators that made a cello bob back and forth in time to the music it was trying to play.

Key word—trying.

Player cellos, like violins, were also never intended to be a thing. This one she had named Brutus, and it was always a pain in the ass. This was her third time trying to keep it running, and she decided she needed to size up the drive shaft. It kept sheering off. Wood or copper wasn't going to do it, she needed steel. Or to think of a new solution altogether.

"Hi, there."

She looked up and smiled at a tourist who was leaning on the railing. It was beginning to creep into the slower season, so there were no longer guided tours, and people were allowed to wander the building at their leisure.

The man was about her age, with dark hair and bright green eyes. He was smiling at her warmly, leaning over so his elbows were propped up on the wood. It didn't escape her notice that he was attractive. He had that kind of cut jawline that turned people's heads.

"Hi," she said back to him.

"You part of the exhibit?"

She laughed. She had heard that joke a thousand times, but she learned to laugh at it every time. Tourists never did realize they weren't as clever as they'd like to think. It was really quite rare that anybody came up with anything unique. "No, sorry to disappoint. I'm here to fix these silly things."

"That must be an immense amount of work."

"You've got that right." She held up the sheered copper pin.

He whistled. "Ouch. I wouldn't think it had that kind of torsion. I guess it is trying to push a cello around. Not exactly precision equipment."

That caught her attention, and she looked at him with a raised eyebrow. "You know your stuff. Yeah, I'm debating between replacing the linkage with a clevis and a shackle instead of a through-bolt. It won't move as well, but that should account for some of the twisting."

The man was smiling broader now, and he propped his head up on his hand as he watched her. "You could drive it with a ball joint."

"Are you an engineer?"

"I am. Are you?"

"Nope, making this shit up as I go."

"That's most of engineering. Don't tell anybody else that. They'll catch on to us."

"Far be it from me to trigger the fall of civilization. 'What do you mean, pressure fit translates to cram it in there?' Wall Street would crash."

The man laughed. "You sure you're not an engineer?"

It was rare to talk to someone who knew anything about what she was doing. She waved him over the railing. "Come on and take a peek."

"Really?"

"Yeah. I promise you know something I don't."

Without missing a beat, he slung one leg over the railing and then the other and walked over to sit beside her on the ground. Looking down into the hole, seeing all the moving bits and pieces, he groaned. "Holy shit. That's a mess. Is all this custom?"

"It was built in 1901. They didn't have McMaster catalogs back then."

He laughed and, fishing through his pocket, pulled out his phone and flicked on the flashlight. He peered into the hole.

"What's your name?"

"Phil."

"Alice." She held her hand out to him. He took it, shook it warmly, and the smile that lingered on his face was a little sweet. He looked back down into the mechanism.

For the next few minutes, they bantered about how the thing operated. He gave her some suggestions, and she reached for her notepad and pencil. She began to jot down notes. It wasn't long before he had her notepad and he was drawing out ways she could fix Brutus the Cello once and for all.

It made her wish she had any clue what she was really

doing with the machines. She always thought of herself as fairly smart until she met someone who was *actually* smart. "Where're you from, Phil?"

"Boston. I'm a teaching assistant at MIT."

She laughed. "Ah. That'd do it."

"That'd do what?"

"That you're making me feel like a moron for not having thought of any of this."

"That's part of our job description. It's in the contract we sign. I have to meet a quota or else I get reprimanded." Phil smiled. She laughed, and they fell into a comfortable silence for a pause. "Hey," he started again, "it's almost lunch. Do you want to take a break and go get food with me?"

Huh?

Oh. "Phil, I'm sorry." She held up her hand, showing him her engagement ring.

His face instantly fell, but he shrugged it off. "I'm always late to the party. It's nothing to apologize for. I'd still love to grab a sandwich, though. Maybe you can talk me through some other mechanical problems. I like being useful."

She smiled. He really did seem like a sweet man. "Sure. That sounds nice."

He stood and gave her a hand up. They went to the railing and climbed over it. It was when they were on the other side of the wooden rail that he suddenly wavered. It was like something pushed him. He struggled to maintain his balance. "Wh..."

"Phil?"

He was silent. He looked down at his hands for a moment, turning them over and examining them like he had never seen them before. He flexed his fingers one by one, as if testing how they worked. He brushed his palms down his shirt, smoothing the wrinkles.

It was then that he looked up to her.

His eyes weren't green anymore.

They were blue and light brown.

Phil grinned with a familiar expression that wasn't his own. It was wicked, cruel, and fiendish. "Phil" balled up his fist, and without warning...punched himself in the crotch as hard as he probably could.

The color of his eyes flashed back to green as she watched, and his expression became one of twisted shock, horror, and absolute agony. He collapsed to the ground, holding the source of his pain, and moaned.

"Phil, oh, shit, are you okay?" She reached down to help him, but he shoved away from her.

"Oh, god...oh, god." Wild-eyed, he staggered up to his feet and ran away, limping as he tried to flee whatever madness had just happened to him. She couldn't imagine what he thought had happened. Either he was running to the bathroom to be sick or trying to escape whatever supernatural impossibility had taken over his mind. Both. She voted both.

Ghastly and disembodied laughter echoed through the room, quiet but pervasive.

She clenched her fists, anger flaring in her. Phil hadn't done anything wrong! Storming out of the room, she went up to the fourth-floor apartment, slamming the door behind her as she got up to the top of the stairs. "Julian!"

He appeared in front of her, making her jump. "Yes?"

"Why did you do that?" She was shouting, and she knew he didn't like being yelled at. But she was furious and couldn't help it.

"He was flirting with you."

"And? I didn't say yes! I told him I was engaged. He was just being nice!"

"No man is ever *nice*. Not when a pretty girl is involved." Julian sneered. "He wasn't going to take no for an answer. Engaged isn't the same as married."

"You had no right to do that to him."

"He was a guest in *my* home. I have every right to do anything I want to anybody within these walls!" He snarled. "This is my domain."

She shook her head. "That isn't true. You aren't god here—"

"Yes. I am." He whirled away from her, pacing angrily around the room.

"What you did was wrong. You assaulted a man for asking me out for a sandwich."

"I have done far worse than that in my time. I have done *terrible* things, Alice. I am a murderer. I have strung up people from the rafters of my house for far less than—"

"Wait. What?"

He paused.

Something cold like ice ran down her spine. He turned to look at her, and there was something dangerous and a little insane glittering in his mismatched eyes. There was a frantic quality to him that scared her. She shrank back toward the door.

No.

No. No. He had misspoken. He hadn't meant that. He hadn't implied that he—no. "Julian…?"

The grimace he made was both a prideful sneer and a look of twisted anger and agony. He turned to face her and bowed low and dramatically at the waist. Like he was taking a bow on stage.

As if he had just finished a trick.

"Say it isn't true," she whispered, pleading with him.

He straightened, and his expression smoothed into a

haughty, arrogant, and cruel smile. "I could have forgiven him for dancing with you. I could never forgive him for stealing a kiss from you. They belong to me."

The name left her lips, terrified and broken sounding. "Billy."

17

Alice felt like she couldn't breathe.

Julian had killed Billy. He had possessed him and made him hang himself...because he was jealous of a guy who was barely more than a kid.

It was too much. The air in the apartment felt too close. Too tight. Too hot. She whirled for the door and grabbed the handle. Tugging on it, the door wouldn't move. It didn't even rock on its hinges. The knob didn't even rattle.

"What's this, now?" He grabbed her by the upper arm and yanked her back around to face him. He pressed her against the wall. He was furious. "Where do you think you're going?"

"Away! From here, from you—from—"

"I think not." He dragged her away from the wall and threw her onto the sofa. She landed on it hard, and before she could push herself back up, he straddled her legs and pinned her there. This was a familiar game of theirs, but now it had taken on a whole new meaning.

When she struck at him, trying to claw or punch, he pinned her wrists over her head and glared. "This is pointless! You only leave this place because I allow it. Do you think you can escape me? Oh, Alice, you'll never leave here again."

"Let me go, Julian!" She struggled and kicked, trying to get him off her. But it was like moving a lead weight. Or a car. He was immovable. She realized suddenly that he had only ever been pretending to be mortal. To be normal. He was only ever letting her gain ground in their wrestling matches to enjoy the game. He could crush her in an instant.

He wasn't human anymore. Not really.

"No. Not now, not ever." He growled in his throat and forced her wrists under one of his hands. He balled up the other into a fist, and for a moment she was worried he would punch her. Instead, he took out his wrath on the wall, slamming his hand into it over and over again. "This isn't how this was meant to go. I'm not ready yet! If only I could keep my fat mouth shut for *once,* this never would have happened!"

"Ready for what?"

He glared, mismatched eyes blazing in fury. His jaw ticked, and he didn't answer.

"Ready for what, Julian?"

He ignored her and lowered himself closer to her, his face inching nearer. She turned away from him. "Disgusted by me now? Why? Because I killed one stupid little boy?"

"Billy didn't deserve to die. You know that."

"I've killed a lot of other people for a whole lot less, Alice. You know I've killed people. I've told you as much. You chose to ignore it."

"You said you hadn't done it recently."

"Did you think I'd changed?" He laughed, derisive and

cruel. It was a side of him she had very rarely seen. "Did you think you fixed me?"

"No, but you lied. You said—"

"Define 'recent,' Alice. Hm? Did you mean an hour? A day? A week? A decade? If you had asked me if I had killed anyone since we had met, my answer would have been very different." His fingers trailed over her jawline, turning her head back to face him, forcing her to meet his gaze. "I didn't lie. You weren't specific enough."

"If I had asked you 'have you killed anyone since we met,' would you have told me the truth?"

"Absolutely not." He smiled, the madness shining in his eyes. "But you didn't. Ergo, I never lied."

"Bullshit. You're quibbling—" Her words were cut off as he kissed her. Brutally and rough, taking, not giving, he forced himself against her. He was trying to get a reaction out of her, she knew. His embrace turned desperate, feverish and wild.

She lay there and stayed as stiff and unresponsive as a corpse. As Billy's corpse, lying in a grave somewhere, cold and abandoned. She pictured that poor, smiling, hopeful boy. The one who had seemed so full of life. Lying in a casket, filled with chemicals and painted with makeup to make him look more like who he had once been, not what he now was.

When it was clear he wasn't going to get anything out of her, he snarled and pulled his head back, his face a twisted mask of rage. He looked as though he might strike her, before he dug his fingers into the sofa cushion next to her head instead. "You love me. You love me. You've said it a hundred times. You will forgive me!"

"You murdered him." Tears stung her eyes, and she didn't fight them. She let them roll free and slide the short distance from her eyes to the hair at her temples, following the line of gravity. It was cathartic. She could cry again for Billy. For what he suffered. "He was only a silly kid with a crush. You killed him because he kissed my cheek."

"He had no right—"

"I am not your property!"

Her shout broke him off in shock. He looked at her, his brow furrowed. "Every part of me belongs to you, Alice. Every part. My heart, my body, my soul, this house...my corpse, my secrets, my magic...everything is laid bare before you. I have placed it on a platter at your feet and begged you to deem me worthy. I love you. More than anything else, even myself, I love you. And all I need is that gift in return. To have you as mine, just as I am yours. I am your property, Alice *Strande*. And you are mine."

"No. No more. No more lies, no more sadistic games. You forced someone to hang himself because you were jealous, and you're used to always getting your way. You're nothing more than a spoiled brat—"

His hand latched around her throat. He reeled back as if to strike her with his other fist, and then something in him visibly shattered. His rage fell apart and crumbled. He fell on top of her.

"Oh, no, no, no, no," he moaned in agony and leaned his forehead against hers. "I'm sorry, please, I'm so sorry, Alice, forgive me—please—my father...My father used to call me that. He used to say that to me before he would hit me. After he had punched and kicked my mother until she was unconscious, he would turn on me. He'd call me a brat. He'd tell me I ruined his life. And now, I've become him."

Moisture dripped onto her cheeks. Tears. They weren't hers.

Julian was crying. His shoulders were shaking as he kissed her cheek repeatedly, begging for forgiveness.

He'd been abused as a child. It made a great deal of sense. Like another piece of a puzzle, so much of his psyche clicked into place. His showboating. His need for attention. His disdain for her aunt and uncle.

He was a broken man. And he had glued himself together in the only way he had known how. She reached up and wrapped her arms around him, holding him to her. "I don't know how to forgive you for murder. I don't know if I can." *In some terrible way, I'm to blame for Billy's death. If he hadn't had a crush on me, he'd still be alive.*

"The boy is meaningless. He wasn't anything important."

"Neither am I."

"You are the most important thing in the world." He lifted his head from hers. There was something fragile and raw in his eyes. Exposed. He was desperate. It was as though he were watching his whole world burn down around him.

"To you. I wasn't anything to anyone before I came here. Before I met you. Who will be denied their world because you took him away?"

He recoiled as if she had been the one to strike him that time. He stood from the sofa, pacing away from her, and buried his head in his hands. He tugged on his hair, yanking on the strands, as if doing that might fix whatever was wrong.

She shot up from the sofa and made for the door again. Before she even touched the knob, his words interrupted her.

"It won't open. You can't run."

"Let me go, Julian."

"Never. I will never let you go. Not now, and maybe not until the sun burns this world to dust."

Giving up on the door for now, she turned and placed her back against the wall. "I'll break a window and climb out onto the roof."

"You can't break the glass unless I allow it. Do you think this place has stayed in such pristine condition because I have a crew come through to paint it every year?" He snorted. "Please. I only hire someone to mow the lawn so people don't get concerned." He lowered his hands from his hair and took in a deep breath, letting it out in a long wavering exhale. "Don't you understand?"

"Understand what?"

"Beautiful, brilliant girl. So smart, and yet so short-sighted. All living people really are. You see only what's in front of you, and maybe a step behind. Oh, Alice." He turned to her and shook his head. He lifted his hands from his sides, and as he did, the whole of the building seemed to rumble beneath him. "I've told you, but you don't understand. Not really. I am this house. And it...is me." He lowered his hands and the noise stopped. "I am every mullion, every doorway, and every pane of glass. I am every ounce of wood, every speck of paint, and every piece of tile. I am every bit of plaster, of lacquer, and of gloss. The wires in the walls are my nerves. The copper pipes are my veins. There is nowhere you can go that is not *me*. There is no part of me that is not this place. We are one. And I will never, *ever,* let you leave here again."

Tears were streaming down her face now, and she didn't feel any need to stop them. She shook her head numbly and felt her heart pounding in her chest as if it were going to explode in an attempt to free her from this cell. "Please, no, Julian—you can't. You can't keep me here against my will."

"But you love me. You'll forgive me. It might take time, it

might take years, it might take a century, but you'll forgive me."

A century?

Her mind skipped over that like a rock on a pond. She couldn't focus on it. There was too much. "You possessed him. You made him hang himself."

"It wasn't hard." He sighed. "I don't know why you want to dwell on this."

"I want to dwell on it because it's important! When? When did you do it?"

"Fine." He threw up his hands in frustration and then rubbed both his palms over his face. "Fine. After we were done fucking on the theater stage—the first time, anyway." He was far too eager to point that out. "I left you asleep in bed. He was still in the ballroom, chatting with friends. Once they were gone, I took over his body. I wrote the note. I made him wait in the darkness until everyone had left. I planted his phone on a shelf and hit record. I tied the noose that he placed around his neck, and I forced him to jump over the railing."

She let out a broken-hearted sob.

"I stayed in his body until he was a corpse. He never felt any pain. He watched what was happening as if you were watching a show on television. He never knew a single ounce of suffering."

"You took his life. He had to watch as you killed him!"

Julian pinched the bridge of his nose and looked for all the world like he was trying to argue with a toddler. "He wasn't ever going to leave you alone. As long as he lived, as long as he worked here, he was going to circle you like a botfly. You take pity on those who get no attention from others. It makes you easy prey."

"Do you speak from experience?"

He growled and, storming to a shelf, plucked up a glass candlestick and hurled it against the wall. It shattered, the tiny shards raining down against the carpet, glinting like bits of ice under a winter moon. When he turned on her, his voice was a roar. *"He was just one boy!"*

"Then how many others have there been?" she murmured. "How many people have you killed that one boy is a snowflake in a storm?"

Julian laughed. It was a cruel, frozen, empty-sounding thing. He smiled at her, and she wished he hadn't. The man she saw before her was a visage of the soul she thought she had known. A caricature of the man she had loved. What she saw looking back at her wasn't an alluring promise of pleasure and secret joys in the darkness—it was the maw of the void.

"Do you want to see?" He stepped toward her, ominous and slow. "Do you want to see for yourself how many people I have killed over the years?" He pulled in a sharp breath through his nose. "I suppose you won't believe me if I don't. You never believe a word I say until you see it with your own eyes. Very well!"

She screamed as he jumped toward her, twisting his hands in her hair. She pushed at him, but he wouldn't budge. His breath was hot against her cheek. The smell of cloves was thick in the air as he forced himself closer to her. Two hours ago, she would be aroused. Now she was terrified for her life.

"My Alice. My wonderful, brilliant, *foolish* Alice. Come! Let me show you what horrors I have wrought!"

And with that, she ceased to exist.

More or less.

She didn't know how else to describe it.

Everything...let go. She knew how Loki felt, being

walked through a door. She was all at once aware of herself, and not, at the same time. Julian had dissolved her body like he did so many other things—ghosting her through the walls and floors. It was like being asleep, like flying in a dream. Everything was tangible and not, real and not, as he pushed through everything at a breakneck speed.

She had no idea where they were going. Or what was really happening. When she could feel the world around her again, she staggered and fell, collapsing to the ground in a heap. The floor underneath her palms and her cheek was solid. She could feel the grooves in the shellac on top of the old woodgrain.

For a second.

The world tipped up around her as his hand fisted in her hair. He yanked her up onto her feet painfully. "Come, Alice. Let me show you!"

They were on the second floor. Far away from the apartment at the other end of the building. They had moved far faster and a much farther distance than she would have imagined was possible in such a short span of time.

He's everywhere. He is the house. He can be anywhere and everywhere he wants to be. "Julian, please—"

"No. You asked. You shall see."

A large metal contraption stood in front of them. She'd seen it many times before. It was hinged in the front, the two front doors split open like a morbid version of a chestnut. It was an iron maiden. Both organic in its hand-hammered, hand-forged construction, and rigid and terrible in its austerity. It was a creation of pure death and terror.

Spikes lined the insides of its back and the doors, jagged and sharp, handmade and imprecise but no less terrible. It was the very image of what a human could do to another in their cruelty. There were very few other examples of the twisted soul of mankind than this.

As he dragged her toward it, she screamed.

He meant to put her inside it.

"Please, Julian—no, please—I don't want to die!"

"A shame. Death is so predictable. What's the old joke? Death and taxes?" He cackled. He had no mercy for her. He dragged her to the terrible device and yanked her around to face him. "Do you think I'm a monster, Alice?"

She hesitated.

He shook her once. "Do you?"

"Y—Yes—"

"Good." He leaned his head down close to her lips, hovering a half inch away. "Do you love me?"

She couldn't answer. She didn't know. She did until about an hour ago. Now she wasn't so sure. Now it was all a tangled mess. She was trembling in his grasp.

With a heavy, beleaguered sigh, he shook his head. "Very well." He reached his hand *through* the back wall of the iron maiden. Something clicked loudly. The floor of it dropped open like a trap door. On the other side was an inky nothingness that seemed to stretch on forever, and yet be only an inch deep at the same time.

Before she could say or do anything, he threw her headfirst into the hole.

All she could do was scream as she fell.

All she could hear was his laugh as she did.

18

JULIAN WATCHED the trap door swing shut. It could never be found by outside sources. Not unless he was already long gone from this world. At that point, anyone who found his hidden chambers was of no concern to him.

Alice.

Oh, Alice.

He leaned against the frame of the iron maiden. He didn't worry about the spikes. They didn't bother him, even if he rammed himself at them at full speed. He placed his hand over his eyes, and he wept. Sliding to the ground, he buried his head in both hands and let himself cry.

What have I done?

He fought the urge to follow her. No, she had to learn. She had to see. She had to know the full wrath that he was capable of. He needed to show her who he really was. Not on his best days, but on his absolute worst.

For better or worse, for richer or poorer, in sickness and in health. Aren't those the words? See me at my worst, my Alice. My beloved. See what I hold in my soul, and if you have to look away...then there is no hope for me after all.

Whoever said it was better to have loved and lost was a goddamn piece of donkey shit. He pulled his hands away from his face to look down at his palms. Hands that had done so much. They had created so much beauty and wonder and had knotted so many ropes that lead to death and sorrow.

He did not regret killing Billy. Nor did he rejoice in it.

He didn't think about it at all.

It meant as little to him as anyone might think about swatting a fly. Billy was an annoyance. A tiny, insignificant, and brief irritation. That was all. *Why doesn't she understand that? Because she isn't like me. Because she can't understand what Forever really means. Not now. Not yet. Maybe soon.*

Maybe.

He was sick of maybes. Pulling his knees up to his chest, he bent his forehead to them and hugged himself into a ball, knowing he would look pathetic if anyone saw him. He didn't care. He let his sobbing wrack his chest as he cried. Not for the stupid boy he had killed. Not for himself, even.

But for her.

For his Alice.

And for what she had done to him.

He could have lived a hundred thousand years without ever caring for anyone. He could have been exactly as he was—blissfully ignorant of what he was missing, bored, and alone. But then she came into his world. Then she entered, and he knew what love was. He had thought it a myth or a fairytale all through his life and well into the after. But then she came. And ruined it all.

Or fixed it.

He wasn't quite sure.

This felt like death all over again. He had never cried as

much as he had cried over her. Not since his father had beaten him half to death when he was a child.

Julian remembered the blood. Blood was everywhere. On him, in his mouth, on the carpet, on the walls. On his mother. His father had been beating her. She had passed out, and then Edgar, predictable as ever, had turned on Julian. He was only a boy of nine when he had decided enough was enough.

When he had learned to palm a knife like a magician might a playing card.

He remembered his father lying there on the floor, sputtering and gagging, his mouth pooling with blood. It flooded his lungs, his throat, and was choking him. Good.

Even then, he hadn't cried.

When his mother woke up, she couldn't stop screaming, like Alice was now. Wailing in horror and sorrow, not understanding that what he had done had been the *right* thing. The *just* thing.

His mother had called the cops, not knowing what else to do. Faced with the choice of sending either him or herself to jail...she had pointed the finger at him. At her own son. The police hadn't believed her—it had been 1885, after all. The police were far less trusting of an adult woman than they were of a nine-year-old boy. Such were the ways of the times. He had knelt there, only then crying like a babe, tears streaking through the dried blood on his face, as they carted her away. Committing murder hadn't troubled him, but her betrayal had hurt him.

He went to an orphanage after that. It hadn't taken him long to run away with whatever he could steal to survive. One circus caravan later, and he found himself in the tent of a parlor illusionist and scam artist. Seeing his gift for the trade, the old man taught him everything he knew. His moniker had been *William the Incredible.*

Those had been some of the happiest years of his life. After Julian had moved on, seeking more to learn and more fame to garner, he had never forgotten the old man who had taken him in. In return, Julian provided for the man as he grew too old to perform. When William—whose real name was Bruce, he had learned, much to his disappointment—had died, he had done it with his hand in Julian's.

"William" hadn't cared who Julian was, who he had been, or what he had done. He didn't care that he had killed his own father and that his mother had betrayed him. He only saw a talented boy who was worth teaching a few tricks in exchange for the money his nimble fingers could lift from the pockets of the unsuspecting marks in the audience while their attention was elsewhere.

But it was as close to love as Julian had ever known.

He didn't regret killing his father. Even back then, he'd been certain that what he had done had been the right choice. He always believed every decision he had ever made was the correct one. He had no room in his heart or his soul for doubt. Success didn't come on second-guessing. Success came on the belligerence required to charge ahead regardless, and to look back at mistakes and claim they were part of the plan the entire time.

Now he wasn't so sure.

Alice had stopped screaming.

He had listened to her fall. Listen to her wail and sob.

But then...it had stopped.

That scared him more than her crying. Terror grasped his heart in an icy grip, and he vanished.

Very few times in his life had he ever questioned himself. Only twice. Once, when he looked at the bloody knife protruding from his father's neck as he gasped like a dying fish upon the living room carpet.

And twice...was now.

Oh, god, what have I done?

Alice was falling.

Julian had thrown her through a hole in the floor, headfirst. She hit something metal, and she turned onto her side to try to protect her face, caging her arms over herself. She felt like she was moving against something solid. She had hit a metal embankment, and memories of going down a metal slide as a child flashed back to her.

She could even feel the ribs in the folded metal as her trajectory changed from downward, to mostly downward. She screamed. She kept screaming. The movement seemed like it went on forever.

Right until it didn't.

The slide fell away, and for a moment she was free-falling again. She fell onto something crunchy, like a pile of sticks. She coughed as dust filled her lungs as she tried to fill them with what had been sorely lacking, which was air. Instead, she got a mouthful of grit. She hacked and tried to clear it, but she felt like she had sucked in flour. She tried to get a sense of gravity as she rolled onto her back. Nothing felt broken. Nothing felt harmed.

Whatever she had landed on had broken her fall, crunching underneath her and taking the blow. She wheezed and tried to move, rolling onto her side and spitting to try to clear the junk from her mouth and her nose. When she could finally breathe, she took a few shallow, experimental breaths.

First step was to confirm that she could, in fact, still breathe. Check. Step two was to confirm nothing was broken now that any initial shock might have worn off. Fingers, toes, check. Okay. Step three...was to answer one very important question. Where was she?

Where had Julian thrown her?

Fishing through her coat pocket, she pulled out her phone. She pushed the button on the side and, flicking upward, hit her flashlight. She turned it to the side to see where she was.

And screamed.

Much louder than before.

The empty sockets of a rotted skull were staring back at her, hyper-illuminated by the powerful LED in her phone. Cold and stark, all contrast and shadows, it was like the image of a pure nightmare staring back at her.

She thrashed, shoved herself away, and rolled back onto the pile of sticks.

Sticks.

She turned, and another face was there to greet her in its nearly fleshless grimace. Lips long dried and desiccated were pulled back from yellowed, stained teeth. Shriveled and devoid of the liquid that had given them a human form, they were little more than wax paper pulled over tendons turned to brittle ash and stretched over bone.

Bones.

She hadn't landed on sticks.

She had landed on bones.

In a blind, flailing, graceless mess, she scrambled away from the pile of bodies. Not one, but many. More than she cared to see. She crawled and thrashed until her nails met solid stone instead of the brittle flesh of long-dead bodies and fragile fabric.

Pressing her back hard against the wall, she kept trying to push away from the mound in front of her, her heels digging into the dirt beneath her. Her efforts were useless. She couldn't push through a wall any more than she could will the catacomb-esque jumble of corpses to go away.

But her panic didn't know that.

Somewhere along the way, she had dropped her phone. The flashlight was pointed up at the ceiling, bouncing ambient light off the rough-hewn surface and the walls, reflecting down in too-dim shadows along the chaotic and twisted forms of the long-dead souls in front of her.

Eyeless faces stared at her. Mouths locked open in silent screams, or with their lower jaws missing entirely, the tendons having rotted and dropped away. Somewhere near her was a skull, having rolled there from its owner, gravity taking priority over dignity.

The air swirled with dust. Detritus of rotted bodies and decaying fabric stirred up by her unceremonious fall into their midst.

Julian's victims.

She didn't know how many there were. It didn't matter. There were enough.

One is enough. One is too many.

And I love him.

Or loved him.

She was screaming, weeping, her breaths coming short and shallow, making her feel dizzy and like it was all a dream. Like this was a terrible, surrealistic nightmare.

This isn't real.

She kicked and struggled, pushing her heels against the floor, trying to escape the pile in her continued panic. This couldn't be real. She refused to accept it. This kind of thing only lived in horror movies and terrible novels. Not in real life. Not in *her* life.

It couldn't exist.

But there it was, staring at her, several dozen souls crying out their silent warnings. Telling her to run away—or calling out for her to join them. She wasn't sure which. In this nightmare and in this reality, both were true at once.

She had never had a panic attack before. Not once. Now she knew what they felt like.

The world seemed to be dropping away from her. It was like she was falling down another tunnel. But this time, it was a tunnel of her own making. It was somewhere safe inside her mind, somewhere fuzzy and soft. The horror that was reaching for her, a tangled mass of bodies and limbs, was an illusion. A dream.

She'd wake up soon.

It'd all be over. She'd wake up in Julian's arms, her cat curled up on her lap, and everything would be okay. This was only a nightmare. The air she was struggling for was a trap. It wasn't her friend. The air she was trying to breathe was keeping her stuck in this dream. She let it go.

Nightmares weren't real.

Darkness came for her.

JULIAN APPEARED and looked down at the limp form of Alice. He crouched at her side and pressed his fingers to the vein at her neck. He let out a sigh of relief as he felt the pulse thumping beneath his fingers. Fast, still slowing from what must have been an overwhelming pace, but there.

He shouldn't have thrown her down here. His rage had cooled. In the absence of the hot fuel, the reality of what he had done was sinking in. Bad enough that he had killed the boy, in her eyes. Now he had gone and done *this.*

How much more can I do before you will never forgive me again? Or have I already gone too far?

Tears had taken her eyeliner and sent it down her cheeks in dark streaks. Even like this, unconscious from sheer terror, she was beautiful. Her face was smudged with the dust and ashes of his neglected and abandoned victims. And yet he still marveled at her. *Poor girl. Poor, precious girl.*

"I'm so sorry, Alice. I'm sorry I showed you this. But I can't let you go."

He sought out the source of the light that was illuminating the otherwise impenetrable chamber. He didn't need it to see. He picked up her phone, flicked off the light, and slid the device into his pocket. It did nothing to dull the jumbled faces that seemed to be staring at him, empty in their rot, howling their rage at him.

"Hello, old friends. Good to see you too. Long time, no chat." He sighed. He knew each of their names. He could remember how he had killed each of them. Jonathan, Brien, Leroy, and the rest. Thirty-six corpses lay in his pit. Not a single soul lingered in his walls, though. No, that would take much more work than simply tossing a mound of moldering flesh into a pit. Much more work, indeed.

He looked back to the girl. *Work I am remiss in completing.* Shaking his head, he walked back to her. Leaning down, he scooped her into his arms and cradled her against him. She was blissfully unconscious. *I ask too much of you, don't I?*

He was done with this place. Maybe forever. Disappearing, he took her with him as he drifted back up to his home. He went straight to the bathroom and placed her in the tub. She was filthy. Landing on a heap of long-abandoned bodies would do that to someone. He stripped her clothes gently.

He didn't want to wake her, although he doubted he could manage if he tried.

Running the water, he ensured it was warm before he plugged the drain and began to fill the tub. He soaped a cloth and cleaned her carefully.

He scrubbed her of his sins.

Even under her fingernails that were caked with his disaster. They were not her burdens to bear. *Oh, but they are. That is what marriage is, isn't it? I am her burden, and she is mine. And mine is enough to crush her whole.*

"Mrow?"

Julian looked down from where he was sitting on the edge of the tub to see two little gray paws on the porcelain next to him. Loki was up on his hind legs, peering at him curiously, and then glancing to Alice. The cat leaned forward to sniff his mistress.

Julian smiled sadly and felt a tear slip down his cheek again. Wiping it away with his shoulder, he shook the suds off his hand and reached out to gently stroke the cat. Loki leaned into the embrace, purring loudly. To the cat, everything was now right with the world because "A Human He Trusted" had said there was nothing to worry about.

Trust. What a stupid thing. Trust was only the way to get hurt. That was why animal cruelty was such a sin against nature. Nothing trusted quite like an animal. Julian had murdered more than one person he had caught kicking a stray dog or cat.

Trust was such a rare and precious thing. And Alice had given it to him. Not once, but twice. And twice, he had betrayed her. He rinsed her clean and drained the tub, taking a towel from the rack and carefully drying her.

"I'll make it up to you. I promise. I really promise." He sounded so much like his abusive father it sickened him.

How many times had Edgar said the same thing? How many times had his father bent over the bleeding and weeping form of his mother and promised it wouldn't ever happen again? *"I'll never hit you again, I swear. I love you. I love you, and that's what matters, right?"* The words echoed in his mind like a poison, and if he still had the ability to vomit, he would have.

He had become every ounce of his abusive past, hadn't he?

Lifting her in his arms, he carried her to his bed. He dressed her in her pajamas and tucked her in under the sheets. He crawled in beside her, feeling like a cuckoo in the nest, an unwelcome and venomous snake, but he couldn't help it. He needed her. He needed to feel her against him, and to know she was still alive and, for the moment, still with him.

Four paws padded across the bed as the cat jumped up to nuzzle her, curling up against her arm and under her chin, purring loudly. For a moment, he could pretend everything was normal. That this was any other night spent embracing the things he loved.

I want this forever. I need this.

I cannot let this go.

No matter what it means.

He was not his father. He was not a drunken, abusive piece of shit.

No.

He was far worse.

19

Alice woke to the smell of roses surrounding her. It was at once serene and cloying. Comforting, and yet it brought back memories of the funeral of her parents. That over-saturated sweet smell of flowers when they were either too prevalent or too close. She normally wouldn't have made the association, except for the images in the back of her mind that suddenly came screaming to come to the forefront dragged it up with them.

Bodies.

So many bodies.

Something was on her chest, crushing her. She imagined herself underneath the pile, one of them, her body decaying and rotting alongside theirs. There were too many bodies, lying atop her, sucking out her air. She jolted awake. She reached out to grab anything near her. In the process, she heard a very upset cat meow as she chucked Loki off her chest and sent him hurtling to the foot of the bed.

Sitting up, she struggled to fill her lungs with air. It took her a long few seconds to realize she wasn't in a dark hole—she was in bed. It hadn't been bodies crushing her, it had been her fat-ass cat, who was now sulking at the foot of the bed, his tail swishing, indignantly cleaning his face with his paw.

It was daylight. Sun was streaming into the windows, and by the looks of things, it was well past noon. The room was not well-lit; it was downright cozy. It had no right to look so welcoming. Her life was falling apart. There should be a thunderstorm or a hurricane outside. The weather should have the kindness to reflect what was going on in her mind.

Burying her head in her hands, she squeezed her eyes shut. She tried to sort out everything that had happened. What she had seen had been real and not a bad dream. Julian had hurled her through a hole in the floor and into a pile of his ex-victims. And they had clearly been down there a very long time.

None of them were fresh.

Except for Billy.

How many more had he killed that he hadn't kept? How many more souls had died at his hands that were in their own graves, and not some mass catacomb beneath the building?

Loki padded into her lap, headbutting her elbows, demanding attention. She looked down to the cat and hugged him, petting him, much to his purring pleasure. He might not understand why she was upset, but it didn't matter. He couldn't grasp the enormity of what was going on. But he knew something was wrong, and he knew he had to try to fix it one nose-boop at a time.

"We have to get out of here," she murmured to her cat, not wanting to talk too loudly in case Julian might hear her. She looked down to the pillow as she glimpsed something in the corner of her eye.

There was a rose lying next to where she had been sleeping. It was a real one, not carved out of wood this time. A note was still tied to its stem all the same. She reached over and picked it up.

Loki instantly began chewing on the stem, and she couldn't help but smile at her cat's antics. Her world was crumbling around her, but he had a plant to chew on. Priorities were priorities, after all. She flipped the note over. It was longer than the others he had left before, and she had to unfold it where he had creased it in half.

"I had to take care of some business. The day job calls. I love you, Alice. More than anything in this world. What I did to you last night was inexcusable. It was vile, and I cannot express to you how sorry I am. I cannot ask for your forgiveness. Please, rest. We will talk very soon. All my love, Julian."

Vile. It was an understatement. What he had done—hurling her into a pit of bodies—was more than vile. Having a pit of bodies at all was the first insurmountable problem. The fact that he had chucked her into it was another thing. Two separate, entirely unforgivable things.

Third, if you put Billy's murder on that list.

How many more terrible things had he done that were unforgivable?

I need to get out of here. I need to get in my car and go and never come back.

Scooping up Loki, she draped the cat on her shoulder and went for the door. Trying the knob out of the apartment, it didn't budge. She knew by the fact it didn't even jiggle that it was immovable, even if she had the key.

Julian had locked her inside with more than a simple slab of wood to stop her. He wasn't going to let her go anywhere.

She hugged Loki, taking any comfort where she could,

and didn't know what to do. She didn't know where her phone was. She went to the only landline on the fourth floor but, picking it up, only silence greeted her. No dial tone. The line was dead. Either because it had been cut long ago, or because Julian was keeping it that way.

The message was clear.

Sit tight.

For now, and maybe forever.

Sitting down on the sofa, she hugged Loki and buried her face into his fur, trying to keep herself from crying again. She didn't know how many more tears she could spend before she ran out. The image of those bodies in that place, staring at her, made her shudder.

Loki purred and nuzzled her cheek, trying his little furry damnedest to cheer her up. And in its own stupid way, it was working.

That was until something occurred to her. Something that sank into her slowly like winter cold on a hike. Bits and pieces of what Julian had said to her began creeping together, piecing themselves one by one into a grid. She could see his clues now for what they were. Yesterday had been the last day she would ever try to pretend he was anything other than what he really was—a murderer. A ghost. A monster.

And her fiancé.

And the man she loved. The one who made her happier than she had ever been her life.

The one who had a pit of bodies beneath the house.

The one who had strung up a young boy because he had asked to dance with her, and who had snuck a harmless kiss on the cheek.

The man who made her smile and laugh harder than anyone else ever could. The one who had shown her she might have value—might have talent—where she previously believed she had none. Ever. Anywhere. The one who loved her, and had said the words to her, when no one else in her life ever had.

She didn't know which half would win. But she knew one thing, and one thing only—she might not live long enough to find out.

The pieces of the puzzle clicked together. The picture it formed was more important than how she felt about him. It was more urgent than anything else.

Julian was going to kill her.

She was sure of it.

That was...if she didn't stop him first.

THERE WAS SO much work to be done. Julian had to rush now. There were two days of preparations before he would be ready to perform the ceremony that would make her part of the house and keep her soul within its walls alongside his. He wasn't truly certain it would work for more than one mind—but he was desperate to try.

He could not let Alice go.

Not now, not ever. He would rather lose her in the attempt to secure her place among the rafters and the beams than to see her slip away to old age. Or worse, to panic, fear, and disgust. He had felt her tugging on the door again, trying to find a way to escape. He knew she had picked up the phone in an attempt to call for help.

It broke his heart.

But he wasn't surprised.

If he let her out of the doors now, she would never return. She would climb into her car and flee. He would never see her again. Why would she ever come back to him? He was a demon. A monster. This was why no one had ever loved him before—he wasn't worthy of it. Who could love someone who murdered like he did?

Who could love someone as jealous as he was?

Who could love someone who *threw them into a pit of bodies* in a fit of anger?

Julian had always known he had a temper. It was never subtle. The first thing that went wrong, the first thing that didn't go his way, and he would pitch a fit. He had tried to temper it over the years, and he thought he had succeeded.

Clearly, that had been a lie.

Just as his observed increase in patience had only been the result of his boredom and loneliness, it was now clear that the only reason his temper had improved was simply because he had nothing to be mad about.

He sighed and rubbed his hand over his face, likely smearing white paint on his cheek. It would vanish when he did. The spell etched onto the floor needed new lines. Different lines. He had scrubbed up the ancient stains of his own blood and stripped the white from the varnish to lay down the new symbols.

A different soul, a second soul, required a new twist on his old work.

He looked up at the setting sun that cast the tower of the fourth floor in amber and crimson tones. It was beautiful. The view from up here was spectacular, a full three-sixty vantagepoint on the valley around them and the forest that stretched on in all directions. He wished Alice was with him to enjoy it.

He heard her crying from downstairs. The sound of it triggered his own tears. He wanted to curl into a ball at her feet and beg for forgiveness. For what he had done, and what he was going to do.

If she even could forgive him.

No. I can't think like that. She will forgive me. She will love me again. She must.

Otherwise, he didn't know what to do. He didn't know how he could go on without her. Eternity had never scared him; it had been what he searched for, after all. But now, the idea that he might exist forever without her was sinking talons like sharp daggers into his soul.

He worked for hours, long into the night, the sun replaced with the glow of the overhead lights as he painstakingly laid out the spell. But eventually, he needed to stop to do some more calculations. He had the bulk of it ready, but the details were still not quite finished.

And it needed to be perfect.

Vanishing, he slipped through the floor and back to his apartment. He found Alice asleep on the sofa, the cat on her lap. She looked exhausted and miserable. She had every right to be both of those things.

He felt like garbage. He was. He sat on the edge of the sofa next to her and reached out to pet the cat. Loki purred, rubbed his fingers, then hopped off her lap to go wander off toward his food bowl.

Leaning down, he kissed her while she slept, wishing he were some storybook prince. Wishing that when she opened her eyes, they would be filled with love and hope. Not fear and disgust.

But if wishes were horses, paupers would ride.

And he didn't deserve her love.

But like all things he didn't deserve—he would find a way to have it anyway.

It'd mean his end if he couldn't.

Alice woke to the feeling of someone combing their fingers through her hair. It was one of the most wonderful ways to wake, and she shifted, not wanting it to stop. This felt safe. This felt like love. This wasn't torment, or agony, or fear.

But it also wasn't real.

It was a fading dream. She knew who was sitting near her, stroking her hair. She would never be able to forget what he felt like when he touched her. Instantly, she went rigid. At her response, the fingers stopped.

She opened her eyes and looked up to the mismatched ones of Julian Strande. There was so much hurt in them that she felt something in her own heart twist in response. She scooched up from where she was lying to put her back against the arm of the sofa.

Silently, they watched each other. Each expecting something from the other. For her, she wondered if he was going to pull a knife from behind his back and gut her like a fish. She didn't know what he wanted from her. But what he wanted and what he thought he would get were very clearly different things.

Through the pain in his eyes, she saw the hope. His jaw ticked as he looked down and away from her, seemingly unable to hold her gaze. Shame washed visibly over him, and it looked as though he was on the verge of tears.

She had expected to want to slap him the first time she saw him again. She expected to scream and try to beat him to smithereens. But instead, she found herself unsure of what to say. Unsure of what she even wanted to say.

She was conflicted, to put it mildly.

"I'm so sorry," he whispered. "I shouldn't have killed the boy. I shouldn't have thrown you into that pit. I shouldn't have done a lot of things. But regrets are only that—regrets. I can't change what I've done."

She stayed silent, still not sure what to say. She pulled her knees up closer to herself.

Julian stayed still, looking down at his palms as if picturing what he had done with them. "The first person I killed was my father. He was beating my mother to death. When she passed out, he came for me. Edgar hated me. He despised the fact that I was ever born. He said I was a brat, a freak, and a disgrace. He often said my mother must have slept around, because no son of his would be born like this." He pointed at his eyes briefly, before his hand fell back down. "I was born in 1876. People didn't understand abnormalities like mine. I was a monster the moment I opened my eyes. One day, I had enough. I was nine. I stabbed him in the throat with a knife I hid in my sleeve. That was the first time I ever used sleight of hand. I don't regret killing him. I never have."

He shut his eyes, lowering his head. "My mother told the police what I had done, but they didn't believe her. I was put into an orphanage. I never knew what became of her until the internet was invented. Then I could finally look her up. She was convicted and spent the rest of her life rotting in jail. All six years of it. She died of disease, I'm sure."

"I'm sorry."

"I'm not. They were both terrible people. It took me a long time to come to terms with that."

"What did you do?"

"I ran off to join the circus." He finally turned to look at her, a smirk fighting for purchase through the sadness on his face. "It wasn't so cliché at the time, I promise. There I learned how to be a conman and a grifter. I learned to pick pockets. And I learned the art of magic. Both kinds.

Although my obsession with the *real* arts didn't take off until many years later, when I had the fame and opportunity to find my way into those social circles. They don't look kindly on orphans."

"What're you going to do to me, Julian?"

He looked away from her, and his jaw ticked again. "I'm not going to hurt you."

"I'm beginning to think you have a weird definition for the word 'hurt.'" She braced herself and forced herself to ask the question. The answer wasn't going to be one she wanted to hear. But it needed to be said anyway. "Are you going to kill me?"

"I'm sorry for killing Billy. I lost my temper. I thought I had cooled my heels over the hundred years I've been dead, but I was wrong. I am sorry I threw you into that place." It was obvious he hadn't answered the question.

"Who were those people down there?"

He sighed, and his shoulders slumped briefly before he shrugged them idly. "People who got in my way. One of them was a lawyer, if that makes you feel any better." He struggled to smile again, his terrible humor trying to break through, but it flickered and failed before it could solidify.

"Are you going to kill me and throw me down there?"

"No."

"Are you going to kill me?"

He went silent again. It was as good as a yes.

"Let me go, Julian."

"No." He shut his eyes. "I'm sorry."

"You can't keep me here."

"Yes, I can. Don't confuse 'shouldn't' with 'can't,' dear Alice." He stood from the sofa and walked across the room, running a hand over his hair, smoothing it back. "I shouldn't do a great many things, and yet I do them anyway. You're safe here."

"You have a really fucked up definition of safe too. You're going to kill me! And what...make me like you?"

"Yes."

She tried not to gag. She couldn't help the terrified noise that escaped her throat. "No, please..."

"We will be together. I love you, Alice. What did you think was going to happen? Did you think I was going to let you grow old and die while I stayed here alone in my tower?" He laughed cruelly, mocking her short-sightedness. "Do I look like someone who ever lets anything slip through their fingers?"

"I can't stay here with you. I can't." She stood from the sofa as well, going for the door. She knew it was pointless, but she yanked on the handle again anyway. "You can't force this on me!"

"I can. I will. You'll forgive me in time, and we'll have so much time to talk it all through."

"That's not how this works—"

Suddenly, her back was against the wall, her upper arms caught in his tight grasp. "That is exactly how all this works, Alice! You know what I am. I've told you that I'm a murderer. I've said the words. You refused to accept it. You wanted to blind yourself to the truth. What...did you think you could *change* me?" He laughed again.

"No. I...I hoped that—"

"What, you could temper me, then? Do you think my ego lets anyone do anything of the sort? No, Alice. I am what I am. You need to accept it. You will accept it. You will love me again."

"How can you be so sure?"

"You won't have a choice." He smiled.

"Let me go!" She pushed at him, and he took a step back.

He shrugged again. "Suit yourself. Run yourself ragged if you want. You won't get far."

She heard the door click next to her, and she took the opportunity. She threw it open and ran down the stairs as fast as she could, nearly stumbling and falling down the steep angle as she did. She knew he was right.

She knew she couldn't escape.

Julian was the house. He wouldn't ever let her out the door.

There wasn't any hope.

But I have to try.

20

I really am a monster. Julian had always known it to be true, but here was another piece of proof to stack on top of the pile of evidence that would convict him in any court of man or god.

The love of his life, his fiancée, his heart and soul, was running through the house at breakneck speed. Terrified, afraid, and trying to escape him.

It shouldn't be nearly as much fun to chase her as it was. He wanted to catch her. He wanted to chase her until she collapsed, panting and exhausted, and then rut her wherever she fell. He wanted to claim her again as his, remind her that she wanted him, and kiss her until she gasped out words of love as he took her.

Something told him she wasn't going to be in the mood.

But it didn't stop him from daydreaming.

It also didn't stop him from laughing, cackling in enjoyment, the sound pervasive and total through the house as she ran from him. Each time she would find a door to the exterior, he held it shut. She tried every window, every exit, and none would obey her demands. This place belonged to him, and so did everything in it.

The poor thing was silently crying. She needed every ounce of air to fuel her panic, or else he was certain she would be screaming.

He wanted her to scream, but...in a very different way.

She'd fight him, she'd kick and scream, and she might tell him to stop. If she did, he'd obey. But if she didn't...

His daydream came back to him, and he laughed again. What was the harm in trying?

Run, pretty rabbit. Run, for a wolf is on your heels.

I DON'T WANT to die. I don't want to die. I don't want to die!

That was all she could think as she ran from room to room. All the while, she heard him laughing at her, teasing her.

She yanked on a door.

"Not that one. Maybe the next?"

His voice was nowhere and everywhere, taunting her as she tried to flee. Each door, each window, he would laugh and prompt her to keep trying. To keep running. To keep burning out her candle of hope that was going faster than a firecracker at the Fourth of July.

Behind her, she could hear doors slamming in her wake. Cutting off her path backward if she tried to turn around and go the way she had come. But that wasn't her goal. Her goal was *out.*

Away. Freedom. Safety.

She knew it was hopeless. But what else was she going to do?

Soon, she made it to the front door.

They were both open! She could see the dark parking lot outside, the moonlight shining off the plants and grass that were starting to fade in the early fall air. She could smell the crisp breeze as it wafted through. She ran for freedom, finding the inspiration to pick up speed.

She knew it was another lie. She knew it was only Julian tormenting her.

The doors slammed shut as soon as she reached them, and she smashed into them at full force. She pounded her fists into the wood, sobbing.

"Please, please, let me go—"

"No. You came down the rabbit hole into my wonderland, and now you can never leave."

Resting her head against the door, she tried to think. She tried to sort out her thoughts and come up with a plan. She couldn't escape by running away, but there had to be other options. *How do you fight a ghost who controls everything around you? How do I defeat him?* She had to incapacitate him, or...or something. There had to be a way.

Creak.

The sound triggered something primal in her. Something that reached into her psyche and plucked some sort of chord. It was the reminder of trauma.

Creak.

Rope. Stretched rope, straining under its load, swinging. She turned and looked up to the railing where Billy had died. Not by suicide, as everyone had been led to believe, but by murder.

And there he was. It was a lie. An illusion. A shadow. A featureless apparition of a boy swinging from the noose that had ended his life. But the silhouette was enough to pull a scream from her throat. She ran. This time, not to escape from the house—but from the terrible effigy.

"Run, my pretty little rabbit! But you cannot hide from me."

She turned down a corridor and ran into a wall. The impact hurt, as she hadn't been expecting it. There shouldn't be anything there. She had walked down this hallway a thousand times, and she knew where there should be walls! She took a step back and stared at it in awe and horror.

It was as though it had always been there. A broken-sounding noise left her as she turned from the intruding wall to run back the way she had come. But she pulled up her steps as quickly as she had started.

Julian was standing there, smiling. A wicked kind of glee shone in his eyes. Normally, that expression promised dark pleasures she would let him unleash on her quite happily. But now, it came with another, far more visceral threat. He was going to kill her.

"Please, no—please, I don't want to die—" She shrank against the wall that shouldn't be there, and yet was. It was impossible.

But he was the Impossible Julian Strande, after all.

And this was *his* house.

"I'm not going to kill you. Not tonight." He stepped toward her slowly. "My work isn't done yet. You have another day or two before it happens."

"Is that supposed to be comforting?" She tried to sound angry. She sounded desperate.

"Yes?" He shrugged. "I don't really care what it sounds like. Come here, Alice." He held his hand out to her. "Come to me. Let me kiss away your fears."

"No!" She ran, dodging around him, escaping his reach. He laughed at her pathetic effort, but she didn't care.

"Just give up! Where do you think you're going to go?" he called after her. His ghastly cackling sent a shiver up her spine as she tore away from him as fast as she could. But she knew he was right.

There was nowhere to go. Nowhere to hide. Nowhere to escape from him. She had to outsmart him.

But how did somebody outsmart a magician, a madman, and a genius? One who could control the world around her? In this place, he truly was a god. How could she outsmart someone like him?

Play to his ego. That's how. Hubris is his weakness.

Her legs were burning. Her lungs were on fire. She couldn't keep this up for long. She ran through a hallway that was meant to lead to a flight of stairs, but as she rounded a corner, she pulled up short. She found herself once more not where she should be, but instead in the large room where Julian kept all his favorite stage props.

The box he had locked her in that night was by one wall. There were dozens of tricks lining the walls, set up like the museum that it was. She skidded to a halt and turned to try to run away. The door she had come through slammed shut in her face.

So did the only other door out of the room. It was exactly like it had happened before.

She knew what he was planning, and she swallowed the rock that had crawled up into her throat. Only Julian would be capable of that kind of leap of logic. *I'm running for my life, and he wants to remind me how much I like a little fear.* This was different. Very different.

"Gotcha."

The voice in her ear made her scream. She whirled and staggered away from a laughing and very victorious-looking Julian. He took a step toward her, and she took one back. The smile plastered on his face was predatory and vicious, like a wolf before a meal.

And she was the snack.

"Let me go."

"Why?"

She furrowed her brow. "Why? What the hell do you mean *why?*"

One step forward from him, and one step back from her. "I meant exactly what I said. Why? Why should I let you go?"

"Because I asked. Because this isn't right. Because you can't kill me."

"Can't is different than should, remember? I shouldn't kill you, maybe. Fine. But I'm going to. Not tonight. Tonight..." He raked his gaze down her body, dark smile unflinching. "Tonight, I have other plans."

She shook her head and retreated another step as he kept stalking her, his shoes clicking on the wood floor. The echoes were ominous, and she broke out in goosebumps. "I—"

She screamed as something snapped around her ankles. She looked down and watched as chains wrapped around her like snakes and pulled her clean off her feet. She landed roughly on the ground with an *unf* as the chains yanked her backward.

"I love being a ghost." He snickered.

She rolled onto her back and tried to kick the chains off, but they were cinched tight. They were dragging her across the floor to a table that sat underneath an overhead rectangular frame. It was covered in spikes. The table was full of holes. The spikes were meant to fall and skewer whoever was chained to the surface. It was another escape trick.

Tonight, she might not be so lucky. When the chains yanked her to the base of the large metal table, they stopped. But the lack of movement didn't last for long. Julian fisted her hair in his hand and pulled her to her feet. Throwing her onto the surface, she struggled against him. But it was pointless. He was too strong.

She couldn't fight him.

Not like this.

But it didn't stop her from trying. When all was said and done, she was lying on her back, staring up at the enormous grid of long, deadly, solid steel spikes overhead. Light shone off their wickedly sharp tips.

Her hands were shackled over her head, and the locks were far out of her reach. There would be no getting free. Not unless he let it happen. "Please, please—no, I don't want to die—" She was crying again. She might not have stopped.

Julian crawled onto the table over her, caging her in with his arms on either side of her. His brow furrowed. "Sssh, Alice...calm down." He leaned closer and began to kiss her tears away. "Shush. It's all right."

"No, please—"

"I told you I wasn't going to kill you tonight. And certainly not like this." He lowered himself to an elbow and stroked his fingers across her cheek. The touch was gentle, soothing. A far cry from the creature that had been hunting her. "I thought you liked our games."

"This isn't a game anymore..."

He kissed her cheek, slow and sensual. He kept at it for a long time, until her crying stopped. Damn her to hell, but his touch was calming her.

Play to his ego. Let him think he's winning. Let him win this fight, and you'll have another chance later. Sure, it might be half an excuse, but anything worked for her.

"Everything is a game. Life, death, it's all the same." He placed another kiss against her cheek. Her heartrate had slowed, and she was trembling in the absence of adrenaline. "I promised I would never hurt you, and that wasn't ever a lie. I never want to bring you pain, and I never will."

He turned her head to face him, and his mismatched eyes were burning with love and lust in equal measures. His gaze was thick with desire, and she knew what he meant to do. And god help every part of her twisted mind, she didn't know if she wanted to tell him to stop.

Holy shit, she was an idiot.

The monster over her was going to kill her. Maybe not tonight, but very soon. But the feeling of him hovering there was twisting a knot in her stomach that was reacting to the familiar promise of pleasure and delight.

He was a monster she loved. Somewhere, somehow, she still loved him. She didn't know if she could accept him or forgive him. But it didn't make it untrue.

Their game had taken on new meaning, but the dance was the same, and her body reacted to it exactly the same way it always had.

Fighting him isn't how I win this. It'll only dig my grave faster.

He kissed her, seeing her hovering on her own knife's edge of desire. It was slow at first, tender, gentle and exploring. Giving her every chance to bite him or to rip her head away and scream at him to stop.

But she didn't.

She didn't want to.

I love him. He's a monster, and he's going to kill me, but I love him.

That made her twenty-seven thousand kinds of stupid. But she had enough fear for a lifetime, let alone one day. She couldn't take it anymore. The running, the crying, the screaming. She wanted the man who made her feel safe, who made her smile and laugh. She wanted him to make it all okay again.

And if she was going to survive this—if she was going to stop him—he needed to trust her a little. He needed to give her enough freedom that she could come up with a plan. If she fought and screamed, he'd chain her up in a closet and leave her there until he was ready.

So...it was smarter to play along.

That was the excuse she was going to tell herself, anyway.

He was kissing her like a prince, coaxing her into responding to him. It wasn't hard to fake it. She didn't have to. He was cradling her cheek gently in his hand as he poured every ounce of love he owned into his embrace. It was a promise and an apology all at once.

Gradually, the embrace became more forceful. He pressed harder against her, his love becoming need, becoming a nearly frantic desperation as he slipped his tongue past her lips and to tangle with her own. He moaned in bliss as his fingers began to slide down her cheek, down her neck, drifting lower inch by inch until it settled over the swell of her breast.

When he kneaded her in his hand, she arched into him with a gasp. He let out a purr of approval in his throat as he lay down against her, resting between her legs, ravaging her mouth with his.

The prince was gone, and the lust-drunk conqueror had replaced him. Slowly, he ground his hips against hers, pressing himself against her core. She could feel his desire, already eager from chasing her through the house. Her fear fueled his desire, and to be honest, it was the same for her.

She didn't try to stop the moan that escaped her as he

began to press against her in a slow tempo, miming what was to follow.

He broke the kiss, leaving her to fill her lungs with a gasp, as he watched her writhe beneath him. There was no taunting smile, no teasing, no goading over his clear victory over her. She saw only love and desire there.

"I need you, Alice. I need you more than you can ever know."

He pulled her clothes from her, piece by piece, using his abilities. Soon she was lying naked beneath him. He sat up, kneeling between her legs, and began to wander his hands over her, stroking every inch he could reach. It felt different than before—it felt like he was worshipping her. Savoring everything he could.

She squirmed, her body reacting to his closeness with an undeniable fire. He always knew how to push her buttons. It seemed it didn't matter when or why; he could trigger that part of her with effortless skill.

She watched with her own anticipation as he undid the buttons of his white shirt and slid it off. He was so beautiful. So perfect. She watched the muscles of his chest shift as he tossed the fabric aside, leaning back down over her. His mouth caught one of her already hard nipples between his teeth and began to lick and torment her, soothing and teasing.

He went on, stoking the fire that was already raging, until her breathing was short and shallow again, this time for a very different reason. She shivered, yanking on the restraints that held her wrists over her head, clenching her fists for lack of anything better to do.

Julian kissed his way back up her body, resting his weight on his elbow to undo his fly. She felt him there at her entrance, teasing her, going no farther just yet. Hovering close to her, he kissed the corner of her mouth once before she heard a click from over her head.

The restraints were free. She pulled her wrists out of the binding and looked up at him, confused. Then she understood. He wanted to see if she'd fight now that she had a choice. If she'd slap and claw at him now that she could.

He hooked her knee over his arm and lifted it, opening her to him. His other arm was behind her neck, cradling her, watching her with eager, mismatched eyes. "I love you, Alice…I love you so very much," he whispered.

She took in a wavering breath and let her hands settle on his shoulders. She slid one of her palms to cup his cheek. She looked into those burning eyes, and she knew her words weren't a lie. They never would be. No matter what he did…no matter what she had to do to survive…it didn't make them untrue. "I love you, Julian."

He pressed his hips into her. He filled her slowly, tenderly, rocking himself into her as though he wanted to make the moment last a hundred thousand years. And she wanted the same thing.

She wrapped her other leg around his waist and pulled his face down to kiss him. In this moment, he wasn't a monster trying to kill her. He was a man making love to the woman he adored. She could pretend that was all he was, even if it was only for the moment.

He took the invitation to lengthen his movements, slow and meticulous, enjoying the dance for the dance's sake. It seemed neither of them was in a rush to see tomorrow. This moment was about love. And it was real.

She really did love him. She loved a murderer. She loved a monster. She loved a man who had filled a pit with victims. She loved a demon that was plotting to kill her. She loved a man who made her smile and laugh and feel special.

She loved a man who could bring her more joy than she knew was possible. They were both at the same time. She invited him inside her. She wanted to feel him. She wanted the pleasure and the ecstasy they found in each other.

Tonight, she was with her lover.

Tomorrow, she would try to destroy him.

21

Julian never understood the phrase "making love" until that moment. He had always thought it was a pathetically gentile way to say fucking. But when his Alice had lain there beneath him, accepting him for what he was, holding him, caressing him, gifting him with breathless sighs of pleasure and contentment as he took her, he knew there was, in fact, a difference.

Fucking was grand, and he would do it a million times and never tire of it.

But that had been something different. Something significant. Something that had wormed its way into his heart. He had shown her every ounce of what he felt for her. He had kissed and caressed her until they both peaked, a silent, gentle, delicate release that felt fragile. It wasn't the roar of the ocean that took them both beneath its currents.

Truth be told, he preferred that.

But last night had been a treasure and a gift, and he would hold it in his mind forever. She should have been a weeping, frightened, terrified mess. She should have screamed at him to leave her alone. She should have pushed him away.

Instead, she confessed that she still loved him. And he would make sure she never, ever regretted it.

She lay in his arms now, asleep against his chest in their bed. It felt like the world had righted itself. The last twenty-four hours had been an abnormality. A lover's squabble. A rather unique and explosive one, but he was never one to do anything by half.

He wanted to kiss every inch of her beautiful naked body. He wanted to make her unravel on his tongue, on his fingers, on every part of his body he could utilize. He would make sure she never regretted the decision to surrender to him.

She had given up everything to him, and he would repay her in kind. This house was part of him, and he was part of it. Soon, they would share it. Their souls would be tangled together, inseparable as the roots of two ancient trees. To rip one away would be to destroy them both. They would be indistinguishable.

He could think of nothing else he could want more in this universe or any other than to give her all of himself. To lay himself at her feet and profess his words of undying love and devotion. Most couples might say that to each other—but he meant it quite literally.

When he carried her up to bed, she curled against his shoulder and snuggled into him. They did not speak. They did not need to. Anything that would come out of his fat mouth would only ruin the moment. She was tired. Overwrought. He had terrorized her again, and she needed rest. She would need it for what was to come.

He nuzzled into her hair, kissing the top of her head. "I promise it won't hurt, Alice. It'll be peaceful and painless.

You'll fall asleep in my arms like this, and when you wake up, a new life will be ahead of us." He whispered to her, keeping his voice low, ensuring not to wake her.

She shifted but moved closer to him. The sound of his voice had drawn her into him, wrapping her arm over his chest and hugging herself to him. It had been a perfectly guileless, honest movement. Free of lies, free of tricks, free of thoughts, he had spoken...and she had reacted.

If he could have loved her any more than he already did, he would have in that moment. He smiled dreamily and leaned his head back against the pillows, surrendering to the happiness that washed over him.

He wasn't alone anymore.

Alice would be his forever.

Everything was going to work out.

ALICE WOKE up in the arms of the man she loved. Maybe she should let him kill her—clearly, she was too stupid to live. *I never said I was smart, and I never said I was sane.* Now she could add "a good person" to the list of things she was pretty sure she wasn't.

But when he had looked down at her last night with so much emotion in his eyes, so much need, and hope, and adoration, she hadn't been able to turn him away.

He was so strangely fragile. She knew if she had, she would have shattered him. And despite everything he had done, and despite everything he was planning to do, she... didn't want to hurt him.

But she had to.

It was either that or let him kill her.

And she did not want to die.

It had been her last chance to be with the only man she knew was ever going to find his way into her heart. After this, she couldn't imagine how she could recover emotionally. How the hell could she ever open herself up to another person after all this?

Yeah, so, my ex-fiancé was a murderer. He killed a bunch of people, and then tried to kill me. Did I mention he was a psychotic, super-powerful ghost? Where're you going? Hey, come back! It was so awful that it kept her from laughing at how absurd it would be. No, she would find a way to stop Julian, and then she would go commit herself into a psychiatric hospital for a long, long time.

She shifted and picked her head up to look at him. He was feigning sleep, lying there with his eyes shut, a wistful smile on his face. She knew he was faking it, now that she knew he didn't actually sleep. He probably didn't want to ruin the moment.

Too bad.

"Is this the morning you kill me?"

"Are we playing *Princess Bride* quotes?" He opened his eyes and focused on her. "Because if so, that isn't right at all."

Sighing, she went to push away from him. He caught her in his arms and pulled her back.

"Stop." He frowned. "I'm sorry. My humor is awful. You know that."

"I asked you a question."

"Not this morning, no. I have some more work to finish before we can begin."

She cringed and recoiled. This time, he let her go. She got up to pull on some clothing.

"I thought you accepted this was going to happen. I thought last night..."

"I don't have to like it. I don't have to be excited. I don't want to die." No, she hadn't accepted any of it. But she didn't lie, either. It was his favorite trick—the half-true half-answer. He was a good teacher, and she was fast to learn.

"It won't hurt. I promise. You'll fall asleep, and when you wake up, you won't be dead—you'll be more alive than you've ever been. We'll be together." He was standing at her side then, and she jolted at the sudden movement. He was clothed. He urged her to turn to him, and she finally relented. Wrapping his arms around her, he pulled her up against him. "I love you."

"I love you too." It was true. She didn't have to lie. She placed her palms against his chest and fought the tears that were stinging her eyes. She shook her head, forcing them away. No. No more tears. "I'm scared."

"I know. It's okay to be scared." He leaned in and kissed her forehead gently. "But I have you. I'll catch you. I'll always be here for you."

Those words, she believed. He honestly thought he was doing the right thing—that this was the only way to be together. He wasn't really wrong. She knew some day she would grow old and die, and he wouldn't. Maybe he was right. Maybe she had been happy in her ignorance.

It didn't mean she was going to let him do it. Not without trying to stop him. She leaned her forehead against him and tried to pretend nothing was wrong. This may be one of the last times she would ever get to hold him.

He stroked her hair soothingly and kissed the top of her head. "I should go. I'm close to being done. Eat some breakfast, pet your cat, and try to relax. I'll make us a nice dinner, we'll drink a bottle of wine, and by midnight, our new life will begin."

"Are you going to poison the wine?"

"No." He paused. "Maybe." He paused again. "Good guess."

She wanted to punch him and laugh at the same time. But she was too much of a conflicted mess to do much of anything at all. She took a step away from him, nodded, and wrapped her arms around herself. "You should go, then."

He sighed, dreary and defeated, and shook his head. "I'm sorry. It wasn't supposed to be like this."

"What was it supposed to be like?"

"I hoped you would be...excited."

"To die?"

"To be with me."

She cringed. The way he said it felt like a slap in the face. She turned and walked from the room, unable to take it anymore. She wanted coffee. She wanted something normal. And then, she had to come up with a plan.

She had the start of one, but it was simply that—the start. "Can I walk around the house?"

"No. I'm sorry. The museum is open, and I can't have you warning the staff or frightening guests. I don't want to make you my prisoner, but for now, I don't have any other choice."

You could let me go. She didn't bother saying it. She nodded weakly again and went about emptying the coffee machine to fill it and brew herself a cup.

"I'll be back later. I love you, Alice. I'll be in the tower. Yell for me if you need me."

She nodded but didn't have the strength to respond. He vanished a second later, and she knew that was the last time she would see him before he either came back to kill her, or she found a way to stop this madness.

Sitting at the kitchen table with her mug of coffee, she shut her eyes and tried to think. Loki hopped up on the table and nuzzled up against her hand. Distractedly, she petted him. She didn't want to think what would happen to her cat in all this. She didn't think Julian would hurt him—it was clear the ghost adored the fluffball—but she didn't know how any of this was going to end. Not well, no matter what.

"I'm so sorry, chonko." She sighed. "I know you don't understand anything of what's going on. I don't know how we're all going to wind up on the other side. I'm sorry." She leaned and kissed his head. The cat purred and rubbed his head on her cheek. He sat and swished his tail around his feet, simply happy to be near her.

If only she could be an indoor cat. It seemed like a simple life. Eating, sleeping, crapping, hunting, sleeping, eating, and so on. None of this kind of madness. None of this kind of tragedy.

She put her head down on her arm and tried to focus. She tried to pretend it was all another puzzle. One more thing that needed to be solved.

Step one, she took stock of what was at her disposal. She counted through the things in Julian's fourth-floor apartment and ticked them each off her list as she did. Weapons would be pointless. She couldn't fight him, and even if she did, she couldn't kill what was already dead.

Fire extinguisher. Useless.

Books. Useless.

Piano. Useless.

Furniture. Useless.

Wait.

Books.

She lifted her head and shot from the table and ran into the parlor. Digging through the shelf, she gasped in relief and excitement as she found Julian's journal. He had put it back with the rest. He had taken her notes, but he had kept this in his apartment.

She had a chance!

She had translated every word of this thing. She had pored over every page. She might not have the translated copy anymore, but she didn't need them. She could have basically recited it all by heart. Dropping it onto the table, she started to frantically flip through the pages.

It was a spell book.

And spells were real.

And there was one she remembered seeing. It had been the basis on which he had built the rest of the house. It was only a small piece of the complicated magic he had woven to accomplish his goal. But for her, it would be plenty.

There it was. She placed her fingers against the symbol inked onto the page. There was no telling how long it would last. She wasn't a powerful magician. In fact, she'd never even attempted anything like this before. But it was the only shot she had at survival. It was the only shot she had at getting out alive.

It was her only chance to destroy Julian Strande.

All she would need was half an hour. Just enough time to get her cat, her bag, and flee. It only had to last that long.

It was a spell to trap spirits. She pulled the furniture out of the center of the parlor and pulled up the rug that covered the wood floor. She had to work fast. She didn't know if Julian was spying on her, but she couldn't be sure he wasn't. If she took too long, he might peek to see how she was doing and discover what kind of stupidity she was attempting.

Digging through a kitchen drawer, she found a piece of white chalk. Using that and a piece of string and some tape, she traced a perfect circle around a point in the center of the room. She began copying out the symbol on the page, erasing the lines several times before she knew it matched. Any wrong mark might ruin it.

Or she assumed so.

She had no fucking idea what she was doing.

Glancing at the page, she read the garbled mess of gibberish beneath it. She hadn't memorized the code, but the cadence of the symbols sparked her memory. She needed something of his to summon him. Jogging into his bedroom, she fetched the silver cigarette case that had his monogram etched onto the face of it. Once she placed it into the center of the symbol, she took a step back and braced herself.

It was probably going to fail.

And if it did, he was going to be mad.

Fuck him. He's trying to kill me. He doesn't get to be mad when I try to stop him.

She rolled up her sleeves and knelt at the edge of the circle. Placing her hands on the ground within the first ring, she shut her eyes and said the words that she remembered were on the page.

Pain.

Pain screamed through her mind like hot iron. She cried out and nearly fell over. She pressed her palms hard against the wood and felt something wet pool beneath them. Wet and hot. When she opened her eyes, blood was pouring from her hands. The liquid was tracing the white chalk circle, spreading out at an unnatural speed.

The cost of magic was a little bit of life.

Julian had said as much.

She didn't pull her hands from the ring. This was the price she was supposed to pay. When the blood connected around at the other side, the circle flared to life. It glowed with a strange and unnatural source.

She heard a scream.

Julian hit the ground hard in the center of the ring, spasming in agony as something wracked his body.

The flare of light cooled but didn't disappear. The symbols were idly glowing. The deed was done, and the spirit was trapped.

She lifted her hands from the circle and looked down at her palms. It was as though someone had dragged a knife hard across both of them, cutting her deep. They stung like a bitch. But it seemed she wasn't the only one in pain. Julian's thrashing had stilled, but he was shivering, a sweat on his brow. He pushed himself up onto his hands and knees, and then transferred his weight to his heels.

"Well played, little Alice...brilliant, beautiful girl. Well played." His voice was shaky. She had wounded him. Summoning and trapping a spirit wasn't comfortable for either party, it seemed. Mismatched eyes opened and met her. There wasn't any anger in his expression. There was... awe. Admiration. When he glanced down to her wounded palms, his look was one of concern. "Please, don't ever touch that book again. I couldn't handle knowing you whittled away your life like I did mine."

"I don't ever plan on using it again."

"Good." He shifted and sat with his legs in front of himself. He looked around at the chalk symbol around him. "Impeccable. You really are a wonderful student. Go bandage your hands. I'm going nowhere."

"How long does this last?"

He shrugged. "Until you release it, or you get too far away, or you die." He looked back to her. "It will keep draining your life with every second that passes. But you're strong. You'll last a while, I expect."

That wasn't comforting. "I won't need it for long."

"Good. Go wrap your hands. I can't stand to watch you bleed."

She stood from the floor and decided she should do that anyway. She went to the bathroom and, finding two rolls of gauze, wrapped up the wounds on her palms. She looked like a fighter. Too bad she didn't feel like one. She began packing up her things without going back to see him. She shoved as little as she could survive with into her bag. She had to cross through the parlor to get Loki's kitty-carrier.

"What're you doing?" Julian asked. He had one knee bent, his arm draped over it. He had sat there, looking utterly casual and unconcerned, right up until he saw the bag in her hand.

"Leaving."

"No!" He shot up from the ground. "No. Alice—don't go." He stepped to the edge of the circle, and it flashed bright white, sending him staggering back from the invisible barrier. He hissed in pain and swore loudly. "You can't escape me. The spell will shatter before you set foot outside this house. You can't drive faster than I can fly, and my power reaches to the edge of my estate. The driveway is a mile long. Do you think you can really win?"

She paused, watching him. He was right. Well, at least about his speed versus hers. But she wasn't sure about the magic circle. "You're lying."

"Am I?" He reached out his hand and pressed it against the physical barrier. He snarled in pain, his lips pulled back into a grimace, but he held firm. The barrier crackled and sparked, arcing with something like electricity.

Something felt like a vise clenching around her heart,

like a hand was buried in her chest, squeezing the life out of her. She felt dizzy. It hurt. Her heartbeat was slowing. She struggled to stay standing and fell to her knees.

Julian pulled his hand back from the barrier. "See? A spell is only as good as its master, and a cage is only as strong as its slave. I can break this spell—and you with it. But I don't want to. I don't want it to go this way. Let's order some Pizza Pit, or Chinese food, or cook a lovely meal, and drink some wine, and...please, Alice. I love you. Please. Not like this."

He was on his knees now on the other side of the barrier from her. The feeling of the metal claws in her heart had ended as soon as he had removed his hand, but she was still catching up. He inched as close to her as he could.

"If you leave this building, I'll kill you. Drop the spell, Alice. This is large and dangerous magic you've used. This isn't some simple conjuring spell. You're going to burn yourself out in an hour. Let it go. We can work something out. Do you need more time? A year? Two? Ten? I can wait. I can learn to be patient. Please. Let's talk this through."

"Shut up." She groaned and finally lifted her head, glaring at him. "You're lying. The instant I let you out of there, you're going to stab me to death."

"No." He paused, and when she glared at him, he growled. "Fine. Yes. But it won't be a knife. It'll be poison. I didn't want you to go into this afraid. If you can't accept it willingly, then I can do it when you aren't suspecting it. If everything had been ready last night, it would've happened then."

She shut her eyes tight and ran her hands through her hair. She squeezed her fists in the strands, tugging on it, trying to use it to speed up her brain and force her to focus.

"I hoped I wouldn't have to do this," she murmured. "I

didn't want to hurt you. Let me go, Julian. Let me walk out of here and set me free."

"No."

Her shoulders slumped. Pushing to her feet, she wavered for a moment before she steadied herself. "Fine." She walked away from him. Heading to the door to the stairwell down, she twisted the knob. It opened obediently. Julian's magic was dampened when he was in the circle. Good.

"Where are you going? Alice!" he shouted helplessly from the other room. He sounded like he was on the edge of a panic. "Alice, come back!" He was afraid. That meant that she had a chance.

"Goodbye, Julian," she said back to him, feeling her heart beginning to break. She was dying from the magic, and if that didn't kill her, sorrow might. "I'm sorry. I love you."

It was either him...or her.

22

SHE COULD HEAR Julian screaming for her as she descended the stairs into the rest of the house.

Alice had to work fast. She didn't know how long the magic would last. She didn't know how long she could keep it going. She could feel something cold working its way into her, icy and foreign. Her clock was ticking.

Pushing past the guides and tourists, she ignored them all. Her hands were wrapped, her palms were bloody, and she was sure she looked like a disaster. She didn't have time for them. Halfway to her goal, she reached out and yanked a fire alarm box, setting off the screeching of the system. Everyone needed to get out. Everyone else needed to be safe.

Her life might be over. Her chances were slim, and she had to take them even though she knew it likely was going to end poorly for her. But that didn't mean everyone else had to follow her down.

Not to mention the fire alarm might not be a mistake. It might be a little premature.

She went down to the basement as quickly as she could

and locked the door behind her. The plan in her head was clicking together with alarming speed. Adrenaline was fueling her, and she knew what she needed to do.

There was a generator there meant to run the house in the case of a power outage. She took the can of gasoline that was kept next to it and shook it, glad to hear the slosh. She went to the workshop and found a grill lighter and one of her lockpicking sets.

And then she walked up to that old piano set into the wall. The door to Julian's mausoleum. She placed her hand on the keys and played the combination of notes that would trigger the lock. On cue, it sprang to life. The morbid, minor key song had always sounded eerie and tragic. And now, it was a funeral dirge.

For her, for Julian...for the love they had shared.

The whole house answered. The building itself was one massive calliope, after all. It must have sounded like mayhem to everyone upstairs. She couldn't care less. She let the music wash over her. It resonated in every beam and joist of the house. The piano slid back and away, and she saw the stairs which led up and into the tomb. The sun was still cheerily shining, once more ignoring the dire nature of her dissolving world.

She climbed the stone stairs, focusing on putting one foot in front of the other. The magic was clawing at her deeper and deeper. The farther she walked from the source, the more it hurt. But in a few more minutes, it'd all be over.

If this works. I don't even know if it will.

This might not have anything to do with how the magic functions.

But I have to try. This is my only shot.

She reached the top of the stairs and quickly walked to

Julian's glass casket. When she saw it, she nearly dropped the can of gasoline.

There wasn't one coffin.

There were two.

His was just as she remembered it but pushed a few feet to the side to make room for its pair. It was an identical match to his. Save for two important details. One, it was empty. Two...it had her name on it.

AS. Alice Strande. He had already called her that before, and it seemed he was intent on making good on the threat. The two letters twined around each other like vines, mimicking his own Art Nouveau logo.

Her heart pounded, even if it felt like she was in a pressure chamber. Even if she felt like everything was clenching down around her, it struggled to beat harder in her panic. She knew he was planning to kill her, but seeing her own casket brought a broken sob out of her.

Shaking her head pitifully, she let the tears streak down her cheeks as she tried to focus on what she had come to do. She walked to Julian's casket and easily picked the lock at the head and the foot of the beautiful piece of craftmanship. He had made his own casket. Of course, he had. And then... he had clearly toiled to make an equally masterful one for her.

She lifted the lid, and it creaked on hinges that had not been used in a very long time. Unscrewing the top of the gas can, she went to go pour it into the box. She was going to burn his body, and if that didn't destroy him, she'd burn the building down too.

Looking at him, he could be sleeping if it weren't for how pale he was, or how blue his lips were. She reached out and touched him, stroking his hair. "I'm so sorry, Julian...I love you. I really do. I can't...I don't want to die."

She stroked the backs of her knuckles down his cheek. He was ice cold. He had been dead for a long time, after all. She swallowed the rock in her throat and tried to keep herself from sobbing. She could do that in the car on the way out.

Lifting the can, she got ready to pour the gas. She stopped, as her gaze fell on a plastic toy in his dead hands. A meaningless trinket she had printed from her machine. The octopus she had given him. It had meant so much to him—that stupid gift—that tiny bit of kindness.

He wasn't shown kindness frequently, was he? The masterful magician, the charismatic fiend, the frightened child who had been beaten until murder was his only choice. The jealous, beautiful, terrible creature she had fallen in love with.

Do it. Do it. Don't be so stupid. Do it!

But she couldn't.

She simply couldn't. She put down the can with a hollow *thunk* and collapsed to the ground, weeping.

She let the magic fall away. She released the spell that was lingering in the back of her mind like she was holding on to the string of a balloon. It shattered, and she felt like she could feel warmth again.

It didn't take long for him to find her. She felt someone kneel in front of her. Hands settled on her knees. She didn't look up. She didn't want to see.

"It wouldn't have done any good." He lifted one hand to stroke her hair gently. "Burning my body wouldn't have hurt me. I just keep it because I'm sentimental. You would have had to burn the house to the ground."

"I was going to try that next," she murmured, feeling as broken as she sounded. Broken, and defeated.

"I doubt you would have lived that long. That spell you

cast is a deadly one. Come. It's time to end this." He took her wrist firmly in his hand and stood, tugging her up with him. She shook her head, fear gripping her through her grief. "Stop fighting, Alice. It's over."

It's over.

Her life was over. She let out a wail, and her knees gave out. He reached down and picked her up in his arms, seeing that she wasn't going to be able to stand on her own.

She felt him slip them both up and through the glass. For that moment, she was flying. Soaring over the roof of the house as though she was already dead, and her soul was sailing away. But then she saw where he was taking her.

The tower.

Passing through the windows, she felt gravity take over once more as he returned them both to solid form. He placed her on her feet in the center of the circle. She shook her head weakly, silently pleading with him. He stroked her cheeks gently before cupping her face in his hands and leaning in to kiss her.

"It'll all be okay soon. Don't worry." He kissed her forehead and slipped something into her hand.

Looking down, it was a bottle. Small, brown glass, and filled with some liquid she couldn't identify. A cork was in the top. Around the neck was written a little note. *"Drink me,"* it read.

"I couldn't help myself."

She would have laughed, or glared, or done anything at all if horror hadn't kept her from it. She shook her head weakly again. "Please...please no, Julian—"

"Drink it. We'll watch the sun set, and then we'll be together. All this will only be a memory. We'll look back on this and laugh at how silly it was."

"I can't—I—"

His temper snapped. "Drink it!"

She recoiled from him, taking a step back.

He was shaking, he was so angry. He schooled his features back into a gentle smile and chuckled. "Sorry. You know how I can be. This is not how I wanted this to work out. Drink the bottle, Alice. It won't hurt. It won't feel like anything at all. You'll drift to sleep. That's all."

"I—I—I can't—"

"I can make you. I could possess you, and make you watch as you drank every ounce. I could make you lick up the last drop and smile as you did it. *Drink the poison, Alice.*" The last words came out as a seething hiss.

Once more, she shook her head. It was barely any movement at all. But she couldn't do it.

He snarled in rage. Before she could react, he grabbed her by the arms and forced her to the ground in the center of the circle. She screamed and fought, but he pinned her easily, trapping her arms underneath him.

He pulled a switchblade from his pants pocket. It was a little white-handled one. She recognized it. It was the one he had given to her from his collection. He flicked the blade open, and she screamed again.

"Enough!" He covered her mouth with his hand and tilted her head away, pressing her cheek to the floor beneath her. It revealed her throat to him. She wailed against him, muffled and hopeless. "Stop crying, Alice. Stop. I didn't want to do this. I promised I'd never hurt you. You're going to make me break my vow."

All she could do was sob.

He leaned down and kissed her cheek. "I love you, Alice. I love you, and I'm sorry."

He straightened. She squeezed her eyes tight and waited for the pain.

She waited to feel the burning sting and agony as the steel slipped into her throat. She waited for the taste of blood she knew would follow. She waited for it to flood her lungs. Hopefully, shock would set in quickly and it would be over.

None of it came.

"No!" With a sound that was a cry of heartbreak and rage, his hand left her mouth. She looked up to him as he hurled the knife across the room. It hit the floor and clattered to the ground.

He shoved away from her, standing, and walked a few paces away before collapsing to his knees. He put his head in his hands and doubled over. "I can't do it. I can't. I promised I wouldn't ever hurt you. Oh, Alice. Oh, god, what have I become?" His shoulders shook. He was crying.

She scooted away from him as far as she could, her back against the wall. She was shivering from fear and adrenaline. She didn't know what to say. She didn't know what to do.

"Go."

Her heart seemed to stop at that one word. But from shock, hope, or what, she didn't know. Many things at once, she suspected.

"Leave me. Leave here. Take your things, and never look back. Burn this place down on your way and end me, if that's what you want. I don't care. Go. Leave me." Julian seemed to cave in on himself at the words.

"I—"

"Go!"

At his scream, she jumped an inch in the air. Without any other options, she did as he had ordered. She stood on trembling legs and went down the stairs without saying goodbye. She put a disgruntled Loki into his carrier and grabbed her bag. She made her way down the winding stairs and out of the house, passing all the exhibits and pieces of curio she had come to know so well.

When she came to the front door, she paused. Her hand hovered over the knob. Opening it, she looked out at the parking lot. The fire alarm had stopped screaming. Julian had probably silenced it before coming for her in his mausoleum. The parking lot was empty, save for her car.

The moment she stepped over that doorway, Julian would be alone.

Forever.

JULIAN SAT in the center of the circle, his head bowed, his hands over the back of his neck, using the weight of them to curl himself farther into a ball. He hadn't stopped crying. He didn't know if he ever would.

He had felt the front door open. He had felt it shut. She was gone. She had taken her things, she had taken her cat, and she had left him. That was all he knew, and that was all that mattered.

He was alone.

He deserved to be alone.

He would never touch her again. He would never hold her. Kiss her. Make her laugh. He would never see her smile. He would never impress her, annoy her, frustrate her, or comfort her. Alice would leave this place, live her life, and die somewhere he could never reach her.

In this place, he was a god. But his power was only ever that. Wherever she might go, he could never know. He would read articles, he would search the internet for her, he would wait for her obituary someday. He would learn of her husband, her children, and all the people she left behind when she passed as a comfortable old lady.

Or perhaps he had shattered her psyche. Perhaps she would run away and die alone and cold. He hoped not. He wished her happiness. He wished her love. She deserved what he couldn't give her—a family, a life, and hope for the future.

Not death. Not an eternity of nothingness. Of endless murder, lies, and deceit. A fathomless sea of tricks, shams, and illusions. She had opted not to burn the building down as she left, and he found himself disappointed. Maybe it was time. Maybe he should go find that gas can and do the deed himself.

Who am I kidding?

I'm a coward. I always have been and always will be. I'm afraid to die.

And so was she. No wonder. He had asked her to do something no person should ever be forced to do. *And yet I've done it so many times.* Like that stupid boy. He had killed the annoying little shit to keep him from ruining everything. And yet, by doing so, Julian ruined everything instead.

Like he always ruined everything.

He would stay here in his tower and weep until the world crumbled to dust. That was how it felt, anyway. Perhaps he'd finally descend into madness and let his sanity crumble. It was a better way to spend the rest of time, aimless and devoid of humanity.

When a hand settled on his shoulder, he froze.

Impossible.

He wouldn't let himself hope. He wouldn't let himself pray she had come back to him. She had come to say goodbye, that was all. She couldn't live with the guilt or lack of closure. She needed to put the period on the end of the sentence.

Someone sat at his side.

He had been so focused on his pain, he hadn't even felt her approach.

Refusing to lift his head, he stayed as he was, his eyes shut. He wouldn't look at her, see the pain and the betrayal and the hurt in her eyes, and know he had shattered the only love anyone had ever felt for him.

He felt her lean against him. She was so warm, so perfect, and he tried to cherish every spare second she chose to spend with him before she left him forever. She had come to say goodbye properly before she left. She wanted closure. That was all. There was no other reason she would come back.

"Julian..."

No. No he wouldn't look. He wouldn't reach out for her. He wouldn't cry, or beg, or plead with her. No matter how he wanted to fall at her feet and kiss them and swear he wouldn't hurt her, wouldn't kill her, and would worship every second she stayed with him.

He couldn't handle the pain when she inevitably said no.

"I'm scared."

Her voice was soft. Strained. Something was wrong. He looked up at her then, hearing the fear in her voice. She looked odd, and there was something glassy about her eyes. She was looking down at something in her hand.

The bottle of poison.

If his heart still beat, it would have hitched.

The cork was gone.

It was empty.

"Alice...?"

She blinked, and a pair of tears streamed down her cheeks. "I'm so scared."

Instantly, she was in his arms. He pulled her close to him, sitting her in his lap. He held her head against his chest, and he kissed her forehead. "Ssh, it's all right. I love you. It's all right. I have you." He wanted to ask why she had done it, but he didn't dare.

But she knew him too well. "I couldn't leave you," she whispered. She tried to look at him but didn't seem able to focus. "I couldn't destroy you, and I couldn't leave you. I didn't know what else to do."

"It's going to be all right. Everything is fine." He stroked her cheek gently, soothingly, cradling her. She was still crying silently, and so was he. Neither of them cared. "I'll always be here with you. Alice, I love you—I love you so much."

"I love you." She was already fading. The poison worked quickly. It would pull her off to sleep before it did its job. He would hold her until her heart stopped. He would stay with her until the deed was done. He would not leave her alone for one split second.

He kissed her. He embraced her with every ounce of love he owned. She was too weak to return the gesture, and it was okay.

There was a quiet sound of glass on wood as the bottle rolled out of her limp fingers.

Cradling her dead body in his arms, he wept.

"I love you, Alice...Now and forever."

EPILOGUE

"*The Amazing Alice Strande.*"

That was what the poster read.

She didn't think it looked anything like her. She shook her head as she looked up at the painting depicting her upside down, hanging from her ankles, the giant swinging spike walls of a machine called The Beartrap that were about to crush her if she didn't escape in time. It was the same deadly trick he had strapped her into that night on the stage. She'd never forget. It made her blush every time she performed it.

In the poster, she was wearing a skimpy outfit. One she'd never wear in real life. No matter how badly Julian pestered her to do it.

And he did know how to pester.

"What?" Julian asked from the top of the ladder. He had just finished hanging it. "Is it crooked?"

"I don't look anything like that."

He leaned out from the wall and peered down at it. "I think you look great."

"My boobs are not that big."

"You're upside down." He hefted a pair of invisible boobs in front of his chest. "Gravity." He climbed down from the ladder. "I love it."

She put her hand over her eyes and sighed. He really was impossible. "Of course, you do. You painted it. I'm not wearing that outfit tonight."

"Oh, come on! It'll be false advertising otherwise." He wrapped his arms around her waist and pulled her flush against him. "The crowd'll love it."

"No, you'll love it."

"Both can be true. They aren't mutually exclusive." He flashed her that trademark smile and leaned in to kiss her. "C'mon. Wear it. It'll be fantastic."

"I'll wear it after the show is over. How's that?" She poked him in the chest.

"Deal! Progress is progress." He kissed her and let it linger for a long moment before breaking away. The love in his eyes took her breath away.

Well, not that she needed to breathe anymore.

Not really.

But she'd never get used to *not* breathing. She understood why it was so easy for him to waltz around like a living person. It had been ten years since she died in that tower, and it only felt like ten days.

The first time he had trapped her in the underwater tank to prove her fear of drowning was pointless, he had laughed as she struggled and smacked against the glass. Sure enough, she hadn't drowned.

Couldn't kill what was already dead, after all. But it took a lot of adjustment. She didn't know if she'd ever get used to walking through walls or feeling the whole house like she could feel her own hair on the back of her neck. Easy to ignore, impossible to notice, until she stopped and thought about it.

And with it, was him.

They were bound together. They might as well be one soul now. It gave her a kind of bravery she didn't know she had owned. It was the only reason she agreed to headline a show. He had trained her every day for years, and she finally agreed she was ready to stand on her own. Not as the assistant, but as the master.

"Let's practice the Snake Box one more time." He let go of her only to take her hand and pull her toward the entrance to the theater. The lobby was being decked out for the event. It was her first show, and it was a big deal. They had several VIPs from Vegas and Hollywood coming to see the performance.

Not like they would be able to figure out half the tricks. Not being able to die took a lot of the risk out of escaping from giant spinning sawblades or reciprocating saw Julian was going to use to "cut off her head."

Her head would come off, all right. But not in the way they all thought it would.

"It still feels like cheating."

He glanced over his shoulder at her as he led her to the stage. "Of course, it is. It's entertainment. We aren't trying to say we're saints and talking to god. We're telling people it's a trick. The only difference is, it isn't a trick in the way they think it is."

She sighed. He was right. Julian could have started a cult in his honor, gathering people in his house to worship him. He was getting his worship in the form of applause instead. It was the more benign of the options for someone with his ego, she had to admit.

She narrowed her eyes at him. "You like practicing the

Snake Box so you can shove me into a tiny space and feel me up."

"And? No one's around. Maybe I'll do more than feel you up this time."

He had never slowed down. And neither had she. Not once in ten years. Without any of her mortal limits, sex between them had become...well, wild put it lightly. Supernatural would be a little too on the nose. Indescribable was the only word she could pin to it.

One thing she learned was that Julian had an infinite imagination, especially when it came to ways to be sick and twisted. And she never told him no. Even when he was holding her ghostly severed head in his hands.

That had been weird.

Good. Very good. But very weird.

She asked for warning next time he decided to try that.

He was still very clearly the one in charge of the house. She was still coming into her own. His powers were far more practiced, far more skilled than hers, and honestly? She never once refused him.

Lifting the top of the box, he looked down into it and sighed. "You. Out." He pointed. "Git."

A large, fluffy gray cat strolled leisurely out the side of the box, phasing through it as though it wasn't even there. He stretched, yawned comically, and sat to lick his paw and wipe his face.

She chuckled and leaned down to scoop up her cat. "Hey, there, chonko."

Loki had died six years ago. It had made her question everything she thought she knew about animals. The poor, elderly animal had scratched at the door of the stairs to the tower and howled until she finally opened it for him out of curiosity. He had limped up the steps, arthritis having plagued him in his later years.

He padded into the center of the circle, lay down, and died in her arms. Julian had wept like a child there beside her, and they held each other as they mourned a creature who had been family to them both.

It was two days later that she woke up with him pawing her face and meowing loudly for food.

Julian had laughed, scooped up the animal, and danced around the apartment calling him "his little fluffy warlock." Loki's reaction was to insist loudly on having breakfast. Julian had no explanation for the cat's reappearance, except that the floor of the tower was still painted with the design to imprint her soul onto the building's makeup when she passed. The cat was her pet, and so he might have been able to follow.

He admitted it was only a theory. But he was so happy that he never really questioned it, and she felt the same. Her cat had learned how to walk through objects and adjusted to being a ghost far faster than she did. The museum had become haunted by a Maine Coon as of late. People would see him perched up on calliopes or case-works of various nickelodeons. A few lucky patrons or guides would even be able to pet him and get a purr and a nuzzle, only to have him vanish when they weren't looking.

Or when they *were* looking.

Loki didn't give two shits about maintaining the illusion of being alive. And no amount of lecturing the cat did any ounce of good. He was living his absolute best afterlife, and the fluffball continued to drag in birds or critters from outside.

The mouse problem in the house had basically been

eradicated. Mice had a hard time escaping from a cat who could hunt them *inside* the walls of the house.

Loki planted a single paw in the middle of her forehead as she held him. That was his favorite thing to do. She kissed it and set him on a table nearby. He lay on his side to watch them practice.

He had waltzed on stage a few times during a performance, not caring one bit about the people watching. Many of the newer posters for the shows contained a leaping cat for that exact reason.

Ten years had passed. Ten of the happiest years of her "life." Existence. Whatever. She was still Alice, and he was still Charles. Her aunt and uncle had both passed away, and there was a little bit of relief in her when they did. The lies became so much easier after that. Soon, they'd have to change names to keep up appearances, but they had another decade or two before it would get awkward.

Walking to the box, she shut the lid and hopped up on it to sit there. She waved Julian over to her. He obeyed with a smile, and she pulled him to stand between her legs. She folded her hands behind his neck and smiled at him.

"What?" He lifted a hand to rest the pad of his thumb against the hollow beneath her lower lip. "You have that look again."

"I'm reminiscing."

"About what?"

"The day I first came here. When I met Charles."

He snickered. "Remember when you thought you had cheated on me with me?"

She jabbed a finger into his chest. "That was still mean."

"But it was really good, though."

She hooked her ankles around his legs and used them to pull him closer. It had been good. The fear had faded over the years, especially since she knew he couldn't hurt her. But the excitement and anticipation never faded.

"Admit it." His hands trailed to her hips and pulled her up against him. "You loved it."

"Fine."

"And you love me, my Amazing Alice Strande."

There, in the center of the house, in that thirty-foot gap in the plan that only she and Julian knew the answer to, lay her body. It was in a glass casket with those initials on it. She had accepted her new name when she had woken up in his arms that day, cradled not body to body, but soul to soul.

She had become Alice Strande, and she had never looked back.

She leaned up to hover her lips over his, close but not sealing the kiss. Not yet. She loved to tease him. He loved being teased. She had played her own games with him over the years and found him eager to surrender to whatever she wanted to do to him. And oh, she had a lot of payback stored up.

"Say it," he murmured.

She smiled and nipped at his lower lip before she gave in and whispered, "I love you, my Impossible Julian Strande."

ALSO BY KATHRYN ANN KINGSLEY

Harrow Faire:

The Contortionist

The Puppeteer

The Clown

The Ringmaster

The Faire

Immortal Soul:

Heart of Dracula

Curse of Dracula

The Impossible Julian Strande:

Illusions of Grandeur

Ghosts & Liars

The Cardinal Winds:

Steel Rose

Burning Hope

The Masks of Under:

King of Flames

King of Shadows

Queen of Dreams

King of Blood

King of None

Queen of All

Halfway Between:

Shadow of Angels

Blood of Angels

Fall of Angels

ABOUT THE AUTHOR

Kat has always been a storyteller.

With ten years in script-writing for performances on both the stage and for tourism, she has always been writing in one form or another. When she isn't penning down fiction, she works as Creative Director for a company that designs and builds large-scale interactive adventure games. There, she is the lead concept designer, handling everything from game and set design, to audio and lighting, to illustration and script writing.

Also on her list of skills are artistic direction, scenic painting and props, special effects, and electronics. A graduate of Boston University with a BFA in Theatre Design, she has a passion for unique, creative, and unconventional experiences.

Made in the USA
Columbia, SC
02 September 2024

41524815R00153